J. MICHAEL STRACZYNSKI'S
RISING STARS

"Someone's killing the Specials," Dr. Welles said. "We have to find out who, and, maybe just as important, why."

"You've always been fair and honest with us, Doc. You've always tried to protect us from the outside, and from each other. Now it's my turn. I'll find out who's doing this."

"Then what?" Welles asked, a little slow on the uptake.

"I'll stop him. Any way I have to."

My visit with Dr. Welles confirmed my worst suspicions.

First, that, toward the end, Peter Dawson lived the loneliest kind of life. He had become a fatality on the crash site of his most cherished dreams long before he was murdered. It was too bad. He had been a sweet kid who'd never hurt anybody. Though impervious to pain, he'd actually squirm at the sight of blood, and cried whenever anyone got hurt severely. It galled me he had been denied any chance at redemption.

Second, that the killer was one of us.

J. MICHAEL STRACZYNSKI'S
RISING STARS

Book 1: BORN IN FIRE

ARTHUR BYRON COVER

ibooks
new york
www.ibooks.net

DISTRIBUTED BY SIMON & SCHUSTER, INC

ibooks, inc.
24 West 25th Street
New York, NY 10010

The ibooks World Wide Web Site Address is:
http://www.ibooks.net

ISBN 0-7434-3512-5
First ibooks, inc. printing July 2002
10 9 8 7 6 5 4 3 2 1

Edited by Karen Haber

Special thanks to Matt Hawkins
and Frank Mastromauro

Cover art by Gary Frank and Peter Steigerwald

Illustrations by Keu Cha & Jason Gorder

Printed in the U.S.A.

ACKNOWLEDGMENTS

The author would like to thank J. Michael Straczynski, the creator of *Rising Stars*, and Harlan Ellison, for putting their heads together and thinking of me; Karen Haber for figuring out what I really meant to say; Byron Preiss and Steve Roman, for putting up with me; Susan Ellison, for something that has nothing to do with this book, and Kathryn Drennan on general principles; Richard McEnroe, for pitching in at the shop; the author's agent, Jonathan Matson, for his infinite patience; the author's beloved wife, Lydia, for saying, "Get to work"; and all the friends and acquaintances the author has made at the Dangerous Visions Bookstore, who emphasized that it was about time he did something.

PROLOGUE

Sergei Goncharov, Russian cosmonaut, awoke with a start. He'd been dozing off, dreaming he was sleeping in his luxurious new three bedroom apartment, and had forgotten he was in the midst of his second orbit around the Earth. For a moment he was afraid; not everyone had come back alive from the journey he was now undertaking, and he was not sure he liked how the tin can he was floating in had been welded together.

He felt a muscle spasm in his back. He was going to be cramped like this for another entire orbit. Why couldn't the scientists redesign these capsules? They still mistook men for chimps. . . .

Then he couldn't help but grin. He was where he'd always dreamed of being. So what if not all his comrades had returned from their journeys? The job wasn't going to any safer just because he'd taken it. He'd always known where all the bodies were floating anyway.

In any case, should the worst happen, his family would be taken care of by a state grateful for his sacrifice, and not even death could rob him of the vision of Mother

1

Earth below. She was a beautiful, glorious garden of life. What was the word the Americans called it? An Eden . . . ? Sergei felt himself on the verge of tears, just looking at her through the tiny portal window. He would have been on the verge of a spiritual epiphany, that is, if the state had acknowledged a connection between mankind and the ineffable. As it was, he had no words to describe how he felt, no words other than humble and insignificant that is, two feelings he wasn't used to having.

The South American landmass came into view. So green and inviting . . . like so much of the Earth he had not yet seen. He yearned to travel down the South American rivers, and stand on its tallest mountains. Hmmm . . . Perhaps if he defected. . . .

But wait—! What was that?

A tiny pinprick of light. In the upper reaches of the stratosphere. It was moving beyond his range of sight. Damn those scientists and engineers—they would let a man travel into space and not provide him with an adequate porthole, so as to deny him the full view? It was their revenge, for not being able to go themselves.

Suddenly, Sergei gasped. His pulse quickened. The pinprick of light had shifted, began going in a slightly different direction. Now he could see the pinprick had a tail of light streaming behind it, and was beginning to turn yellow.

It was a comet! And it was headed toward . . .

Sergei couldn't resist a smile.

The comet was headed toward North America.

1

THE BIG FLASH

This is the story of how it happened, of how it came to be, and how it could have been. This is the story of a select group of individuals who were made from the stuff dreams are made of, and of how they lived and died. This is the story that asks the question: Was the existence of the Specials the result of blind chance, a typical random unprecedented phenomenon that surely must occur in the universe from time to time? Or was their existence the result of physical manipulation by an ineffable, unfathomable, supremely vast intelligence, not unlike the ones you find in Lovecraft and the Bible? I can only report the story. You'll have to decide.

The name is Simon, John Simon. The others, thinking they have a sense of humor, have always called me "Poet." And I am a Special.

This is the story of how the Specials came to be, of what happened to us and some of the people we knew. This is the story of how we loved and how we fought, of where we did right and where we went wrong. This is the

3

story of the world we touched and the places where the world touched us.

And all the terror and beauty and death that happened during the spaces in-between. . . .

Rick Cobham couldn't believe his good fortune. He was working as a stagehand at a rock festival at the Atlanta Speedway, helping to set up and break the equipment of a succession of singers and bands, many of whom formed a significant part of his record collection. These were his musical heroes, the people he'd have gladly emulated if he'd been fortunate to have been born with musical talent.

Already, during the past two days and nights, he'd been standing behind the back of the stage, stoned out of his mind, listening to Janis Joplin, The Grateful Dead, Blood Sweat & Tears, Led Zeppelin, Joe Cocker, and about 25 other top acts. The music hadn't stopped the entire time, and neither had Rick. Some of the roadies had given him pills to help him stay awake; he didn't care how hard he crashed, when he finally did. He knew this was the high point of his life so far, and he didn't want to miss a minute of it.

Right now he was listening intently to the Byrds. They didn't sound the same as they had when he first listened to them, when he was in high school. The band had started its career doing folk rock and psychedelia, but now it was into this country thing that was really good, but sounded too much like the music the rednecks had listened to in his hometown for him to be comfortable with it. Of course, only one member was the same—and he'd changed his name from Jim McGuinn to Roger—so that might have had something to do with their new direction.

Someone bumped into him. Biff.

"Hey! Watch where you're going!"

Biff, a long-haired hippie dude who had a face that looked like it had been put together by a committee, didn't even look at Rick as he said, "Sorry, guy."

Rick tried to control his temper. The moron didn't even know who he'd bumped into, his eyes were fixed so solidly on—

The sky.

Rick looked up. He experienced a profound sinking sensation, like his stomach was a rock being dropped down a well.

The music had stopped. Roger McGuinn whispered, "Far frigging out" into the microphone. The crowd was quiet. Everybody else was looking at the sky, too.

Looking at the comet.

Rick had never seen an actual comet before. It struck him that this one was awful big.

Indeed, its glorious silver and gold plume was lighting up the arena and the crowd like a rising sun.

The year was 1968. It was the year the Chicago Police presented such memorable urban hospitality to the protesters on the streets outside the Democratic Convention. It was the year Tom Wolfe's *Electric Kool Aid Acid Test*, a seminal work of mod literature masquerading as journalism, was published. This was the year Dr. Christian Bernard, a prominent surgeon who, by the very fact that he lived in South Africa was also a prominent beneficiary of apartheid, transplanted a human heart into a patient. 1968 was the year of the Beatles' "Hey, Jude" and Simon

& Garfunkel's "Mrs. Robinson," from the movie *The Graduate*. It was the year of Stanley Kubrick's *2001* and Sergio Leone's *Once Upon a Time in the West*. It was the year Martin Luther King and Robert F. Kennedy were assassinated. It was the year newly-elected President Nixon promised "to bring us all together," a task at which he proved to be an utter failure.

But those historical milestones of 1968 paled into insignificance when compared to the fact that during that year mankind was forced to face, if only for a moment, his metaphysical impotence in the wake of an indifferent universe. Luckily for mankind's collective peace of mind, the theory that global warming caused by a major meteor impact resulted in the extinction of dinosaurs had yet to be developed (but when it did, many had to face the trauma of the event all over again).

Not only that, but 1968 was the year I was conceived. By itself hardy a momentous occasion, but it did have consequences. Profound consequences.

Dr. William Welles sat on his balcony trying to read a science fiction novel. His heart wasn't in it; the words on the page seemed just that—words on a page. He sighed, put down the book, and took a sip from what was, perhaps, his fourth martini of the night. It had been a long night, and he'd lost count.

And why not? He deserved to be off his game a little bit. His latest girlfriend had just walked out on him, and only because he'd slipped and used the name of an ex-girlfriend instead of hers. He couldn't even remember whose name.

He tried to put things in perspective. In a few years he wouldn't even be able to remember what the girl who'd just walked out on him looked like. The pain he was feeling right now would be of little consequence to him. That's because he'd already felt it a hundred times.

Even so, he was becoming tired of it. Could it be he wasn't being properly supportive or considerate toward his new partners? As a practicing psychologist, he naturally had to attend an hour of personal analysis each week—he'd have to ask his own shrink about it.

Oh well, tomorrow was another day. And, as he liked to say, "another day, another conquest."

Gradually Welles noticed something amiss in the sky. The horizon was beginning to glow a bright yellow. Yet the time was only three. Furthermore, he'd seen his share of sunrises in his day, and this one was happening unnaturally quickly.

Then of course there was the fact it was originating from a southeasterly direction.

Welles stood and gripped the rail so firmly his knuckles turned white. One of his patients—a veteran of the war in sunny Southern Vietnam—once confided that no one in active jungle duty ever made fun of someone who'd soiled his pants while in a firefight—nearly everybody had done it, at least once. You wouldn't have been human if you hadn't.

Welles had the feeling humanity in general would be sharing a similar sentiment in the years to come. He knew he wasn't going to laugh at anybody.

J.J. "Bud" Jackson held a cinderblock over his head and hurled it into the window of a liquor store. He was going to get good and plastered later on—he didn't care if he was at home or on the street—and there wasn't a thing anybody could do about it.

Ignoring the encouragement of a handful of people behind him, he elbowed his way through the others who'd taken advantage of his initiative and headed toward the liquor department. He grabbed the first three bottles in his reach, put 'em under his arms, and left the same way he got in. He paused and tried to figure out which way to go.

People were swarming in and out of the other shops, and were disappearing into the crowd. A few men were loading a sofa into the back of a flatbed truck, and a dental office was being hit by a Malotov cocktail; the bottle crashed through the office window and the flames spread over the floor and onto the walls with the splattering of the gasoline that had been within the body. On the opposite end of the street, people were running away from the oncoming police cars.

Bud ducked down an alley and ran. A residential area was dead ahead; with luck, the streets would be relatively empty. Realizing he was alone in the alley, Bud put two of the liquor bottles under one arm and hastily opened the third. It was vodka. He took a big swig and felt the burn going straight down his throat like liquid hot chili peppers. He coughed and leaned against the wall.

Tears were running down his eyes. The amorphous rage which had motivated his recent behavior was giving way to sadness. His life had always been hard but never before would he have stooped to stealing. Oh well, it was all the man deserved—the white man, that is, the white man who provided the liquor, the white man who owned the store, the while men who sat at the counter, and the man who shot Reverend King. No, he took it back. It was *the least* they deserved.

Damn, it was getting light. Was the fire from the

dental office spreading that quickly? He didn't feel hot.

He realized things had quieted down. Being closer to the residential street, he walked out there and found himself paying no attention whatsoever to his theory that it would be less crowded than the business street. There were people there, but they were paying as much attention to him as he was to them.

Which is to say, none at all.

A few moments ago Bud had wanted to burn the ghetto and the city to the ground. Now he was repenting such sentiments. Because for a few moments, it looked like it was actually going to happen.

A low persistent rumbling accompanied the huge fire streaking across the sky. Somewhere nearby a radio was playing, and the local DJ had selected a song for the occasion: Jefferson Airplane's "Have You Seen the Saucers?" Normally, Bud preferred soul music, but this time he thought the DJ had made a good choice.

Things on the streets still remained quiet after the fire had disappeared over the horizon. The Police refrained from arresting people, because the rioters were trying to make themselves scare as discreetly as possible.

Including Bud. He even dropped his precious liquor bottles.

Like everyone else, he had family and friends to get back to.

Elsewhere, there were pile-ups on the freeways and streets, most of them minor, but not all. Accidents happened everywhere, of course, on the well-lit city streets and on the dark country roads. Drivers couldn't help looking into the sky when they should have kept their eyes on the road.

Lovers found their passions immediately deflated, while those who were sleeping were roused by the sound or the light, and people working graveyard shifts ceased performing their tasks and walked outside, to watch the sky.

Military bases went on red alert. The National Security Council immediately began gathering data, and a man was sent over to awaken the President. It was too late. President Johnson was already awake, sitting outside the residential quarters, wearing only his bathrobe and drinking a beer, gabbing nonstop about the end of the world.

He wasn't the only one.

My mother was making love. Making love with *someone,* naturally, the main question being *who?*

Where would be a secondary question.

Needless to say, I never really pressed the issue, but as I was the last Special to be conceived—probably—and the last to be born, definitely, I can only assume the answer to the question would be determined by the state of Mother and Father's marriage at the time.

By the time I was old enough to notice such things, and to realize they were different because most adult couples were able to get along with one another in front of other people, the state of my parents' marriage was roughly analogous to the state of the U.S. Navy the morning after the Japanese attack on Pearl Harbor.

So, it happened one of two ways. The first, and the more conducive to my general feelings of self-worth vis-a-vis my entrance into the world, was that Mom and Dad were together. The details of their encounter, I, as their son, would rather not speculate on, but I would imagine their lovemaking included a certain amount of love, tenderness, and mutual respect along with all the other ingredients.

If so, it could have been the last time, which brings me to the second way:

It starts with Dad, drunk, passed out in bed, with a cigarette burning in an ashtray and watching a bad television show on the tube. In other words, his usual condition: Dad, dead drunk and unaware that he was alone because his wife, my mother, was stepping out on him.

Either way, my mother had just helped make the beast with two backs, and her partner had just helped her to make me. For all I know, the couple might have been too busy to notice the comet hurtling toward their general vicinity. In any case, Mother never mentioned it to me.

Everyone who was there in the small Midwestern town of Pederson agrees the light was blinding—it was like a gigantic lightbulb flash, though it lasted for an entire twenty seconds. For a long time the religious believed it was the literal hand of God, come to smite the simple sinners of Pederson the same way He'd smited the cities of Sodom and Gomorrah. Those who managed to stay their religious fervor for the duration of the experience said that the light was cool—it generated no heat—and those who compared notes afterwards discovered the illumination was the same regardless of one's proximity to the presumed point of impact. And everybody agrees that the comet disintegrated the moment before it actually touched the treetops it should have already been torching. Disintegrated like the Tunguska comet that flattened Siberian forests for miles around in 1908 and caused such a far-reaching light in the night sky that one could read the newspaper on a London terrace by the glow.

But the most interesting thing about what happened is what *didn't* happen.

For one thing, the trees did not burn.

The roads did not melt. The streams did not boil. The chickens did not bake and the cattle did not roast.

The people did not melt. Their houses were not flattened. A crater was not formed, a world-spanning cloud of dust and debris did not erupt into the stratosphere and cut off the majority of the sun's rays for decades, thus ... thus ... doing what? Creating what sort of condition with what sort of effect? The theory of global warming, plus the theory of how the dinosaurs became extinct because of it, did not exist in 1968. In 1968, most paleontologists still believed the dinosaurs were warm-blooded and there was such a thing as a brontosaurus.

However, the paleontologists, along with everyone else, believed the comet should have pounded the entire town of Pederson into dust—just for starters. The fact remained that when the comet disintegrated, nothing happened.

Other than the flash, which almost immediately became known in popular parlance as the Big Flash. The most common image of it, the one that sticks in people's mind even though it isn't strictly accurate, is the painting that was used on the rush issue of *Time* magazine, showing a group of kids playing sandlot baseball, stunned and transfixed, looking upwards at the sky, while the comet hurtles directly toward them. Those kids in that picture represented an entire community where everyone should be dead, but where everyone was alive. No harm done.

Something should have happened.

Something did. But no one knew that, yet.

*　　*　　*

Funny, I can't think of the Big Flash without thinking of Renee Cabana. She was a red-haired, pony-tailed skinny rail of a girl, gangly and awkward. We were both ten at the time I'm thinking of.

Renee had the gift of visions. Usually she couldn't see them herself, but everybody around her saw them as plainly as you could see a movie screen. Renee had the ability to warp the fabric of light cast during various times past and different spaces. But she had no control over what time, place, or event she summoned, nor could she control the duration or the range of the vision. Sometimes the visions lasted for five seconds, sometimes for up to an hour. Sometimes only those right beside her saw them, sometimes only those within a hundred yards. Like I said, she had no control. Renee was like the idiot savant of time machines.

But it did make her interesting to be around. One day the girls in the john felt they were doing their business in the midst of the carnage of the firebombing of Dresden. I and several others had already seen Cornwallis surrender to Washington at Yorktown, Elvis gyrate his hips on *The Ed Sullivan Show*, and Ed Gein put on a grotesque mask made from the skin of one of his victims, to name just a few. Usually we didn't know beforehand who the subjects of the visions were, and of course occasionally the subject was a plain, normal, not-famous individual going about his or her business. Some of the kids made it a point to do research on their own to find out who we'd seen.

Usually those of us within Renee's range saw things from a normal vantage point, close to the ground. On the day I'm thinking of, we had a somewhat higher perspective. The girls screamed, and the boys wanted to. I dropped the book I was reading.

We were three hundred miles high. Looking down on the awe-inspiring Earth from a stationary position in a vacuum, from a standing, immobile position. My book remained at my feet. It floated with me.

"What's going on here?" Chandra demanded. Her dark eyes flashed. She had the tone of one who fully expected to be paid attention to; all the boys were interested in her, even then, at that early stage of their emotional development.

"It's okay," said Jason. "We can still breathe." He was always the bravest of us, even then.

We should be freezing, I thought. We stood in virtual orbit. The Earth rotated majestically below. A fire was just beginning to ignite in the sky. A fire connected to the tip of a plunging comet. I knew instinctively that Renee was enfolding us in the temporal reality of 1968. This wasn't just any comet with a three-mile diameter plunging into the stratosphere. This was *the* comet that had caused the Big Flash.

We didn't see anything abnormal either. Once we were a little older and could investigate comets for ourselves, we had no choice but to conclude the comet responsible for the Big Flash was, as far as appearances went, just another comet. There was no reason why it shouldn't have destroyed Pederson in an instant.

No good reason, anyway.

I did notice that whether the comet passed by or through a cloud, the cloud remained undisturbed.

An important clue, perhaps, *why* the comet's disintegration defied all known laws of both physics and common sense.

Particularly the *for every action, there is an equal reaction* law.

Scientific theories abounded in the wake of Earth's non-impact with the comet. One of the most common postulated that the comet had not existed in our own universe, but actually originated in another, parallel dimension, or an alternate reality, or even a mirror universe, that had somehow broken through into ours. The break had not lasted long, when viewed from the cosmic perspective; indeed, by those standards, its existence lasted less than a fraction of the duration of the blink of an eye.

Religious theories abounded, as well. Most of them had to do with the ineffable hand of God, or the Sword of Allah, striking down the infidel or non-believer. And there were philosophical theories, particularly New Agey ones, about how the purity of Gia had resisted the forces of negativity from another universe.

On the other hand, a lot of people didn't give a damn. As soon as the excitement died down, they went about their business, figuring the only true thing that could be said about the Big Flash was that it was gone. Over. Finished. Kaput. A Big Flash no more.

I don't know about the scientists, the religious folks, and the philosophers, but the common folk couldn't have been more mistaken. In a very real sense, the Big Flash wouldn't be over for decades.

One more thing. Now you know why I associate the Big Flash with Renee. It was she who had been responsible for my most vivid mental picture of it. Poor Renee. She didn't last very long, once the real trouble started. She was one of the first to be gunned down at the massacre. But now I really *am* getting ahead of myself....

2

THE SQUARE ROOT
OF ZERO

It was as if an atomic bomb had gone off in Pederson and left everything standing. Nothing like it had ever happened before, obviously, and chances were (people hoped) nothing like it would ever happen again.

Before the Big Flash, Pederson was a combination of a small manufacturing city, a farming town, and a business community. The people who owned the factories, the big farms, and the banks tended to live in outlying suburbs. Most families were white and had lived there for at least three generations, though after World War II some black and brown people moved in and proved themselves adept small businessmen and shopkeepers.

Outside of town lived a slew of small farmers—the size of the average farm was about 200 acres, I'm told—and they grew soy beans and corn, mostly. All in all, I'd say the city was pretty normal, though probably wealthier than most cities of its size. It had its society people, its church folk, and its low-class roustabouts, of which I'm sure my mother was one, for a while. Doubtless the Pederson community was also enduring the social change and evolution the '60s are famous for, with kids growing their hair long, doing drugs, experiencing the sexual revolution, etc. And who knows? If it hadn't been for the Big Flash, I might have been a normal kid fated to grow into a normal adult; probably the most rebellious thing I would have done would be listen to punk rock music.

But by the day after the Big Flash, it seemed tourism would become the new local industry. Scientists, reporters, and the National Guard were the first to swarm into town, followed by the doctors, the psychiatrists, those who would one day be known as environmentalists, and last but not least, the seekers: those who were embarked upon spiritual journeys or merely sought answers to metaphysical questions or personal dilemmas. The seekers thought Pederson had been sanctified, somehow, by the ineffable hand of the cosmos. And who is to say they were wrong? Though others would denounce the events of the Big Flash as a curse rather than regard it a blessing.

In any case, within a few years Pederson was a changed community. The easy social familiarity people once had while walking the main thoroughfares was gone, replaced by the brusque politeness of anonymity. Souvenir shops opened, selling items relating, however vaguely, to comets and the Big Flash. NASA opened up a research/public relations center, and even built a telescope and an auditorium where a laser show ran continuously. For years.

Then there were the motels. Roads that once wound through open prairie or between fenced farmland were now blighted with establishments that went by names such as The Flash Inn, The Comet Tavern, and Motel Slipstream. But that change was benign compared to the garish presence of adult entertainment, which brought its gentlemen's clubs and their neon lights shaped in the nude female form. My favorite sign was a place that proclaimed its "Live Nudes"; that always amused because I wondered why anyone would want to see a dead nude. Just goes to show you what I knew.

Other than that, life was normal for the good people of Pederson. For the next few years anyway.

For me, normalcy was pretty disappointing.

There's a picture of Mother and Father with me while she was still in the hospital. Father looks like hell, blurry-eyed, stubbled, and distracted, as if he wished to be somewhere else, already, while Mother appears radiant, as if she had just made the most beautiful baby who'd ever lived. I'm asleep, content, in her arms. She says I wouldn't smile, not even when the photographer tickled my toes, thus proving how serious I was, even then. I always thought her observation ridiculous. Who ever heard of a newborn smiling just because a stranger was tickling his toes?

Of course, my response to the requirements of having your picture taken was no different six years later, when a photographer was shooting for the yearbook of our first grade class. I can't say I'd been looking forward to it—all the other kids seemed to enjoy coming to school in their Sunday-go-to-meeting outfits. Somehow I always knew that dressing neat in the traditional manner just wasn't my style, though of course I had no idea what it was.

The photographer was a young man named Gilbert Jones. I remember him wearing jeans and a lumberjack shirt. I wouldn't smile for him either.

Mother decided to explain. "You may as well give up. He never smiles."

The photographer laughed as he made an adjustment

on his camera. "That's okay, it's a challenge. I've never met a kid I couldn't get to smile, sooner or later."

"Are you a clown?" I asked. Not smiling.

"He doesn't even laugh at cartoons," said Mom.

"A kid who doesn't laugh at Bugs Bunny?" Gilbert Jones said, shaking his head. "That's sad."

"You don't know my Johnny. He's been a serious boy ever since he was born. He's different that way. At first we thought maybe there was something wrong with him, but the doctors say he's perfectly healthy. Just quiet."

"From what I'm seeing, he's just a boy of few well-chosen words. That's a lot different than being quiet."

"I'm sure he'll grow out of it."

"Could be worse. He could be autistic." He took the shot. "That'll be fine, John. You can go now."

I went, even though the only place to go was the hall. We—the kids and I—were waiting there to have our pictures taken because outside a storm raged. The sky was as dark as night and the rain pounded against the roof like a million drumming fingers. A few of the boys were pushing each other around. My mother went over to take care of it and I went to the window to watch the world. This was the first torrential downpour I'd ever seen. It was mysterious and quietly terrifying.

Because of a trick of the light, I could see my reflection in the window. I had rarely looked at myself until then, I mean, truly looked at myself. This time I found myself wondering, just who *was* this kid with the dark eyes and the perpetual frown? Was this really me? I messed up my hair. My mother had trimmed it just before this session, had cut the bangs so they were all even, but that was too much order in my personal appearance to suit me. Even then, I'd aspired to a certain amount of untidiness. It's a character trait I'm certain I was born with, because I certainly had no rational reason for it. It was the way, I felt, that was all.

Outside, the rain kept coming down like a million buckets, over and over. I listened to it intently. It made a thousand echoes, and I imagined I could hear every one. I was very serious about it. If I'd been questioned by someone—*did you really hear every echo?*—I would have insisted it was the truth. Furthermore, the echoes came in waves . . . they rumbled deep inside my chest.

Behind me, Matthew Bright's mother, a birdlike brunette who had lots of energy and who always seemed to be around whenever there was the slightest deviation from the school routine, was handing over the info card to the photographer.

"He's a fine boy," she said eagerly. "I'll just know you'll take a good picture of him."

"He is a good-looking lad," said Jones, not really caring one way or the other. By now he only had the energy to be professionally nice.

Matt was the only boy wearing a tie; earlier he'd showed us—proudly, again and again—how easy it was to tie the knot. He was a freckled-faced kid who sat on the stool before the screen and stared with an utterly guileless confidence at the lens. It didn't seem to bother him that his mother was simply making the process take longer; guileless confidence was practically his first and only trait at this stage of his life.

"He's never been a bit of trouble," said his mother. " And healthy! Not a sick day yet. We're very lucky."

"I'm sure that'll come across in the picture," Jones said slyly.

Lucky was how I heard *my* mother also describe Matt;

one day she'd learned about his penchant for climbing that train trestle near the mines. She and Dad talked about it once, upon a rare occasion when Dad was sober and acting civilized toward her. Mother remarked that while adventurousness might be normal for some children, Matthew was taking it to extremes.

Maybe so, but I'd never had a sick day either, and I'd climbed the same trestle once, when no one was around to watch, just because I wanted to see if I could. When I reached the top, I looked down—a hundred feet below a polluted stream trickled between the wooden posts—and for a moment contemplated dizziness, and nervousness, and possibly even a potentially dangerous clumsiness. But only for a moment. Otherwise I'd accomplished the feat as easily as Matt had.

And there was Joshua—white-haired, snotty Josh—who, when three years of age, had gotten on his roof with a lawn mower and pushed it off, presumably to hear what it would sound like when it crashed. Mary Lesh could already speak three languages. Samson Biggs was an expert juggler and card magician. Paula Ramirez was real quiet, quieter than me, but she had a serene, even-handed personality; Stephanie was soft-spoken and shy. Everybody picked on Willie, one of the black kids, and Lee Jackson didn't like anyone to touch him, not even the nurse. That was my crowd, my definition of normal.

Just then everyone was distracted by the grandest, most prolonged roll of thunder we'd ever heard. A few girls shrieked, and the boys laughed nervously. I was fazed not a whit—I'd seen the lightning strike in a field across the street and had expected the sound. But the intensity of the rain had practically doubled since I'd started watching it, and that bothered me a great deal.

Matt's mother, meanwhile, prattled on.

A distinct drip could be heard despite the staccato noise on the roof.

A puddle had begun forming on the floor near the door to the infirmary.

A thunderclap erupted, practically overhead this time. The whole building shook. Everybody tried to shrug this one off; nothing was wrong. It's just been close, that's all.

I, on the other hand, didn't feel so sure. I seemed to be the only one who noticed the rivulets of fresh rainwater creeping across the upper doorframe.

The puddle got bigger. I distinctly remember this was my first time witnessing such a phenomenon. Mom'd always put buckets under leaks. I knelt and touched the water, then tasted it on my fingertip. Probably wasn't such a hot idea. Schools were typically insulated with asbestos in those days, and the kids hated sitting in one part of the auditorium, where it was believed the insulation directly above was somewhat compromised.

Another flash, the closest yet, and then a spectacular thunderclap. The building rumbled again. Only the rumbling was different, this time. More severe. The previous rumble had rattled me from the neck down. This one rattled me from the toes up.

I looked at the ceiling. What I saw made my jaw drop.

The adults weren't paying any attention. Neither were the kids. I was the only one who knew. I was the only one who could say anything.

But there wasn't time. The roof started making noise, all on its own, and that was more than enough to get folks' attention.

The roof was buckling. It was later determined that

lightning had struck a tree and split it in half like a wishbone. The impact of the branches and trunk against the roof had magnified certain structural deficiencies which should have been taken care of long ago—thus inoculating the janitors, the principal, the teachers and the school board all from being solely responsible for the problem. They were all a part of the problem, and hence could be held equally blameless.

That was the official word, anyway, the one the media accepted. The Pederson school system was fortunate indeed there were a lot more important matters to be investigated in the wake of the incident. Their negligence came in under the radar, so to speak.

Those were later considerations. At the moment I was focused completely on the big chunk of ceiling disengaging itself from the rest of the roof.

It was coming down. And was going to land right on Matt and his mom.

Glass from breaking fluorescent lights rained all about, the gasps from the kids seemed to suck the air from the room, and Jones accidentally knocked his camera stand over.

The camera flashed just as it hit the floor, just as Matthew caught the chunk of roof. It had already struck his mother on the head and knocked her to her knees. She was dazed, to be sure, and must have thought death was but a instant away. I knew we kids had just missed seeing something horrible.

Instead we saw something amazing. Matt had caught the chunk of roof with the instinctive, casual confidence of a major league ball player, and stood holding it *with one hand* and a big grin on his face. Sure, he was only holding it four feet above the ground, but that was more

than enough room for the photographer to grab his
mother by the hand and pull her out of there.

Once Matt was sure she was safe, he turned toward a
corner, made certain everyone was out of the way, and
threw the chunk there. We were only barely paying attention to that. We were too stunned to move or think.
The rain was pouring in, twice as loud, and roll after roll
of thunder rippled across the sky like waves across an
ocean. The rain drenched us all, and a thin wide river of
blood flowed from a gash in Matt's mother's head.

She looked back and forth from her son to the chunk
of roof a few times, then she fainted. Jones tried to catch
her head. Too late. It made a loud noise against the floor.

Matt didn't seem concerned. He had this impish light
in his eyes. He looked as proud as a pony. He looked
around as if to ask, *What's next?*

No one had any idea.

3

TROUBLEMAKERS

The Big Flash did not alter the fundamentals of human nature; it merely brought those fundamentals to the fore. The human race was already at war when Matt revealed his powers; two great superpowers were waging a proxy global conflict while their people feared the conflict might escalate into a direct war, possibly resulting in nuclear annihilation. Just the sort of thing that brings out the paranoia in men of power.

And no President was more paranoid than Richard M. Nixon. Immediately after the photo of Matt catching the roof was published in the newspaper, he announced a plan to deal with Matt and the other children—"Specials," he called them—who had thus far revealed abilities that hitherto were thought to be solely the province of dreamers and comic book artists. In the view of the Nixon administration, the problem of what to do with the Specials—a sudden wild card in the history of the human race—superceded the Cold War, the conflict in Vietnam, and his new-found diplomatic ties with the Red Chinese.

The plan consisted of a study to confirm the

commonly held (but ultimately true) suspicion that the emergence of the Specials was related to the Big Flash, a survey to determine who was likely to become a Special, and then send them all to perpetual summer camp.

Well, summer camp was what the Nixon administration called it. Others, particularly many of our parents, called it isolation. Quarantine. Segregation. The Nixonians said it was for our own protection—they said we needed to learn about our powers so we wouldn't accidentally hurt ourselves, but everybody knew people were afraid of us. And a few niceties such as an individual's civil rights couldn't be allowed to interfere with public safety, could it?

Deputy Director Parker Paulson of the FBI became the man in charge of the Specials program. At first the press thought he'd risen to his position in the law enforcement bureau solely because of his ruthless and efficient managerial abilities, but the truth was eventually revealed that he was one of the boys who had had no problem going to the now-deceased J. Edgar Hoover's house and helping the old queen out with his Sunday gardening. It was the one certain fast track to promotion in that organization. Within a few months of the so-called crisis, however, Paulson proved himself adept at the job. He'd learned much from the mistakes of the cold warriors who'd served in government before him. He knew how to sugarcoat the most controversial policies, he knew how to flatter Congress and manipulate the media.

In his autobiography, Paulson is hard at work in his office when dawn comes to Washington D.C. He implies he is working on some grave matter of national security, such as tracking student protestors turned bank robbers, kidnappers, and car bombers, or a crazy right-wing racist group set on assassinating a kindly old Southern preacher. Either way, Paulson had already established himself as a straight shooter in a capital of moral ambiguities. If he'd had his way, he would have busted Jane Fonda for collaborating with the enemy, told ex- Vice-President Agnew to his face that he was a nattering nabob of negativity for taking bribes while Governor of Maryland, and would have convinced President Nixon to come clean on the Watergate affair.

That is, if anybody would have listened to him. But when he saw the picture of Matt in the morning paper, after having stayed up all night working on some criminal that may or may not have had something to do with national security, he picked up the phone and said coolly, "Mackie—it's me. Get the director on the line. It appears our prior assumptions were incorrect. We have a problem in Pederson."

Then he just sat there, his coffee untouched, the phone still cradled between his neck and shoulder, his eyes on the paper. Leaving the reader with one unmistakable impression: Paulson was the right man for the job.

Within six hours of Jones' photograph of Matt appearing in *The Washington Post*—it'd been an exclusive—the reporters, law enforcement officers, tourists, and spiritual truth seekers (not to mention those who needed some heavy lifting to find buried treasure) had descended once again on Pederson, Illinois.

As it was, the American people treated those suspected of being Specials *and* their families with all the kindness and consideration and good manners one normally associates with a mob of paranoid, frightened villagers from a *Frankenstein* movie. Nixon took advantage of the

American people's fears and issued an executive order enabling the FBI to examine 1968 tax returns so it could be established, quickly, who'd lived in Pederson at the time of the Big Flash, which children had been born during the next nine months, and where the couples were currently residing, regardless of the state of their marriage. Every parent—and in a few cases, grandparents or relatives—with custody of a suspected Special was informed in no uncertain terms to make the child in question available for testing at the local Pederson hospital for as long as necessary.

And they were to report there immediately.

Paulson emphasized the point when he was asked a few questions by reporters during the press conference Nixon held to introduce him and his role to the American people. Helen Thomas of the *Post* asked Paulson about the children's inalienable rights. "Let's make sure they're *human* first," said Paulson. "Then we'll see if they can have any rights."

At the same time, my mother waited patiently at the reception desk while the pretty black nurse at the desk answered a question on the telephone from Lee Jackson's parents.

"I'm sorry, Mrs. Jackson, it's very important you come in as soon as possible, no later than tomorrow at three. If you need a ride, I'm sure we can arrange for someone to pick you up and bring you here." Beat. "I understand, but if you'll read the letter you received, it specifies that this is a mandate from the Department of Health. It's really for your safety and the safety of your child."

"Excuse me, nurse, I don't understand the reasons for all these questions," Mom said. "They seem a little personal."

"I understand you may feel uncomfortable," the nurse replied. "But it's necessary in order for us to most accurately determine the date on which your child was conceived. don't know for a fact yet, but it's possible the flash six years ago may have had some unforeseen effects on any children who were *in utero* at the time. We need this information in order to determine which children may have been affected, so we can monitor their condition for any adverse effects."

"But what if I don't want to provide all this information?"

"Well, you'll have to talk to my supervisor about that. I can't force you to comply. I can certainly pass along your objection."

"That would be fine."

"But you must understand that this is important to the wellbeing of the child. If you aren't interested in his wellbeing, I'll have to mention that in my report. I can't say for certain that the child welfare division will take your child away for his own good—but I can't say they won't, either."

Mom pondered the implications, I'm sure.

"I'll have to be . . . discreet," she said. "There may be some complications about the date of conception—well, if not the date, then other factors."

"Of course, honey. I know all about the sexual revolution."

Mom raised an eyebrow.

The nurse looked at her coolly. "I read about it in *Newsweek.*"

"My husband, Evan, he thinks . . . it happened after a difficult time we were having. Will this information be private?"

"Of course."

Yeah, except when the government threatens to leak to the press a few speculations regarding the identity of your biological father in order to keep your folks and other parents in line while they go about exercising their constitutional rights. The Feds didn't, but only because they figured out in advance, for a change, that a public relations disaster would have been the result.

"Do you have a pencil?" Mom asked.

"Of course," said the nurse, her tone solidly in the comfort zone.

"When can I see John?"

"When we're done with him."

While my mother waited outside in the lobby, my fellow Specials and I were being examined—poked, prodded, questioned, and observed—by a crack scientific team composed of both American and Soviet experts. Many of the Soviets were psychics. President Nixon, on the advice of former California Governor Ronald Reagan, whose wife recognized the potential of psychic research, had requested their presence. There wouldn't be any security or spying problems because every room, including the bathroom, was bugged six ways to Sunday, as Mother used to say, and a small army was stationed just outside town, in case things got out of hand.

I can't say I was only too glad to oblige to help the experts with their research; I did as I was asked, without enthusiasm. I showed them what little talent I appeared to have had at the moment: the ability to make my fingertips glow blue. For a long time it was all people thought I could do.

When Matt caught that chunk of roof, it was as if a switch had been thrown in the rest of us. Those who had already discovered their abilities were more than willing to show what they could do. Mostly.

Stephanie refrained. They asked her time and time again, politely, pleadingly, and threateningly, to no avail. It wasn't that she was shy, bashful, or afraid. She was simply—in today's parlance—wound up too tight. She dealt with the doctors' "requests" by saying "no" and looking away from them—indeed, I don't recall that she ever looked anyone in the eye, not during those early days.

But Stephanie was the exception. More often than not, the kids whose abilities had kicked in were proud of what they could do. Jason—blonde, crew-cut, blue-eyed Jason, who even then possessed the surety and confidence that would serve him in dubious stead during the decades to follow—was happy to bend pipes of solid iron and to bench press 200 pounds. Not bad for a five-year-old. He could even crush a lump of coal into dust (but not, it seemed, into a diamond, much to his dismay; he *so* much wanted to emulate his favorite comic book character).

I happened to be sulking (as usual) nearby when a lady doctor said, "You're being very helpful," to him. Jason just smiled and said politely, "Thanks. My folks said it was okay if I talked about it, since everybody else was being asked. I like being strong. But my Dad said it was important not to misuse it. He said I've been strong for a long time, even right after I was born. So for as long as I can remember, they've been teaching me to use it right."

A nice speech. Today I detect parental prompting there. His parents had the attitude of people who'd just seen their baby strangle the two snakes who'd just crawled into his crib. I wonder sometimes just what role one's parents played in the nature of the unique talents possessed by the individual Specials. That is, if a Special's particular power was already determined by the combination of his genetic make-up derived from his parents and of whatever contribution the Flash made, or if the pivotal experiences of one's early psychology were ultimately responsible. It's that old nature/nurture conundrum, Special style.

Joshua's parents seemed to make a fine argument of the potential effect of the nurture side of the argument. Joshua's ability was one thing, but what they read into it, and how they molded him as a result, was another thing altogether.

Josh's old man was Reverend Samson B. Kane, a holy-roller preacher in the Midwest, (in)famous for his ability to speak in tongues and to handle snakes. Reverend Kane claimed to be the direct descendant of a Puritan adventurer who'd vanquished all sorts of heinous evil around the globe during the late 17th century. He knew this because he claimed to have seen visions of this past life. But no concrete proof of this earlier Kane individual existed, apparently; whenever closely questioned on this matter, Reverend Kane promised to provide such proof, but he never did. He liked to tease his congregation with hints that God was going to grant him a revelation that would put all doubts about his certitude in this matter to rest, but just as soon as it seemed he was about to say something specific, he turned over the service to his wife, Wendy, who played the organ and conducted the choir.

I don't believe Beelzebub himself could have kept the Kanes from personally showing off Joshua's talent. The doctors doing their preliminary interview only had put pencil to clipboard—and didn't even have time to ask the first question—when Reverend Kane launched into a rap about the morning when they had just finished putting some fresh flowers in the private home chapel. "We were sitting there in morning prayers when we looked at Joshua and there was a light—"

"A brilliant, heavenly light," put in Mrs. Kane.

"It came out of his hands and the table began to rise up into the air, six inches at least. We knew then that our boy had been touched by the Lord." Beat. "Go on, Joshua. Show the doctor the power God has given you."

And Joshua, sitting on a folding chair, held his breath, closed his eyes, and tilted his head toward, presumably, Heaven. A beautiful blue iridescence emanated from the entirety of his body, casting a thousand shades and shadows throughout the room. Slowly he rose into the air.

The doctors were very impressed, but they had to ask Joshua to turn it off because his blue glow was diluting all the other light in the room and it was difficult for them to work.

"Isn't it fantastic?" the Reverend asked one of the doctors. "Isn't it proof of the power and glory of God?"

"You mean, because he can levitate and cast a blinding blue light?" the doctor asked, somewhat dryly.

"Yes! Yes!"

"Well, it beats what Madame Blavatsky said she could do, I'll give him that."

"Heathen bastard!" exclaimed the Reverend, stomping off. As far as I know, Reverend Kane never explained, to himself or anyone, if Joshua's powers were a direct gift from God, why the powers of the others were not quite so holy in nature. But even he, as he and his wife were leaving, paused to take a close look at Elizabeth Chandra, who was just sitting there waiting her turn to be examined and did not claim, indeed, would not know for years if she had a Special talent. The implications were there, however: a girl of six, and all the adult males kept glancing at her; even the boys, who until then had treated her with callous indifference and/or contempt typical of the opposite sexes before the hormones kicked in, kept trying to sit next to her and talk. The attention made her blush, but at the same time I could see she enjoyed it. This was just a foreshadowing.

Speaking of shadows. Randy Fisk claimed not to know what his ability might be, yet, but whenever he got tired of the questions, he found it easy to slip away from the doctors—without even leaving the room. Things were so weird that day that no one even noticed. That should have been a clue. Renee accidentally provided a doctor with a glimpse of the execution of the Romanoff family in post-revolutionary Russia. A doctor who just happened to be taking a cigarette break near Lee Jackson blinked in surprise because it was burning without any help from the unstruck match in his hand. Willie, fat, round, and black, doomed to be an outsider before he indicated he was a Special, floated six inches off the ground, no higher, no lower. With him it was always six inches or nothing. Then there was Gretchen, who could make her skin transparent; and Buzz, who could solve complex equations in his head; and Olaf, who could read a book blindfolded by running his fingers across the type. Pretty nifty, but in later years he had trouble suspending his disbelief, so he got reader's block and had an ability he didn't care about, one way or the other.

And there was Paula. She would grow up to be sweet, enigmatic, spiritual, sensual Paula Ramirez. But at first she was like a gifted autistic child. A Doctor Clark had been interviewing her in a private room when a supervisor noticed, through the one-way window, he had been alone with her without either one speaking for quite some time. Paula was just staring at the wall, while Dr. Clark stared at her with a rapturous expression not unlike the one exhibited by Reverend Kane before the sarcastic doctor had rained on his parade.

The supervisor asked Dr. Clark to come out. When Dr. Clark complied, the supervisor pointed out that he hadn't moved or said anything for a long time.

Dr. Clark cleared his throat. I couldn't tell if he was embarrassed or simply sheepish. Either way, he was having a hard time coping with reality. "It's Paula Ramirez," he said. "She was singing to me."

"If she was singing to you, why didn't I hear anything through the intercom?"

Dr. Clark shrugged. "I don't know."

"Well then, what did she say?"

"I don't remember. All I do remember . . . is that it was beautiful . . . beautiful . . ."

The entire week was filled with events like that. Hints, revelations, and mysteries, all wrapped up in over a hundred children who in a parallel, alternate universe were living normal lives, playing tag or sandlot ball or with dolls, just learning how to enjoy being alive. The kind of life I would have had too. I used to wonder just what might have happened if Mother had waited one more night to step out on Dad, the night after the Big Flash had come and gone. Would I have been a happy child? One fated to grow up and marry and have children? Maybe join the Army or the National Guard, but certainly go on to have a varied and rewarding career as a poet-in-residence at a succession of well-funded universities where it would be possible for me to have a healthy heterosexual relationship with a number of intellectual beauties who could see past my cool Byronic exterior and understand the sensitive inner me? Indeed, what of sort woman might I have loved, in another life? I suppose people always ask themselves that, whenever they have regrets about time lost, or spent unwisely.

Too bad all such speculation is in vain . . .

"We've identified 115 children we believe were *in utero* at the time of the Flash," Paulson said, during a routine meeting of the Council for the Containment of Specials. "Allowing for a margin of error in either direction, and a certain latency period that seems to vary from one subject to another, there could be as many as 120 and as few as 97."

"As few or as many *what?*" said General Baxter. "I mean, what are we talking about here? These are children, but we're talking about them as if they're criminals."

"Not criminals," said Paulson firmly. "But they do represent a potential hazard. We know that most of them are stronger and smarter and more mature than children at that age could possibly be. Others seem capable of directing energy in ways we're still trying to understand."

"But they're just children!" protested Council member Henry McCain.

"Didn't you ever see *Children of the Damned*?" said the Secretary of H.E.W., who was sitting in. "They were just children, too!"

Paulson ignored that remark, because in his mind a more accurate analogy was to be found in certain black and white Roger Corman horror movies. "They are children for the moment. But they will grow up. What they grow into may, in time, represent a threat. How big or how small a threat, there's no way to determine without further detailed analysis."

"Another thing," said McCain. "They're going to go to college someday. What if they want to attend Harvard? Or Berkeley? Can we really afford to have a gang of Special radicals running around?"

"We'll make sure they go to nice conservative Southern schools, if it comes to that," said Paulson. Paternalistically. As if he really did have our welfare at heart. "Think about it—there are now children in existence who can bend steel in their bare hands. Who can start fires. Who can telepathically transmit music to an audience of her choosing. Do you know what the Commies could do with a mind like that? Just think of it: a mutant Joan Baez! The possibilities for successful leftist propaganda are enormous! Which is why I believe that in time, given the abilities involved, the temperaments and difficulties of children, and the currently uncontrolled situation, the justification for what we are doing will attend to itself, soon enough."

"Then what do you suggest we do in the interim?" asked the General.

"Since the parents believe that we're looking out for the health and safety of their children—which is true, to a certain extent—we may as well continue along those lines. We don't know what hit Pederson. The world's greatest scientific minds can't agree whether it was a natural phenomenon, or some kind of radiation, or something manmade. We don't know what kind of long-term health issues might be involved either. I'm sure the parents want us to do everything we can to find out. So

we'll take a page from the way we handled polio inoc-
ulations back in the '50s: encourage cooperation rather
than forcing the issue. We can offer to provide free testing
to insure the health of the children and give the parents
some well-deserved private time with the normal part of
their family. Not only that, this way we can assure them
they will be safe if their child has some inherently dangerous ability he or she is unable to control. It'll be a
totally voluntary form of isolation and examination. One
that will clearly be their patriotic duty to acquiesce
to. . . ."

4

SUMMER FUN ALL
YEAR LONG

When Snappy the Clown—or was it Snuffy?—showed us around Camp Sunshine for the first time, he thought we were in the third, maybe the fourth grade. The truth was we were just beginning school. My fellow Specials were to be the only school chums I ever knew.

I remember. His name was Slappy. I don't know whose idea he was. Probably Paulson's. He only lasted a morning, long enough to show us our rooms (boys in the cabins on the north side of the hall, girls on the south), the classrooms, the rather well-equipped, well-stocked infirmary, the not-so-well-stocked library, and the gym. I think he was supposed to show us around the playgrounds, the golf course, the river, and the wooded acres that were part of the compound, but he was drinking so much of his "vitamin juice" that by the time he was done showing us the interiors, he was just too damned tipsy to do much more than stand up straight. He was very upset that the guards were standing outside the building, but that was all right with us, because we were upset about the guards, too.

39

Poor Slappy. He soiled himself profoundly when we rushed him. We were like a mob straight out of *Lord of the Flies*. Adults had taken us away from our homes and families and here was an adult who was afraid of us, whom we could take it out on. The fact that Matt and Jason could bang their fists through the door he tried to hide behind only increased the joy we felt in releasing our rage.

Fortunately the guards rescued him. They distracted us with milk and cookies, and thus prevented our story from turning into a tragedy before its time. We never saw Slappy again after that, although Link, who had a special sense of smell, once swore, much later, that they stood near one another at a Seattle bus station. I'm certain that had Slappy known he'd accidentally gotten that close again to a Special, he would have embarrassed himself a second time then and there.

We laughed about Slappy all day. It eased our trauma of homesickness. Having Slappy there was a big mistake on the Feds' part, because it had given us an opportunity to bond and to think of ourselves as a unit. Not super-powered freaks, although some of us were that. Not cast-offs from the human race, though already some of us were thinking that was a blessing in disguise. And definitely not the fractionated social hierarchy one finds in all schools at all levels. We were a unit. We were *Specials*.

Slappy the inebriated clown had been afraid of us.

And the guards didn't exactly exude confidence around us either.

Don't misunderstand me. Traditional social factions started the very next day. Tentative friendships were born, and more than a few rivalries seeded. But the memory that we'd gotten rid of Slappy right off the bat was always something we had in common, no matter how bad it got, how much we loved or hated one another, or how miserable we became during any given situation. I'm projecting backward of course. We were kids then, and couldn't have articulated such a statement even if we'd been able to recognize it was happening. But it had happened, which might explain why we were always sympathetic to Lee Jackson. We might not have approved of what he did, but we could understand why.

Heck, we probably would have reacted exactly the same way.

Funny, one of the guards was listening to Emerson, Lake and Palmer's version of "Rodeo" on the radio the morning we talked at the picnic tables; funny, because during my later incarnation as a rock fan, I learned Keith Emerson had played bass with a guy named Lee Jackson, when they were both part of the Nice. *That* Lee Jackson was no relation, though. I checked on the internet not so long ago. I did learn a certain Stonewall Jackson was one of our Lee's ancestors, which may explain why it didn't take long for the stubborn streak running through his family to once again put the kibosh to the notion that you can always trust the government to think of everything.

They could have asked us. Those of us who'd gone through kindergarten with Lee already knew what to expect: you could try to make friends with him but it wouldn't do any good. You could be nice to him and invite him to play in games, but he'd just say no and watch from the sidelines. You could be mean and pick on him but he never took it badly and indeed, he was so bleak in general that picking on him just wasn't any fun.

He didn't laugh when the rest of us laughed and he didn't misbehave either. Even I, the great iconoclast who held everything back, reacted more than occasionally to outside stimuli. The poor kid was like a sick kitten, a five-ounce ball of pain with a perpetual black cloud over his head.

Adults noticed, but they couldn't do anything about it. Encouragement and engagement were equally ineffective. I know now that social workers suspected his parents of abusing him, but they could never prove it. His parents cared, they watched out for him, they tried. But they wanted Lee to attend an internment camp for the Specials about as much as they wanted a vacation in warm, sunny Southern Vietnam. They didn't want Lee out of their sight. They also had no choice. For three weeks they missed Lee and kept expecting to see him in the next room at every turn. Then they noticed there were no more small electrical fires and the car had stopped overheating. They had started to relax . . .

Not that we kids were any better at diagnosing what was wrong with Lee. But then again, he had problems that were way off a normal kid's radar screen.

On the second day, during lunch outdoors, Willie immediately pegged himself as the guy who always got everything wrong. "I hear we're gonna be off from school for as long as it take 'em to figure out what's wrong with us."

"We have to go to school!" said Matt. "What you think those blackboards are for?"

"I hear football teams use 'em too," I said awkwardly. I didn't want to talk to other kids but I figured I had to try. "Maybe they wanna see which ones of us can turn pro when we grow up."

They all looked at me like I didn't know what I was talking about. I flipped Matt a bird, just like I'd seen Dad do a couple of times when he was driving. I didn't know what it meant, just that it was bad. The other kids looked at me as if I was just weird; they had no idea what it meant either.

"Dad says this is no school neither," said Jason. "He thinks it's a plot, that the government is up to something."

"What's a government?" I asked.

"I don't know, but Dad doesn't like it," Jason replied.

"*My* dad says there's nothing wrong with us, neither," said Randy impishly. "We're just special."

"My mother tells me all children are special," said Willie.

"Your mommy!" I said. "You listen to your mommy?" So did I, actually, or I got my butt whipped.

"You're not so special," Jason taunted.

"It's true I can't do anything special yet," said Willie. "But I will someday. Dad tells me so!"

"I think it's God's will we're here," said Josh. Even then, we found the wide, wild look in his eyes both stupid and disturbing. Sorry, I guess even back then I had an instinctive dislike of religious fundamentalists. Of course, none of us realized how much Josh was imitating his own father, because he acted in front of us the way he was supposed to act at home. "We've been touched by God."

"Who's he?" Matt asked.

"Some big guy who's in charge of stuff," said Willie.

"He's more than that!" said Josh. "He's everywhere! He's everything!"

"Then what makes him different than a rock?" I inquired.

"It's what my father says!" Josh replied.

"Sure, Josh, cool," said Randy, leaning toward the embryonic holy-roller. Lee was sitting at one end of the table, trying not to draw attention to himself. Randy stared at him like a mongoose about to snap up a snake. "Lee," he said. "Hey, Lee!"

Lee looked up from his half-eaten sandwich. Peanut butter and mayo. We'd all picked jelly. "What?"

"Is there anything to do around here?"

"I don't know. Why are you asking me?"

"I just figured you'd know. You've been here before, haven't you? When it was an actual summer camp—"

"—And not an internment camp!" exclaimed Jason.

"What's that?" I asked, but neither he nor anyone paid attention to me.

"Yeah, I've been here before," said Lee sullenly. "I didn't like it."

"What's not to like?" asked Matt.

"I just want to go home. I don't want to be here. I don't."

The rest of us laughed at him. All except for Willie, who nodded in agreement. I noticed Lee was looking at something—no, someone—in the distance. Standing in the shadows of a cabin doorway was a large, rather imposing adult. His name was Manfred, but his nickname was Manny. Turned out he'd been a counselor when Sunshine had been a real summer camp, and his parents owned it, so this was where he lived. Since he couldn't be counselor or a teacher here, he was the on-site handyman. Guess a lot of things broke around the camp.

Now if it seems I remember an awful lot about those first days at Sunshine, it's because I do. I've had a lot of help. A few Specials had the power of flashback and vision, like Renee, and Andy Shea became a world-renowned mentalist during a period when it was desirable in certain fashionable circles to know a Special personally. I was the only Special who ever had a Q&A session with Andy, though. He did help me recall, most vividly, certain important episodes of my formative years.

What happened with Lee was a big one. It affected us all.

But at first we were too busy adjusting to our new routine to worry too much about him. Mornings and early afternoons were taken up with classes and the rest of the day with physical education. The adults ran us ragged. One day it might be several back-to-back games of volleyball, another it would be swimming lessons, followed by a game of water polo, and another it would be wrestling, the real kind, with the boys against the boys and the girls against the girls. We were constantly choosing up sides, and even teamed up for the wrestling matches.

One would have thought they wanted us to grow up hating each other. I don't know why they bothered. We Specials weren't exactly immune to the vicissitudes of human nature. Most of us grew up detesting someone, without outside interference.

At the same time the adults acted as if they wanted to make us the healthiest, strongest gaggle of happy mutants possible, and have us bond like a brotherhood of warriors. Not that we noticed much at the time. All I noticed was that at night I was too tired to miss home very much.

The boys soon realized that picking on Lee wasn't much fun, because he barely responded to their taunts. But as Willie seemed to ask for it whenever possible, they turned their attention to him. Willie was a lot more receptive than Lee.

A few of the girls tried to make friends with Lee. Indeed, he was more apt to be on a team where a girl was captain and got to choose who was on her side that day. He was a decent teammate but you can't say he tried hard. And he always played really badly when he noticed Manny was watching.

Manny's chores were nearly always over by the afternoon. He'd often spend them watching us play. When we asked why, he'd say he was curious about us, like any "normal" person might be, and wanted to be watching whenever one of us did something; that way he'd have something to talk about in the outside world. I realize now his answer wasn't meant to be funny or friendly, it was meant to prevent us from noticing he watched Lee while he was talking to us.

After a few weeks our parents were allowed to visit on Saturday or Sunday. Their choice. They couldn't take us off the grounds—the government promised leaves of absence in the future, but claimed the situation was too much in flux to risk it now—but they were allowed to bring us care packages: food, books, and toys. All of which we had to share, but that was all right. A few nights a week we watched movies in a tent, and we were allowed to watch television in the various lounges, provided we didn't argue over which station the set should be on. Most of the movies were Disney films, though I'm grateful that after we were little older, we were exposed to westerns and Harryhausen films. We even got to watch a few Hammer and Corman horror movies, though to make it up to the girls, we sometimes had to watch movies about horses. I must admit, it didn't make any sense at the time. Why dream of someday riding a horse when someday you might be flying?

Lee's parents were about as friendly as he was. At this early stage of the game, most parents were trying to get to know a few of their kids' peer group a little bit. The Jacksons pretty much ignored us. They were too busy making a fuss over Lee. He didn't seem to like it very much—getting attention bothered him—but he didn't squirm as much as he obviously wanted to.

Lee shared a cabin with myself, Matt, and Randy. He had the lower bunk bed closest to the door. The night it happened, it was lights out, and the rest of us were trying to sleep. At least we were at first. Lee was sobbing. He was sitting on the edge of his bed and just sobbed and shook. Matt asked him what was the matter. He didn't say anything.

"Say, Randy," I asked, "what do you think *his* problem is?"

"I dunno. I heard the doctors saying they couldn't figure out what he could do that was special, even though he was born right in the middle of all of us. Maybe—"

"Hey!" Matt exclaimed in a whisper. "Somebody's coming!"

Somebody who had tripped on the steps.

Lee immediately got quiet, and froze completely.

The door opened.

Manny stood in the doorway, waiting. I could smell the alcohol on his breath from my bed.

Lee's tiny hands clinched into fists as he got up and walked toward Manny. He flinched the first time Manny tried to touch him on the shoulder, but did nothing about it the second time.

They walked away.

"What's that all about?" Matt asked.

"I dunno," said Randy. For a know-it-all, he sure was missing a whole lot of scraps of information. "Maybe they're taking him for more tests."

"This late?" I asked.

"Maybe they don't want to be seen. Maybe Lee's embarrassed because he can't do anything special. Maybe that's why he doesn't like that counselor."

"He's not a counselor," I said emphatically. "He's a handyman."

We argued about that for a while, until the inevitable distraction. Even today, I find it difficult to accept how supremely dim we were. Sure we were kids, but we should have known something bad was brewing.

One can imagine all too easily what happened next. Manny escorted Lee to his cabin and put *both* hands on the boy's shoulders. He might have said something like, "Did you miss me? I missed seeing you. Did you miss me?"

And Lee wouldn't have said anything.

"Well?" Manny probably responded. A little angrily. "Say something."

And Lee did finally say something. Probably. He probably said:

"Burn."

And Manny did. His skin burst into flame as if he'd taken a skinny dip into the fires of Hell itself. Within moments—a few painful moments during which he'd screamed uncontrollably—he had burned to a pile of ashes. All that was left of him was his right foot (the sneakers in perfect condition, though the edges of the shoelaces were singed), the ring finger of his left hand, and his teeth. But that wasn't all he left behind. A smoky, ripe stench permeated the room until the grime and soot were cleansed, several days later, from the walls and ceiling. Not to mention the legacy of having been the first murder victim to die as a direct result of his encounter with an irate Special.

In the months to come three other boys stepped forward to recount their victimization by Manny. The authorities figured the sonuvabitch got what he deserved—and if Lee had only shot the guy, he would have had to do some time at your friendly neighborhood asylum, but that would have been it. Lee had, after all, done the world a favor.

Unfortunately, Lee had treated Manny to a case of human spontaneous combustion. He'd done just what Paulson and all the other government creeps guarding mundane human freedoms had been afraid of. He'd done just what they wanted. He'd given them an excuse.

Lee was a tough kid. He might have been afraid, but he kept a cool head. No one knows for sure how long it'd taken for Manny to burn, just as no one knows how Lee slipped past the guards outside the camp perimeter. He must have made it home pretty fast though, because by the time the authorities reached his parents' house, they were long gone.

His folks must have suspected something like this might happen, because they'd obviously been prepared. The automobile registered to Mr. Jackson was left behind, and the family dog had been given to a neighbor the same week camp had begun. The house showed no signs of a hasty departure.

That was the night everything changed. In his autobiography Paulson recounts being in bed with a righteous babe who may or may not have been his wife (he was pretty vague on details about his personal life). She was sleeping with her head on his chest while he heroically smoked a cigarette. The phone rang.

"Yeah. Paulson here."

Beat.

"I see . . . Any sign of the boy? No, no roadblocks yet, but notify the local PD and our people to keep an eye out. Having him loose gives us the justification we've been looking for, but we don't want to get sloppy and miss a chance to recover either."

Another beat. Paulson listened intensely.

"Right. And button down the camp, effective immediately. Nobody gets in or out. Especially out. Set up a meeting for tomorrow morning with the attorney general. Let's get the wheels in motion."

He hung up, and put out his cancer stick. Ms. Babe nuzzled against him sleepily. "Everything okay?"

"Couldn't be better. We got what were hoping for a hell of a lot sooner than we figured. It's true what they say: Patience is its own reward."

"That's good," she said. "Anybody die?"

"Evidently." He lit another cigarette and blew smoke at the moon.

Twenty years passed. Lee spent it with his family on the run, laying low, living underground with the remnants of violent student radical organizations. During that period Lee's parents passed away, and he was on his own. He shouldn't have been. The Feds should have helped him. They should have put out bulletins that they understood he'd been afraid, that he'd been abused by someone he should have been able to trust, that he would have treatment, sure, but that society would have ultimately forgiven him. But that sort of Christian compassion wasn't part of the Nixonian/silent majority agenda. And Lee knew it. During that time, he refrained from using his talent, at least in ways that would have drawn attention to himself.

The next time Lee used his talent, in a public way, it changed things even more.

At camp we could not have guessed what shape our lives would take; the patterns of force that would form our futures were already in motion.

Some of us would embrace what was coming.

Others would deny it, for as long as they could.

Some would become stars. Or comets, burning out all too soon. Or clowns or businessmen or heroes . . .

Or criminals or killers.

The force affected us all in different ways. But we can't blame that for what happened. In the final analysis, our free will was infinitely more free than that of mundane humanity.

We knew each other. Good, bad, or indifferent, we grew up together, knew each others' secret names and hidden faces. There's been a lot written about what happened, and why. Which is why someone has to set the record straight. Someone has to tell their story.

Someone has to speak for the dead.

Throughout our lives, we had been preparing for disaster from outside: from a hostile world, reacting in fear to what we could do. But when the killing came, none of us could have predicted where it would finally come from. We didn't know, could never have guessed, but we should have.

Because like all true evil, it knew our name.

5

CAN'T TOUCH THIS

An old homily would have us believe all people are special, that the uniqueness of each individual contributes to such a wide, wild diversity of human existence that we should rejoice simply because it is so. I'm sure this idea comes as a great comfort to the homeless schizo getting high from crack and booze on the street, or the poor bozo born with something less than the proper allotment of ten toes, ten fingers, two arms, and two legs, not to mention the occasional person who is so butt ugly he, she, and most possibly it couldn't attract a sex partner at a pitch-black orgy. Some people, through no fault of their own, are fated to swim through the algae that lies at the bottom of the gene pool.

Then there's the case of Peter Dawson. Near as I can tell, in his life he accomplished absolutely nothing. His last day on earth did nothing to mitigate that record, however slightly. Walking home from his day job as a security guard at clothing sweatshop, he refrained from smiling at children playing in their front lawn, pretended not to notice a little old lady who needed the door opened for her at the supermarket (where he was making a pit stop for beer), and thought absolutely not at all about his sins and omissions of the past, or how he might make tomorrow a little more interesting or rewarding than today. If he had any regrets, it was that chocolate bars didn't taste as pure and dark as they used to, and Coca-Cola hadn't ever fizzed right since they let the local bottlers assume more control of the ingredients. He'd stopped wishing he had someone to come home to a long time ago.

"When did he die?" Dr. William Welles asked.

"Between ten and eleven last night," said the small town police officer. "You sure he's one of *them?*"

"He's one," said Dr. Welles. He was sitting in his kitchen, looking down at the papers the police officer—call him Officer #1—had pulled from a drawer and left lying around. "Only the 113 who were affected by the Flash were given identity bracelets like this."

The bracelet was silver, rectangular in shape, and was marked with a bas-relief of an exploding celestial object of indeterminate nature. Of course, it was what was inside the bracelet that was significant.

"You say that there badge has a humming device in it?" asked Officer #1.

"That's a *homing* device. Any member of the group who leaves Pederson has to wear it, so we can track their movements, make sure they check in with the local authorities."

"Yeah, that's what the chief said when we found that on the body. He called the 800 number and punched his way through the phone tree until the computer told him to contact you," said Officer #2. "So here we are."

Dr. Welles cocked an eyebrow. Officer #2 was paying

a lot of attention to the photographs on the kitchen wall. Photographs of Flagg, Ravenshadow, Matthew Bright, etc. Photographs of people who meant a lot to Dr. Welles. "Is there something you're curious about?" he asked, in friendly tones.

"Do you know Flagg? And Chandra?" Officer #2, eagerly. "Oh, man . . . did you see Chandra on TV the other night? She's gorgeous. You ask me, she's the most gorgeous woman in the world."

Welles couldn't help shaking his head. "Everybody says that. Hell, *I* even say it. Because that's what she is: The most beautiful woman in the world, to everyone who sees her, regardless of the medium. It's her gift." Beat. "And sometimes, I think, her curse."

"Do you think she's really that beautiful?" asked Officer #2. "Or is it just an illusion perpetrated by the force?"

Dr. Welles shrugged. "Doesn't matter. All I can say is, if we tried to judge her as objectively as a champion at a dog show, she has a lot of points."

"I don't get it," said Officer #1. "If this Dawson guy was one of the Specials, how come I never heard of him before?"

Again, Welles shrugged. "Most people aren't familiar with *all* the Specials. And frankly, a lot of them don't make good copy in the supermarket magazines. I'm afraid Peter was one of those."

"Where do you fit in with all this?" asked Officer #1. "Your chief didn't really prepare you for this interview, did he?"

Officer #1 wiped his brow sheepishly. "One or two things might have slipped his mind."

Welles smiled. This man might not appreciate having

it pointed out that he wasn't up to speed on this assignment, but in his favor he refused to blame it on his superior officer. "I came in near the beginning," Welles said. " Or at least as close as anyone ever got to the beginning." Beat. "Aren't you going to ask why you haven't heard of me?"

"You keep a low profile?" asked Officer #2.

"To a degree. Plus, Paulson and his crew do a pretty subtle job of dissuading reporters and gossip columnists alike from revealing personal data about government employees when it comes to writing about how the Feds have dealt with the various dilemmas posed by the Specials down through the years. And personal profiles are downright discouraged."

"I don't like reporters very much," said Officer #1.

"We think they're a menace to society," said Officer #2.

"It's probably a good thing," Welles said. "If any one of them had asked me, I might have let it slip that while, sure, I was motivated by a sense of altruism and my fundamental decency, a part of me was equally motivated by a desire to make a mark in the history of my profession. Not just to do well and be successful, financially and otherwise, but to ensure my name would forever be associated with a conceptual breakthrough that would make those of Freud and Jung seem like high school term papers in comparison. Call me egotistical if you will, it was still my dream."

"Does seem a little extravagant," said Officer #1, sitting down and crossing his legs. He had helped himself to some coffee.

Welles nodded. "The parents of the affected kids had gone to court to keep the government from taking their kids away. Times were turbulent. Public opinion was divided—people got angry over the Lee Jackson case, just like they got angry over differences of opinion regarding the Vietnam War or civil rights. There were demonstrations, and arguments, even among friends, occasionally became so violent district attorneys had no choice but to charge the survivor with involuntary manslaughter. The parents' case was going all the way to the Supreme Court, fast-tracked by the immediate need for a resolution while the kids were still, well, kids.

"I was a pediatric MD in New York back then," Welles said. "Even then, I was more interested in child psychology than just doing straight general practitioner work, so I like to believe I followed the case with a little more passion than most who were merely curious and/or afraid. I was as surprised as everybody else—and by everybody else I mean the entire planet—when the Court decided that certain parental rights could not be curtailed until it could be determined whether or not the kid in question posed a clear and present danger to the community. Well, they closed down Camp Sunshine in an instant, and had the politicians scrambling for cover. The Ford campaign kept alluding to the Lee Jackson case, while Jimmy Carter kept harping on Ben Franklin's old quote about how those who give up freedom for temporary security deserve neither. The Representatives and Senators running for reelection were falling all over themselves trying to introduce bills that showed, if nothing else, they were ready to move on to safer topics. Nothing passed, that I recall. Luckily for all concerned, the Court had no problem providing a few practical guidelines. The children's mental health was to be monitored at all times by a mutually-agreed on physician.

'Agreed on by whom?' you might ask. I think the administration, a few Congressional committees, and the Armed Forces. The parents had no say-so on *that* matter. Naturally I applied for the job."

"I remember," said Officer #2. "I did read something about you once. In *Newsweek*."

"But you noticed, no pictures. I'd done a fair amount of work for the government on child welfare cases, sometimes even *pro bono*, for the benefit of the families involved. That had given me the reputation of sticking my nose into other people's business occasionally, and that of a troublemaker who didn't mind getting into a bureaucrat's face when it was necessary. I figured my name would probably come up in the discussions, but I never thought I'd actually get the assignment.

"I guess that just goes to show you how wrong a guy can be sometimes. Turns out the Feds needed someone who had a rep as a child advocate, not because they wanted a pain-in-the-ass on the job, but for political reasons, to mollify the pundits and critics. I'll never forget the day the FBI agents arrived at my office to take me to my appointment. I was checking this girl's ear infection and they just showed up like the men in black, ready to whisk me away to another planet. They scared the bejeezus out of the girl . . ."

"Were you afraid, Doc?" asked Officer #1, dipping a cocoa wafer stick into his coffee.

"On one hand, I was looking forward to the job. And on the other hand, yeah, I was afraid of it. These kids were unlike any in history, they were living embodiments of daydreams and nightmares. Whatever force had affected the children of Pederson, I wanted to understand it. I wanted to help them adjust to life in a world of people like us—"

"You mean mundanes?" asked Officer #2.

"Sure, that's what the Specials call normals behind our backs, but they're just as human as we are, and are prone to all the traits we associate with humanity: trust, reverence, fear, an ability to love—"

"And a capacity to kill, isn't that right, Doc?" asked Officer #1.

That brought Welles up short. He nodded half-heartedly, then looked down at Peter's ID bracelet. At the picture of Peter. Poor, overweight, broken-down Peter. Being a Special had been in the final analysis the only unique thing about him. Other than that, he had been a totally average individual. If you'd subtracted his powers, somehow, from his life, that blandness would not have hindered him. Indeed, it would have enabled him to at least find a measure of contentment in the mere fact of his consummate mundaneness. But the addition of his powers to his personal equation created the formula for a personal tragedy of Chekovian proportions. His loss was no big deal in the grand scheme of things. Even so—

"But I also knew that part of my job would be to betray them to the government if I ever concluded they posed a threat to public safety," Welles added. "And to determine how they could be stopped, if it ever came to that. I have adhered to that part of the bargain I've made with my employers, and have always held my duty to my country first.

"That said, I've tried to be a father figure to the Specials, each and every one. Naturally that endeavor has succeeded more with some Specials than with others. You have to understand. When I first got to the school the government had been forced to hastily construct in the aftermath of the Supreme Court decision, I found 113 children who were vulnerable. Scared. And totally alone.

"But most of all, they were amazing."

"I've always followed the exploits of the Specials," said Officer #1. "I guess you can say I'm a fan."

"I've always wondered what it would be like to meet one," said Officer #2.

"Well, I've never wondered what it would be like to investigate a crime scene involving one," said Dr. Welles. "I suppose it had to happen someday—"

"You mean Peter Dawson being murdered?" Officer #1.

"No, absolutely not. Please do not misconstrue me. I did not mean Peter Dawson specifically. Indeed, he was too ineffectual a personality for anyone to work up a grudge against him. In *my* opinion. I did mean, though, that I always feared a Special would be a murder victim someday. Just didn't expect it to be Peter."

"Well, who did you suspect it might be?" asked Officer #1.

"You still don't understand. I was only speculating. Idly."

"I do understand. I want you to speculate. I want you to remember your duty to your country. "

"I speculated about any of them. Or all of them."

"Wonderful. Think anyone could help us?"

Welles thought about it.

"What about Dreamer?" asked Officer #1.

"Lionel Zerb?" asked Welles. "Good question. He can see the residual energy left behind by the recently dead. He found them far more interesting those than of us who were still alive." Welles laughed to himself. "At first we thought he was just distantly daydreaming, but he was listening to voices none of us could hear, emanating from a plane of existence we could not imagine. We can easily imagine it today. I'm afraid my colleagues and I lacked imagination in the beginning. I certainly didn't conceive of a Special who could alter society's concept of the metaphysical while doing only what came naturally to him."

"Think he could help us with this investigation?"

Welles shrugged. "You'll have to ask him. His ability never struck me as being consistent. I don't recall his ever being able to summon someone at will. The spirits of the dead came to him, when *they* willed."

"How did he deal with it?" asked Officer #2. "I mean, mentally."

"Well. Which is not to say the powers of some Specials didn't lead them down sick or twisted, or even just perverse paths. Patrick Ferry could virtually disappear into the shadows, walk anywhere he wanted without being noticed. Of course, the trouble with Patrick was his lack of vision."

"You mean he liked to visit the girls' locker room?" asked Officer #2.

"Yes, how did you know?"

"Because if I was an emotionally healthy 12 year old and could go anywhere I wanted, I'd go there. It's like that movie, *Carrie*. Opens with a vicarious experience. The males in the audience are peeking into the most taboo, yet most enticing place they'd ever want to visit."

"Unfortunately," said Welles, "Pat was programmed to be emotionally immature and never get over his initial—"

"Stick to the subject guys!" said Officer #1.

"It's all right," said Welles, offering #1 another cocoa

wafer stick. He had long since reconciled with his tendency not to stop talking once he got going on the Specials. "You should know that Pat was also inclined toward self-sabotage. He couldn't keep his mouth shut about his exploits. That's when Matt—or was it Jason?—suggested to the girls to redesign the lighting so there were no shadows for him to hide in. Then they brutalized him, somewhat. It was only natural."

"So did you always suspect those two would be superheroes?" asked #2, with genuine curiosity.

Welles recognized the type: a fan-boy, someone who lived so vicariously through his fantasies and hero worship that he was in danger of losing his own moorings in the world. A lot of Specials fans had positions of authority. "No, but I should have. Nor were Matt and Jason the first to indicate the superhero direction was a possibility. Randy Fisk—you may know him today as 'Ravenshadow'—was truly the first. One day out of the blue, he put on what I now recognize as a prototypical version of his current costume, and climbed up on a roof and wouldn't come down. Today his costume arouses fear in some; on that first day, it just looked . . . childish." Welles chuckled. "He said he was on patrol. I must admit, his motivation came as a surprise. I should have known, though. A lot of the kids read comics. The characters provided the young Specials with role models. *Validating* role models."

"So they always knew—" said #2.

"Knew what?" asked Welles.

"Their direction. Who they would be. I didn't know I was going to be a cop until I was 19. If I'd known when I was—"

"Aw, for Christ's sake!" said #1. "You're not going to go all weepy on me again?"

"It's all right!" protested #2. "I took my anti-depressants!"

"Knowing, or even strongly suspecting the direction you're life is going take from the age of six robs the adolescent years of much-needed creative surprise," said Welles. "Poor Willie. Poor, lost picked-upon Willie. He was a pathetic case. Never had a chance. He knew he never would, too. To be the runt of the litter forever. That was his fate. His direction in life: to be a runt."

"Who's Willie?" asked #1, interested despite himself.

"One of the many you didn't hear about," Welles replied, showing the officer a printout of a scan of an old Polaroid one of the kids had taken of Willie as he . . . bugged out.

"He floated away?" #1 inquired.

"Like a balloon. No one ever saw him come down."

Officer #2 whistled. "That's rough."

"What you have to understand about the Specials is that most of them just wanted to live quiet, ordinary lives, didn't want the spotlight. Of course that's impossible, the Feds and social columnists see to that, not to mention their own innate celebrity. But the dream lives on."

"What about the heroes—?" asked #1.

"And the villains?" asked #2.

"I prefer to think of them as the heroes and the ones who didn't turn out quite right. Sanctuary . . . Matthew Bright . . . Flagg . . . Pyre . . . Paula Ramirez . . ."

"What about this Dawson fellow?" asked #2. "What was his power?"

"Peter Dawson is—was—invulnerable. "

"Waitaminnit!" exclaimed #2. "You're saying nothing could hurt this guy? Nothing?"

"I saw a butcher knife in his kitchen," said #1. "It looked like someone had punched a hole in it."

"As if it had been perforated," said Welles. "I understand. He'd probably been slicing a piece of fruit. A mundane man would have cut his finger off."

"You've seen it before?" said #2.

"A few times. In Peter's case, the energy formed an invisible protective shield that covered his skin and lined the inside of his lungs and stomach. It was selectively permeable at the molecular level, letting in oxygen, for instance, but repelling anything toxic. Peter couldn't be cut, stabbed, shot, poisoned, or gassed."

"Didn't stop him from being killed," said #1.

"Jeez, what I would give anyway for that power," said #2. "Can you imagine the sort of cop I'd make?"'

"An invulnerable Keystone cop, I'd bet." said #1.

"You're envious of Peter now, Officer," said Welles, turning on the gas stove to boil more water for coffee. "Nothing could hurt Peter because nothing could get through the energy shield. He couldn't feel knives, or bullets, or broken glass, or nails. My colleagues and I once watched him hold his hand over the flame of an open candle for 30 minutes, and his skin wasn't even blistered. In fact, he only stopped because he got bored with the experiment."

"See what I mean?" said #2. "That'd be great!"

"Except that he couldn't feel anything else, either. He couldn't feel warmth or cold, or the touch of another person's hand. He was totally numb from head to toe."

"Must have made for some lousy dates," remarked #1.

"What about his own hand?" asked #2. "Could he feel *that?*"

"Very funny," said Welles, not meaning it.

"That isn't possible!" exclaimed #1.

"There's a surgical procedure for dealing with chronic pain that involves severing the spinal nerve that carries the pain impulse," said Welles patiently. This wasn't the first time he'd had this particular conversation. "But the nerve bundle also carries touch and sensation. Imagine going through life unable to feel anything. Ever. That's what life was like for Peter Dawson.

"With one exception.

"The process of salivation and chemical exchange at the molecular level during eating meant he could taste what he ate. Taste was the only sensation he could have. So he ate. He ate all the time."

"That explains a lot of what we found at the crime scene," said #1.

"Empty containers for food were all over the place, just casually thrown away in every room," said #2. "And the bathroom was a hygienic disaster area! Someone should have called the Health Department."

"What difference did it make if he cleaned up after himself or not?" asked #1, rhetorically. "Germs couldn't kill him."

"I see you're picking up on the situation fast," said Dr. Welles, pouring the officers some fresh coffee. "I'll be glad to help you in your investigation, if I can, but so far you've withheld one valuable piece of information. I would very much like to know how Peter died. You sure it wasn't natural causes?"

The policemen stared at one another. Their look said it all, but #1 removed all possible doubt from the doctor's mind with the simple statement: "We're sure."

"I don't get it!" exclaimed #2. "If this guy was invulnerable, if he really was a Special, what was he doing working at a service station? And living in a place like that? I mean, with his kind of power, he could write his own ticket."

Dr. Welles couldn't resist a smile, even though he feared it would be misconstrued as condescending. "You'd think that, wouldn't you? When Peter was in high school, he was practically drafted onto the football team. What more could a coach ask for than a linebacker who was invulnerable? In theory, it sounds like having the Rock of Gibraltar on the scrimmage line. But that wasn't the reality.

"I knew Peter was in trouble the moment I saw him run out on the football field for the first time. It was a junior varsity game, the first of the season, in fact. Peter had only joined the team the week before and so was sitting on the bench waiting for the Coach to put him in the game as a substitute, as he'd been promised. I suppose both Peter and the Coach felt his abilities, which I'm certain they kept secret from the refs and the opposing team, might present the home team with a couple of advantages.

"It was the fourth quarter, the home team was down by four points, and a first string linebacker had just gotten the bejeezus whacked out of him when the Coach sent Peter in. Anyone with half a brain could see Peter was out of his league—no pun intended. His knees hit his gut with every step, he nearly stumbled over his shoelaces, and once he got into position, he was lost in the shadows of the opposing team. Turns out the force didn't make him stronger or faster than average. The force just ensured that he wouldn't get hurt when the other side rolled him over.

"Which they did. They shoved him aside like he was a giant Nerf ball." Welles shook his head at the memory. "Peter hit the ground so hard he dented it. The Coach was so ashamed of him he sent him to the stands to sit. Said he didn't deserve to be seen on the same bench as the rest of the boys. Then, when he figured Peter had simmered in humiliation and anger long enough, he sent Peter in for another play. And you know what happened?"

"Peter got the crap knocked out of him," said Officer #1. "Good coffee, by the way."

"Thanks. And you're absolutely correct. Peter's football days were over before they'd even begun. Sadly, that incident can now be seen as a serious trend setter in Peter's life. When he got older he tried to enter law enforcement, starting with the Secret Service. His status as a Special was one factor against him, to be sure, and the fact that he was out of shape didn't help, but the main thing—starting with the Secret Service and going all the way down the line to security guard at a mini-mall or baggage inspector at your local airport—was his supreme lack of talent. There was simply no compelling reason for anyone to hire him in a position of even minimal authority."

"How did he do in college?" asked Officer #1.

"Well, he flunked out."

#2 laughed. "Well, that wasn't going to help him with the FBI."

"Even if his education or lack of one hadn't been an issue, let's just say Peter always had certain problems with authority figures."

"Was he prone to violence?" asked #1.

"Only when he hit someone. He didn't have a lot of strength, but the combination of his weight and his invulnerable skin made for quite a wallop."

"Why didn't he try boxing?" asked #2 slyly.

Welles raised his eyebrows, as if to express disbelief the man asked a question with such an obvious answer. "That wouldn't have been exactly a fair fight. Sure, Peter couldn't be knocked out, but in order to knock out his opponent, he'd have to catch 'em first. And Peter was so out of shape that he couldn't last a round before getting exhausted. But that didn't mean Peter wasn't a dreamer. He took one blue-collar job after another, always waiting for the big break he was certain was bound to happen at any time. The closest he ever came was a commercial spot for an insurance company here in Pederson."

"I saw that!" said #2. "That was him?"

"It was spectacular, in its way," said the doctor. "Holding those live cables, being showered by electrical sparks. He even got to make the pitch: he was invulnerable, but for everyone who wasn't, there was Pederson Prudential, serving southern Illinois for over 20 years.

"The night the commercial debuted, he hired an agent, a manager, a publicist, companions for the night, and waited for the job offers to start coming in from Hollywood. But there were two problems. He was no Chandra, to say the least. If on a scale from one to ten, she's an eleven, then Peter was a minus eight. Second, there was his profound lack of performing ability.

"After that, he left town to find opportunities elsewhere. That's the last I heard of him."

"He never tried to contact you?" asked #1.

"After the Specials turned 21, they were no longer

required to participate in sessions. If, as you say, Peter wound up working at a service station, I'd say he found his proper metier in life. Sounds like he'd finally accepted the fact that putting 'Nothing can hurt me' on your job resume doesn't do much to expand your career opportunities. Now, I've told you everything I know. In return, you have to tell me something. I can't say I was fond of Peter—he tended not to arouse feelings of warmth or animosity, except when he hit someone—but his life was still stolen from him. I'd like very much to know what you've been keeping from the media."

"What's that, Doctor?" asked #1.

"I want to know how he was murdered."

#1 rubbed his chin; he was collecting his thoughts. "Well, seems that Dawson had pulled a few consecutive shifts and got home that night exhausted. He was having a brewski when he fell asleep in his chair. He must have woken up sometime during the process of his murder, but by then it was already too late. His arms and legs had been taped to the chair. He couldn't move no matter how hard he tried. And he couldn't breathe, either. Because someone had slipped a plastic bag over his head—"

"And he hadn't felt it, hadn't known it was there until he'd woken up," said Dr. Welles.

"That's right," said #2. "He couldn't be stabbed or poisoned or shot. But he needed air, just like everybody else. And that's how he was murdered. An invulnerable man, suffocated to death with a plastic bag, something that shouldn't be a danger to anyone over five years old."

"You okay, Doc?" #1 asked.

"You look like you've seen a ghost," said #2.

Welles paused and took a breath. "I'm all right. It's just I hadn't expected him to go that particular way, even though I . . ." He trailed off, and stared out into space, which in his case ended at a corner in the ceiling.

"Didn't a Special die in a car accident a few weeks ago?" asked Officer #1.

"What's that supposed to mean—?" said Welles.

"Just answer the question."

"Yes, come to think of it: Joseph Drake. He had the ability to alter the humidity in the atmosphere."

"Pretty useless power, if you ask me," said #2.

"You wouldn't feel so sure," said the doctor, "if you faced him in a game of table tennis. He could make an air conditioned room feel like New Orleans in the summertime. Had to get him to swear to stop, but I've always suspected that when the stakes got too high, he acted subtly to tire his opponent and rob him of his stamina. Say, you're not implying—"

"The FBI is examining the brakes, even as we speak."

"My God, he was living in the Seattle area, where a man with his powers could help certain controlled substances grow in the winter. Obviously he could have been dealing with some bad people."

"Obviously," said #1.

"Could have been," said #2.

"You suspect the deaths of Peter and Joseph are connected?"

The two policemen shrugged and looked one another in the eye. Then they shrugged again.

"Gentlemen," said Welles, "I am not privy to your silent language."

"Maybe," said #1.

"Possibly," said #2. "Who can say—yet?"

"May we ask you one more question before we go?" asked #1.

"Please," said Welles.

"You said part of your job was to figure out how they could be stopped 'if it ever came to that.' Could you define 'stopped'?"

"I think you know what it means, officer. I don't have to spell it out for you."

"Terminated?" said #2. "He means 'terminated,' doesn't he?"

"Yes," said the doctor, with a distinct lack of feeling.

"You knew," said #1. "You *knew* how he could be killed."

"Depriving him of oxygen was one of several ways. And it's true, I thought of that all by myself. It was in my report to the Court. We had to know their strengths and their vulnerabilities."

"In case they turned into dangerous characters," said #1.

"The information is highly classified," said the doctor. "And it's doled out strictly on a need-to-know basis."

"Where were *you* last night, around 10:00?" asked #2.

Welles cocked an eyebrow. "At my office. Finishing some paperwork."

"Anyone see you there?" asked #2.

"Not that I know of."

"Anything happen recently to make you think Peter Dawson was dangerous?"

"Absolutely not."

The officers walked to the door. "Thank you, Dr. Welles," said #1. "We'll be in touch."

"Great coffee," said #2.

"Not a problem, officers," said Welles.

*   *   *

That's where I come in. I'm still John Simon, the narrator of this journal. I was watching the whole scene on a videotape the doctor had made with one of the hidden cameras installed in his home. I kept remembering a story Piper Laurie told about watching *The Color of Money*, a sequel (made long after the first) to the movie *The Hustler*. Her character committed suicide in the first film, and throughout the presentation of the second, Laurie felt like she was watching something the laws of God and Man normally wouldn't permit her to witness. That's pretty much how I was feeling when Dr. Welles switched off the VCR.

"I can't count how many times these cameras have come in handy," he said.

"You must be kidding," I said. "Do you have some voyeuristic impulse I don't know anything about?"

"No. I am merely a man who has good reason to be suspicious of his government."

"And I am a man who long ago learned to be suspicious of surveillance equipment and all those who depend upon it, both for freedom and security," I said.

"Since you're actively investigating these killings, I thought you'd want to see the tape before—"

"—You edited out the last part of the conversation."

Dr. Welles looked like he'd been pole-axed. "How did you—?"

"I'm sensitive to all kind of electrical impulse. Scanning lines, changing phosphors . . . You made a cut in there. Why?"

"They asked me if there was a Special they might have overlooked who I would consider potentially dangerous— indeed, the most dangerous of all—"

"And you gave them my name."

71

His aura of resoluteness disappeared, and he briefly looked ashamed. "Yes."

"What else did you tell them?"

"That you were a writer and a poet. They weren't impressed, which I guess means they have something in common with *The New York Review of Books*."

That stung. My last serious book had been trashed by William Kristol from the right, and Marc Cooper from the left. The content had been a reflection of my efforts to create a metaphysically sound environmental policy for the human race. I have the feeling both gentlemen mistook my premises as fringe philosophy.

"You know what I mean, Doc. Did you tell them what I could do?"

"No more or less than what I've told others. Just generalities." He did not flinch when I looked him in the eye. "Your main power, the one for which you might be terminated, is still secret, John."

I held up the tape. It needed to be rewound. "Can I take this with me?" Not that he could have stopped me.

"Of course," Doc said. "You understand I had to tell them about you. There's much at stake for me to arouse suspicions toward myself unnecessarily. Someone's killing the Specials. We have to find out who, and, maybe just as important, why."

"You've always been fair and honest with us, Doc. You've always tried to protect us from the outside, and from each other. Now it's my turn. I'll find out who's doing this."

"Then what?" Welles asked, a little slow on the uptake.

"I'll stop him. Any way I have to."

* * *

My visit with Dr. Welles confirmed my worst suspicions.

First, that toward the end Peter lived the loneliest kind of life. He had become a fatality on the crash site of his most cherished dreams long before he was murdered. It was too bad. He had been a sweet kid who'd never hurt anybody. Though impervious to pain, he'd actually squirm at the sight of blood, and cried whenever anyone got hurt severely. It galled me he had been denied any chance at redemption.

Second, that the killer was one of us. Back in the Camp Sunshine days, we talked about how our abilities could be thwarted, as it were, when the adults weren't around. The adults disapproved of such discussions, but they must have known we'd be curious about the limitations of our varied abilities, what we could use them for, and how we might be despite them. We weren't above irony, and often the talk degenerated from a serious discussion to an exercise in imaginative and cruelly ironic scenarios. Renee might walk into a truck while avoiding an oncoming wagon train that was actually part of a vision, or Randy might be shot by a stray bullet while ducking for cover in the shadows of a bank being robbed, or Constance, who could cast temporary "love spells" on others, would fall in love with the wrong man who would stalk her and then kill her, just like a character in a movie. We were a sick bunch, but I suppose every group of kids has its phases. For us, it was a way of defining ourselves, to speculate on exactly what it meant to be a Special.

We also attempted to imitate newly discovered abilities whenever possible—whenever possible being defined as those occasions when the power in question didn't appear too dangerous, or too gross. We tried not to anticipate abilities. The process was too random, too unpredictable. We enjoyed using our imaginations, but there seemed no point turning our minds in that direction. So when Matt discovered he could fly, it was the first time it had occurred to any of us that maybe we'd be able to fly. Practically everyone—save for the most sullen and withdrawn—tried to fly, by jumping out of trees or taking high, risky leaps off the taller diving board at the swimming pool. The medics were fit to be tied that day. As soon as they set one limb, another kid would make another jump, perhaps even the identical jump, with similar results.

Of course, the ability to defy gravity did come to some of the others, but at its own speed, in its own time. Nothing we could do could accelerate the process.

The revelation of Peter's invulnerability—which came, innocently enough, while a nurse was trying to give him a flu shot—inspired the guys to try various stunts, such as holding our hands over a flame or knocking down a wasp nests, to see if we too might be impervious to harm. We weren't so eager a few weeks later, when the downside of Peter's ability was becoming apparent, but for a few days, we daydreamed like crazy.

Oddly, none of the girls tested themselves for invulnerability. They avoided the slightest roughhouse, as if the very concept of invulnerability had aroused an instinctive fear or revulsion. Strangely, Dr. Welles, the one guy I always thought knew the most about the most of us, had no idea why this had been so. In that regard he was as clueless as I was.

The point of all this was we all knew what Peter could do, and what he couldn't do, and perhaps even then some of us had figured out how he could be killed. I must confess, most of us were curious about what would happen, for instance, if a fully-grown Matt and Joshua got into a fight to the death. Who would win? Not that the answer was ever the same. The pendulum kept swinging back and forth.

In any case, we knew some of us would go bad. The laws of science didn't apply to us, so why, the reasoning went, should the laws of God and Man?

We could do as we pleased. Those of us who chose to be righteous, or to have a conscience, or to follow the Golden Rule simply because it was the logical thing to do, knew as well as anyone the importance of the struggle not to test the limits of societal authority. It was a struggle at times difficult to win. And we knew some of us lacked the intellectual or moral fortitude to resist the temptation to stray from the straight and narrow.

Dr. Welles' tape had convinced me that one of us was hunting down the rest. Putting those late-night bull sessions to good use at last.

That's assuming we are talking about just one person. But so far there's no evidence to support the theory we're dealing with more than one person.

Besides, I don't want to contemplate the alternative.

The question now is who, and why?

Followed shortly by, *Who's next?*

6

WHY CAN'T I BE YOU?

John Lennon said that life is what happens to you while you make other plans. Robert E. Howard once wrote words to the effect that man's predilection for war and violence would never end, not while the race the stands. And Raymond Chandler said that down these mean streets a man must walk ...

Things had fallen apart, the center would not hold, and it was up to me to find out why and then do what I had to do to restore order in the world.

Needless to say, I resented it. As the consummate outsider in a family of outsiders, I hardly relished the prospect of dealing with most of these people, who just happened to be my brothers and sisters in the symbolic sense, but I had a job to do, and I had taken the responsibility to heart.

But why? Could I bring myself to admit that I loved my fellow Specials, their virtues and flaws equally, as I might have loved a real brother or sister?

I was about to find out. Peter Dawson's funeral was being held today. In a couple of hours, in fact. I wasn't in much of a hurry. The C.F. Kane Funeral Home was at least sixty miles away, and I was barely pushing my beat-up old Mustang to fifty. The other trucks and automobiles on the highway were racing past me like roadrunners, but I confess, I hardly noticed. I was too busy listening to tape number four of an abridgement of John Rhys-Davies reading *The Rise and Fall of the Roman Empire*. It was a most illuminating experience, especially when weighed against my previous conception of Julius Caesar, defined by the preppie conqueror portrayed on *Xena, Warrior Princess*.

But my spirit weighed me down. The soaring vision of decaying empires, personal decadence, brutish barbarians, and bad government compounded by a poor sense of real politic was crashing under the onslaught of the incontestable fact that one of my contemporaries had died. Yet, for some reason, instead of feeling sad, I felt merely numb.

The day was beautiful, however. Reasoning that it would be easier be remain alone and relatively anonymous in a city, I'd moved to Chicago a few years ago and hadn't spent much time in the rural USA. I'd shut myself off from nature, didn't even go to the parks. Yet today I realized I'd been missing something. The sun was bright and proud, the sky blue and rich, and the lush green fields of grass (some populated with cattle) somehow engendered the feeling, despite all evidence to the contrary, that the world was a safe haven for the noblest hopes and dreams of mankind.

The pungent odor of fresh fertilizer emanating from the fields only added to the illusion of tranquility.

Like all illusions, it proved short-lived. Buildings—farmhouses, barns, storage units—began punctuating the landscape with ever-increasing frequency, reminding me that where the human race was concerned, the concept of tranquility was indeed an illusion. The plains upon which the interstate had been laid gave way to hills and a series of streams that converged several miles to the east. I drove over a series of bridges and ramps. Up ahead, atop the highest hill, a silhouette became visible. I passed a gas station, a public pit stop, a few fast food joints, and some cheap motels that offered vicarious adult entertainment. Presumably actual adult entertainment wasn't too far away, for the discrete debaucher.

The silhouette acquired dimension and began to take the form of the Ravenshadow Castle, which to my way of thinking resembled the Disney Fantasyland castle as designed by an architect on acid. The towers were twisted like candle wax, and the ramparts appeared to have been liquefied during an earthquake. The hill it stood on, I recalled, was artificial, the better to announce the presence of the Pederson Amusement Park, which capitalized on its Special history as much as possible, even to the extent of hiring a handful of Specials to perform for the rubes.

Hmmm. One wonders why Peter Dawson hadn't gotten a job there? The work certainly wouldn't have been as difficult as that which he'd chosen for himself (or which fate had chosen for him), and as I'd known before watching Dr. Welles' tape, he'd demonstrated some interest in show business before. Perhaps it had been a question of what he'd perceived as his dignity . . .

Be that as it may, I was hungry, thirsty, and had to pee. I took an off-ramp and pulled over at a gas station with a mini-mart. As I got out of the car, I noticed a sudden drop in the temperature. Several dark clouds were rolling in from the horizon. I saw a distant flash of light-ning. Even so, it was still possible the coming rain would pass Pederson by.

I didn't mind; it gave me an excuse to put on my duster. Although I liked to think of myself as a modest individual, I had to admit I was vain about my appear-ance. I wasn't the only Special who felt uncomfortable out of my personally designed uniform, as if having super-powers somehow forced one to tap into the racial memory of modern culture, to fulfill certain social expectations.

My personal uniform consisted of my long, dark duster, a generic pair of black boots, black jeans, and a black sweat-shirt with a large white emblem that covered most of the front. (I had several duplicates at home.) I checked out my long black hair via my reflection in the front window. Couldn't be too obvious about it, but I had to admit, I approved of the Byronic, melancholy air I deliberately cultivated.

I walked inside, past the punked-out Gen X'er girl sta-tioned at the counter. I only glanced at her, but she took me in like a samurai watching a sunrise. "Hey!" she said just as I walked into the men's room. I ignored her.

When I left the men's room, she said again, "Hey!"

I walked to the racks of potato chips before I turned my head and arched an eyebrow by way of answer.

"Do you really have to wear that in here?"

"Don't worry, I won't shoplift."

She looked at the security monitor. I wasn't there, though the bag of chips I held was, hanging in mid-air. She gasped. "I know you." She pulled from beneath the counter last week's issue of *People*, the one with a few pictures of Peter Dawson at different stages of his life on the cover. She flipped through the pages till she came to the section with my picture in it. She looked at me, she tapped the finger on the picture. "You're John Simon. The one they call Poet!"

Somewhat crestfallen, I nodded and sighed. Although I'd allowed few photographs to be taken of me down through the years, it seemed the media, whenever they'd seen to use one, always selected the least flattering. *People* had chosen one that made me look like I'd just fallen off the slab.

"Is it true what they say here?" she asked. "That your favorite book is this thing called *The Outsider* by Colin Wilson and your favorite movie is *The Amazing Doctor Clitterhouse* starring Edgar G. Robinson? Never heard of either."

"Each in its unique fashion deals with the relationship between the individual and a society to which he may not be a part."

"I don't believe you. I think you're just trying to be as obscure as possible so you'll impress us with your arcane knowledge." Before I could defend myself, she added, "Is it true what they say here in the personal statistics category, that when it comes to the opposite—or to *either* sex, that you're unobtainable?"

"Sorry, I don't believe my personal life is anybody's business. They jumped to their own conclusions."

"Of course a celebrity's personal life isn't anybody's business. That's what makes it so interesting." She winked.

"I'm not a celebrity."

"Oh please! You're a celebrity, you know it and you like it; otherwise you wouldn't be trying to perpetuate your fame by writing these books. None of which I've read by the way, nor am I in any danger of doing so."

"Well!" I felt the blood warming my face. She'd struck too close to home.

Her grin took the sting out her words. I try not to notice these things, because it makes it that much more difficult to resist temptation, but she *was* attractive. Her shaggy bleached hair, the array of silver studs above her left eyebrow, her white tank top, against her light brown skin, sweet face and tomboyish-yet-killer body, weren't exactly mainstream, but neither was I. She emanated raging pheromones that targeted me like a smart missile.

"Listen to me, John Simon," she said as she rang up my sale. "The fact that you've sidelined yourself in the war of the sexes is more than a waste, it's a goddamned tragedy."

Now I was really blushing. "Are you always this forward?"

"Are you always this dense? Look, why don't you take me out to dinner tonight? With no . . . expectations. Who knows? You might even relax for a second."

"I'm sorry, ma'am, I have previous obligations," I said as she gave me my change.

"If you change your mind," she replied firmly, "then you know where to find me."

"I guess I do."

"Maybe instead of choosing to be a writer, you should have been a Catholic priest," she said as I left, firing another disarming smile.

A few miles down the road I pulled over at a road stop, smoked a cigarette, and tried to get my heart to stop pounding. There were reasons why I had to be a solitary man, as Neil Diamond phrased it, reasons I could confide to no one. Or was I simply fundamentally shy when it came to matters of personal intimacy? Unfortunately, the question of shyness was ultimately immaterial. I couldn't change a thing. I could only wonder how much of it was due to choice.

Suddenly the prospect of attending a funeral appealed to me about as much as choking myself to death with my own intestines. I realized I had something else to do.

Dad sat in the rocking chair on the front porch of his unpainted country shack. He didn't see me driving up the dirt road because he was too busy being passed out.

I got out of the car and slammed the door really loud. He stayed asleep. Or worse. I figured if he was dead, then at least he died with his best friend by his side—a bottle of Jack Daniel's.

I knelt beside him on the porch. The smell of vomit was on his T-shirt. He was even more bloated and red-faced than I recalled. His hair was whiter and his beard longer, much longer.

He started to snore. Just looking at him made me angry. For him, sleeping in an alcoholic funk was business as usual, like taking a sleeping pill. How could I not regard him with contempt? Yet I couldn't help pitying him. Falstaff on his pauper's deathbed had had more dignity.

Of course, Dad still had a few years left to live, unless his liver staged a shut down. I grabbed his shoulder, hard. He started giggling and tried to slap my hand away. "Cyn—stop it—" he said. "You know I can't resist you when you bite me there—"

He opened his eyes, yelped, and jumped out of the chair. "Holy cow! Son! Why—why didn't you—?" Then he realized what he'd said and turned beet red.

Cynthia was my mother's name. I stood there, glowering at him.

Then he laughed. "Sorry, I realize it's embarrassing for children to visualize the exact process that got them into this world. But the fact remains, John, as difficult as it may be for you to believe, there was a time when your mother and I weren't able to keep our hands off each other."

"Was that before or after you consumed your first 1500 cases of Jack Daniel's?"

"During, I think. How is—" he belched "—your mother?"

The truth was, she was having her problems too. "She's doing fine."

"That's great, just great. C'mon inside. I gotta pee."

"You mean you're not going to use the bushes?"

"Not while company's here. You know, it's been five years, at least, since we've seen one another. A man can't help but wonder how his boy's doing, every once in awhile. Can you loan me some money?"

"No."

"Normally I wouldn't ask, but they're about to foreclose on me. I'd hate to lose the old homestead."

The old homestead consisted of this shack, its meager furnishings, a satellite dish, an acre of land, and five rusty automobile shells. Since he'd had that accident at the construction site, Dad had lived off disability, but I knew he'd been drinking the vast majority of his checks, and had probably gotten himself in a financial hole he couldn't get out of on a fixed income.

"No."

"Well, I gotta confess, you disappoint me, son. I don't know if I actually helped bring you into this world, but

I raised you as if you were my own, and you should really help me out in my time of need." He flushed the toilet and walked out of the bathroom. He'd been peeing through most of our conversation inside, only he hadn't wanted to close the door because he didn't want to raise his voice while asking for a loan.

"I can't," I lied. "Right now I haven't got a pot to—"

"Use that," he said, indicating the toilet. "So, let me have a look at you. Hmmm. Impressive. The years are going to be kind to you Specials. If you live that long."

"*What* do you mean?"

"Peter was murdered, you young doofus. The crime is unsolved. It's not exactly the talk of the town—could be bad for business—but everybody knows what people are thinking. Peter didn't have any enemies. He was killed solely because he was a Special."

"And who *do* people believe is responsible?"

Dad shrugged and took a swig from a half-full bottle that had been standing on the mantle. "Damned if they can make up their minds. Some people think the perp is another Special, but he didn't die in a way that any number of organized crime or computer game-types couldn't have figured out. And Peter was known to hang out with gamblers and low-lives from time to time."

"Next thing you're going to tell me is some folks think it was a jealous husband."

Dad shrugged. "Or women. You never know, after watching *The Ellen DeGeneres Mystery Theatre* for a few years."

I grimaced. I'd seen the episode called "The Marcus Welby Murders," but I didn't want him to know that.

"How's the writing going?"

"It's going all right." I was a little distracted. I noticed a few photos on the mantle, near where the Jack Daniel's had stood. They were all in cheap frames, and the glass of one was streaked with grease. One photo was of Mom and Dad in the hospital, with their newborn John Simon cradled in Mom's arms. Another was the grade school photo taken of me just before Matt had revealed his Special powers. A third was of Mom and Dad with me when I was about to graduate from high school, only I wasn't in the photo; I'd been angry at them that day and I'd phased out. The photographer had seen me, but his camera hadn't. "You know that book of poetry I published last year, *Diary of a Bizarro*? There's talk it could win a National Book Award."

"No kidding," said Dad, belching. "I should re-read it. Want some advice?"

"What?"

"Eschew obfuscation."

"Don't you mean 'avoid ambiguity'?"

"A sense of humor would go a long way toward helping you cope with life, son."

"I don't see what's so funny. And who are you to talk to me about coping with life? The bank is about to foreclose your property. You said so yourself."

"Don't worry about me, boy," he said, taking another swig. "I'm like a cat. I always land on my feet."

Noble words, coming from a guy who couldn't always tell his feet from his keister. I turned to leave. All of a sudden, attending a funeral was looking pretty good.

7

THE BIG SLEEP

I was late. Peter's mother—who was his only survivor—had opted for an outdoor service beneath a great tent. It reminded me of when the fair used to come to town. After the service Peter's closed coffin would be lowered into the ground. Presumably there had been a private viewing for those who wanted to kiss Peter goodbye on the forehead or waxed lips or wherever. I found myself wondering how much preservation preparation the undertaker had found it necessary to perform. For although Peter was dead, presumably the force still permeated his mortal shell, blessing it with the same invulnerability that had cursed him during his lifetime. Meaning he would never decay. His body would outlast its coffin, and would remain in the ground until the Earth was vaporized when the sun went nova.

But I'm getting ahead of myself. Before I could attend the service, I had to find a place to park. I eventually did, two miles away from the cemetery. That tent the service was being held in turned out to be big enough to accommodate all the political wings of the Republican Party.

Though Peter hadn't been much of a celebrity in life, he was a superstar in death.

Nearly all the Specials were there, of course. They sat near the front, en masse, segregated from their friends and family. Those who had uniforms were, well, in uniform, even if the uniforms were ostentatious, like Jason's—oops, I mean Flagg's—and seemed too colorful to fit in with the somber mood. Dr. Welles was in attendance, as were several of the teachers and scientists who had worked with us during our childhood and our teens. And townspeople, of course, especially those who simply worked at the amusement park.

Then there were the photographers and the newshounds, the TV folk and a legion of fans who'd just come to town because they couldn't resist the chance for a mass Special sighting. I overheard a few whispering they'd come from as far away as Turkey and Australia. They seemed very excited, and knew the cast segregated up front as well as I did. One young lady attempted to engage me in conversation, but I politely reminded her that this was a somber occasion, and then I made sure to distort any part of my image that might be caught in the tiny camera hidden in her carnation.

The service was delivered by a preacher I didn't know, and as his words were prosaic and vague, I got the impression he hadn't known Peter, either. I assumed Joshua wasn't uttering the comforting words about the mostly-dear departed because of his father's long-standing—and well-known—animosity toward Specials in general. The preacher spoke of Peter's kindness, his work ethic, and how he had never used his power to harm others.

I would have pointed out that Peter hadn't used his power to help anybody either, that he worked only because he couldn't find the way to Easy Street, and that he was polite rather than kind. I would have added that he spent his life desiring what he could never taste, that he never really tried to play with the hand he was dealt, and that he was a materialist who should have found peace and harmony through a spiritual quest. Of course, being raised in a Christian society didn't help. Christianity teaches one to hate and control one's desires; the impulse to sin never really goes away. Whereas Buddhism teaches one to negate one's desires. Maybe Peter should have become a Buddhist; if he'd lived a life without desire, then he might have had a chance to be reborn as a man for whom desire was not a shortcoming.

After the ceremony, while the team of gravediggers was shoveling the soil on Peter's coffin, the police and ushers discreetly hustled the fans off the cemetery grounds. The cameras and reporters were next, and the family and Specials lined up to greet the grieving Mother several yards from the gravesite. She was a little woman, thinned and hunched over by age, with short, thin white hair and a slightly nervous handshake—I could see her hand tremble from a distance. Flagg, his cape billowing in the breeze, stood magnificently beside her, performing the role of surrogate family member.

I was at the end of the line. I wanted to get this part of the ritual over with as fast as possible, yet hadn't wanted to call attention to myself by standing near the front of the line, where Paula and Matt and the other big stars happened to be.

As it was, I stood behind Stephanie and Renee, two of the shyest women in the group, and their husbands. Stephanie had grown into a wholesome brunette, while Renee at this point looked like a nervous bird. Her husband

Alec, a definite jerk, didn't take his hand off her arm during the entire affair. "Hey, John," he said to me, "read your last book of poetry."

I arched my eyebrows.

"Least, I hope it was your last."

"Hello, Renee," I said, ignoring him completely. "How have you been?"

Stephanie and Renee said hello at almost the same time; Stephanie's husband nodded curtly. Then Renee said, "I have been *fine*. Alec sees to that. He helps me control my visions."

"Why would he want to do that?"

Stephanie leaned between us and said, "I've been trying to tell her she could get an honorary Ph.D. in history somewhere." She spoke as if her words were deliciously naughty. I imagine she was quite the wit in Utah, where she'd moved after she'd married pasty-faced Ric.

"Stephanie has a point," I said. "Seems to me the professional historians would pay money to be close to you, Renee, in the hope they might catch a glimpse of their favorite historical eras. I know that I—"

"Absolutely not!" said Alec, as if I'd suggested that she prostitute herself to a bunch of crackheads. "We are going to live a normal life—without any of this Special nonsense!"

Renee looked at Alec with true love in her eyes.

"It's thirty years too late for that, Alec," I said. "You can't pretend to be someone you're not."

"Didn't work for *him*, did it?" he said, pointing at the fresh grave.

I got as far as my first word before Ric stepped between us. "Gentlemen, gentlemen, remember where we are." He nodded to the cameramen, who were waiting for the opportunity to photograph something interesting, a few candid close-ups or, even better, an argument.

I grinned at Alec. Alec glared at me. Renee appeared oblivious; I think the poor woman actually thought she could live a normal life. I noticed her belly was big; what would her firstborn think, I wondered, when he suddenly found himself standing beside a woolly mammoth in the middle of the Ice Age?

Stephanie, on the other hand, was one of the few born within the Force time line who hadn't demonstrated an ability thus far. She'd always seemed open to the possibility, however, and husband Ric appeared to be a decent chap. I worried for them both though; I suspected the odds were against them.

"Isn't he nice?" Stephanie said of her husband. "I'm lucky to have him."

I didn't know if she was trying to convince me or herself. But I was being judgmental. Whereas most mundanes dreamed of being Special—or would have settled for being just exceptional or incredibly talented in a given area—many Specials dreamed of being mere mundanes because they'd seen the price Specials such as Peter and Lee had paid. Even those who seemed well-adjusted, such as myself, had paid a price in terms of isolation and loneliness.

Or was that a choice? I was pondering that very question when I suddenly realized the end of the line had reached the grieving mother. She had swollen red eyes and the attitude that her boy's suffering was at last behind him. Jason's large gloved hand did not leave her shoulder—and she just stood there, waiting—while Jason and I had a brief conversation, which, of course, began with me looking up into his big, innocent baby blues.

"Hello, John," he said in his normal deep, steady voice. "I read your last book of poetry."

"Not you, too."

"I thought it was excellent," he said, oblivious to any anxiety I might have inadvertently displayed. Jason was nearly always oblivious to anyone else's insecurities. Since insecurity did not exist for him, he apparently saw no reason why it should exist for anybody else. "I read it in between comic books," he added with a friendly wink.

We shook hands. Rather, he grabbed mine and immediately crushed my fingers like chicken bones.

"How have you been?" he asked, like he really cared.

But of course he did. The Nexus Corporation paid him to care, and a certain glib concern for others came to him naturally anyway. You know how fabulously successful people are always saying they'd be doing what they were doing even if they weren't getting paid, because they love their work so much? Well, most of 'em are full of crap, but after Jason was hired by Nexus, he acted exactly as he had before. He was a man who got paid—and paid handsomely—just for being his own glib self.

I answered his question the same way I had already fielded the previous queries.

"That's great!" he said, giving me the patented square-jawed grin I'd seen on the Nexus public service spots on PBS. "Say, John, I'd like to have a real chat with you sometime, but I have to take care of Mrs. Dawson here."

"You don't have to," she said, meekly. "You've been great."

"I insist, Mrs. Dawson. Joe! Joe! Could you get the car?" He put his hand on her arm and hustled her off.

She disappeared in the swirl of his red-white-and-blue cape.

Nearby, the rest of the Specials were breaking up and heading off on their separate ways. The ones who strove to be mundane—with the exception of Cathy, I noticed—broke away the most quickly. It wasn't that they disliked us, or were ashamed to be a part of us. Whenever the photographers weren't around they were as cordial and nostalgic for the good old days as you could imagine. But they were like a closeted gay, or blacks passing to be white in 1950s Georgia; they had an agenda that required at least a nominal deception.

Chandra, however, was walking straight up to the photographers. She was followed by about ten or twelve men and not a few teen boys, all crowding hot on her heels. I was amused to see Alec was among them. Renee was obviously waiting impatiently while Stephanie and Ric were saying goodbye to her. Alec glanced at his wife and, if that sudden wided-eyed look of terror was any indication, came to the conclusion that he had succumbed to Chandra's pheromone field way too easily for Renee's liking. Although it was nice to see he wasn't completely dominant in the relationship, I believe she was still being too hard on him. After, I had the dubious talent of being able to resist all levels of pheromones, and even I couldn't help but look at Chandra occasionally.

Joshua was walking besides a well-dressed, older gentlemen, probably a deacon at his church. If he wasn't with his dad, Joshua was with a deacon. It was as if the elders of his flock expected him to lurch into the nearest bar and/or bordello the second he was alone. I wondered if his sex life was as noneventful as mine.

Matt and Randy were laughing at one another's jokes. At least, they were supposed to be jokes. Matt was in uniform and Randy had, for some reason, chosen to wear a coat and tie. I guess he thought he was making a concession to decorum if he pretended to be normal for funerals.

The fliers were all taking off. Wolfboy howled with grief once more, and Connie Whitten was dodging around gravestones so she could reach her car more quickly. I saw Renee get tired of waiting and stride up to her errant hubbie when suddenly I heard it.

Singing. Delectable singing. Devoid of words, somewhat devoid of melody, and completely devoid of sound. You know how Bruchner's symphonies hurl themselves to the threshold of a transcendental conceptual breakthrough of the mystic kind? Or, for that matter, how Bobby Short's rendition of a Cole Porter song evokes visions of wine, sophistication, eloquence, and more wine? Or how township jive from Soweto has an indestructible beat combined with an infectious joy? Combine the effects of all three and you might have some idea of the impact this music I heard only in my brain had on me.

I'd stopped dead in my tracks. I wasn't alone. Only one person could be responsible, and sure enough, not fifteen yards away, Paula walked by, accompanied by a tall and lean manager everybody called the General. The glazed look in his eyes was as apparent as it was in everybody else's, yet he mustered enough self-control to say, "Paula. You're humming!"

She blushed and giggled, then glanced toward her right, at the largest group she'd affected. "Oops. Sorry."

Several "listeners" bowed. A few mimed applause.

"It's all right," said Alec, being pulled along by Renee. "It might get me out of the doghouse—"

"You wish!" Renee replied.

I sighed with relief. In addition to mysterious music that poet laureates had failed to put into words, Paula could communicate her moods, and this time she'd shared a more profound, nobler sense of loss at Peter's passing than I'd been able to muster. And here I was, supposedly the sensitive, poetic, insightful one. Compared to the love she felt for others, I was selfish and insignificant.

I left the funeral feeling emotionally empty and intellectually hollow. True, I was a Special, and had been both blessed and cursed with experiences that had expanded my consciousness in ways Hendrix and Morrison could only have dreamed about, but at the same time so much of my experience in life was second hand, gleaned through observation or through books.

And just as true, the potential consequences of my gaining experience could be grave, and might easily fall on someone else's shoulders. Only a soulless creep would knowingly inflict that kind of peculiar agony upon another.

I had to face it. I couldn't risk being alone any longer. In the final analysis, I was just as human as anybody else.

However, when I returned to the gas station, the girl was gone. I lacked the inclination or the nerve to even ask about her name, much less ask where she might be.

8

WHATEVER HAPPENED TO LEE JACKSON?

I had a dog once, a setter mix, a big, red, dumb dog who was as neurotic as hell, and she liked to sleep in the bathroom in front of the door, so you had to shoo her out before you could do your business in private. But she got old and sick, and she couldn't stand up while she did her business, so finally Mom had to put her down. For two years after that, every time I walked into the bathroom, I half-expected to find her there, blocking the door. She was conspicuous in her absence.

That was pretty much how I felt about Lee Jackson and the funeral. He should have been there.

Of course he couldn't be.

I spent the next few days working things through my head, figuring out the best approach to tackling the mystery of Peter's death. In the Special hierarchy, Peter Dawson and Joseph Drake were bottom-rungers, possessing limited abilities they weren't able to use, for whatever reason, to great advantage. They didn't pose a threat to anyone. Maybe the killer figured that lesser-powered Specials were easiest to kill.

Unless there was some other link between the two victims, besides their common cosmic background, maybe the best thing to do would be to warn all the other low watts in the bunch. Of course, I'd have to warn those who'd yet to manifest an ability too, who were just mundanes waiting to become Special. That could cause general panic, desperation, and myriad mistakes, and for Specials, mistakes tended to be extra costly, especially in the eyes of the law.

Or it was possible my next step should be investigating those among us most likely to have strayed from the path of law and order. That was a long list. Even Matt had been accused of committing a few civil rights violations from time to time, and Flagg—that is, Jason—tended to side with his corporate employers even when their methods were, at best, questionable, and at worst, unethical.

Then again, a methodical approach might cause the killer to think I was actually onto him, which could cause him to err and inadvertently reveal himself, but it might also goad him into killing again. Perhaps not such a good idea.

Actually, most of us have our general movements covered pretty well in the tabloid press, or by the government. I can see a Special slipping away to perform one quick murder, but slipping away for two, especially two that required a certain amount of preparation, just didn't seem likely. Ravenshadow could do it, he comes and goes as he pleases, without being seen, but I know Randy, and although I had no logical explanation for it, it just didn't seem in character for him to kill two of his comrades in cold blood.

Then again, nobody pays much attention to the low watts. The murders didn't require special powers, just special knowledge. Or insight. Perhaps someone had just acquired abilities, or was taking out old resentments on the others.

It was possible that one of the few Specials who had gone completely underground was responsible. Willie Smith was one. There wasn't a one of us who didn't feel bad, to some extent, about what happened to Willie.

We were still kids then, back at Camp Sunshine. Willie could fly but he was never able to get more than a few feet off the ground. Doc Welles figured the problem was psychological, but that was Doc's style: every problem was psychological. I had the feeling that I could enter Doc's office with my arm bleeding at the elbow from a fresh, accidental amputation, and he would tell me I would have to get my head on straight if the bleeding was ever going to stop.

The kids tended to be rough on Willie, me included. Most kids have the capacity to be cruel. We Specials had more capacity than most. No one made fun of a kid because he could fly, or even if he couldn't. But poor Willie could only float. He was like a balloon boy. The kids said he was too fat to fly, and maybe he believed that.

All the adults, especially the shrinks, knew how mean we were to Willie. At times we were like a mob and made jokes at Willie's expense for an hour or two at a time before getting bored. Maybe that doesn't seem like a long time, but when you're a kid and you're all alone and nobody in the general vicinity is on your side, it can be an eternity.

I don't know what we did that day, or what anybody said, that was especially cruel. Maybe it was no more cruel than any other remark, maybe it was even lame. But whatever it was, it was enough. At that moment Willie decided he couldn't take it any more and he stared at us with a glare that even the largest and the most thick-headed found frightening, and he began to float—

—Higher and higher. Straight up, never taking his eyes off us.

We were too stunned to react. Could it be he was floating away from here, out of sight, escaping from the camp? Even those of us who could fly were too astonished to do anything.

He kept on going up, and up, until he disappeared into the clouds. Matt was the first to come to his senses and fly after him, but by then Willie was long gone. That night the camp teachers clamped down, and nobody was allowed to fly for almost a month. I guess they never thought any of us would actually escape until Willie did.

We never found out what happened to him. Specials, reporters, historians, and pundits in general have speculated, sometimes wildly, but no one has ever delivered a satisfactory answer. Willie might as well have gone to Chile or Argentina, for he is truly among the disappeared.

Some of us, as kids, chose to believe he kept on going until he found a place where he could be accepted. I don't know where, unless he found a castle on a floating, deserted island like in Miyazaki's animé classic *Laputa*. Others figured he kept rising until he hit the stratosphere, ran out of air, and died there, that maybe his body is still in orbit somewhere, like that poor Russian cosmonaut who was in orbit when the extra-dimensional comet that brought the force to the Earth arrived.

And maybe Willie was waiting for a chance to get back at us, when no one was looking.

Or maybe not.

It was a typical Monday afternoon for Randy Fiske, a.k.a. Ravenshadow: photographing a bevy of undraped lovelies in his luxurious studio. In addition to the lovelies the studio contained several skylights, a few spiral staircases, and a bunch of abstract statues. I'm not sure what sort of agency he used to contract these women, but then again, it couldn't have been too difficult because he was the famous Ravenshadow, the fabulously wealthy Ravenshadow, the very-dreamy-when-he-wasn't-wearing-his-mask Ravenshadow. I thought I recognized a couple of the women from centerfolds in the men's magazines, but I like to think of myself as too much an effete intellectual snob to say for certain.

In any case, when I snuck in Randy was taking a series of Polaroid snapshots of this very beautiful frail with a pair of green glassy eyes that radiated all the personality of sentient marble. She had her hands over her boobs and, with the exception of an open red robe, wore only a pouty expression I knew I'd seen in print before.

She moved her mouth in another shape, but the poutiness still remained.

She tried again. Still pouty.

"No, that's not it," said Randy.

She tried yet another.

"No, that's not it either . . ."

She sighed.

"Hmmm . . . That's it. Perfect. Hold that thought. Now smile. Smile. Inside, too. "

She did her best. I could almost hear the tiny bowling

ball that was her brain rolling down the empty lane that led to the other side of her head.

"Got it," said Randy without enthusiasm.

"Got what?" she asked breathlessly.

"You."

She sighed again, this time with satisfaction. That had been hard work, changing her mouth around that way. She was relieved not to have to concentrate anymore. She stood and stretched like a cat rubbing its back against the ground. It was easy to understand what he saw in her. "Randy?" she said. "Where are you going?"

"To the loft." He walked up the swirling stairs while he watched the picture develop.

The girls were disappointed. "But you booked us for another hour," one of them said, pouting. "We don't want to leave you unsatisfied."

"You won't. Trust me on that," he said, as if he cared. Randy had always had this Lamont Cranston syndrome— he wanted to attract the ladies while frightening the villains. And if not the villains, then somebody. Today he wore his hair in a ponytail and had on a long gray coat over his usual gray clothing.

I imagine he felt very satisfied indeed as one of the girls wondered aloud if he was really Ravenshadow, because he was only gorgeous, and not nearly as frightening as she'd been led to believe. "Give it time, honey," answered one of the others. "The night's still young."

Randy frowned as the picture became fully developed. It wasn't great, but it would do. The picture was not of her body or her face, but of her left eye. His studio was cluttered with completed works and works in progress— painting, sculptures, charcoal sketches, boxes with objects inside, and collages. The picture of the girl's eyes was slated to be part of just such a collage: an entire canvas filled with women's eyes, a hundred mirrors reflecting a hundred disconnected souls. Most of the eyes were heavily made up with eyelash liner and mascara, but a few were plain and unadorned. Others were bloodshot, or framed severely dilated pupils. As Randy began cutting the photo with a pair of scissors, he said, "You can come out now, John."

"Busted!" I said. "Hello, Randy."

"I've never ceased to find it funny that none of my surveillance equipment picks you up when you come around. And I've got the best stuff. The best. "

"You mean the best Radio Shack has to offer?"

"How come I can feel you when you get here, but the cameras never get anything?"

"I've always had a flair for putting electronics on the fritz. You know that."

He sure did. By now he was barely listening, so busy twisting and turning what was left of the girl's face before the collage, trying to find the right spot.

"You know why I'm here," I said.

"The murder," he replied, matter-of-factly. "You think there are going to be more."

"I do."

"Funny, so do I," he said, but I knew he was really thinking of his collage. "Damn," he whispered to himself. "It's not going to fit. Please fit, I don't want to have to scan this damn thing and PhotoShop it."

"It's only going to fit in the places where you don't want it to fit. That's what makes it art. If it made sense, it wouldn't be art."

"John, I had no idea you were such a devotee of David Lynch movies. Maybe you should have put that in your last book of poems. It would have been at the very least competitive with Jewel's."

"Jewel and I are similar in that we both write in the English language, but that's as far as it goes."

"So what do you want with me?" he asked, absently. "You think I was responsible for the murders?"

"No, you're odd, even by our standards, but you're not a killer. At least not yet. But one of us did it. No one outside the group would know our vulnerabilities well enough to pull off two clean kills."

"I don't know if I should be flattered or not. And why does everybody insist I'm odd? It's because I was the first to put on a costume and deign to fight for truth, justice, and the American way, whatever it happens to be this week, right?"

"You see things, Randy. You're constantly exploring the boundaries of perception, breaking on through to other sides of life and existence. If anybody would know where to start searching for the one responsible, it's you."

"Very flattering," said Randy, concentrating mainly, I'm afraid, on how the new eye would look half-astride an old one in the middle of the collage. "But you don't need *me* to figure that out. Where do *you* think it started?"

"I think with Lee Jackson."

That got his attention. He thought it was funny. "But he wasn't murdered. You saw how he died. It was broadcast on CNN, for Chris' sake."

"I saw it. But I can't help feeling that that's where it all started to go wrong."

Randy laughed. "Remember when *Star Wars* came out, and Doc Welles kept trying to get us to trust our feelings . . . ?"

I refused to allow the conversation to be deflected. "Nobody really knows, beyond general terms, what happened to Lee in between the time he left, and the time he died. I figured if anybody could answer the question, it's you."

"We shouldn't talk about this here. And I could use some air."

"Off to the rooftops, eh?"

"Where else should superheroes converse?" He'd begun putting on his costume, hooking his flowing gray cloak into his shoulderpads. His shoulders didn't need to be padded very much, but as Ravenshadow, Randy was always vain about his appearance. He was a typical Special in that regard.

"What about your guests?" I asked. "Isn't the meter running?"

"As long as they get paid, that's all they care about. They can wait."

"Interesting collage. What's the deal with all the eyes?"

"A philosophical concept—or should I call it an urban myth—I'm trying to reflect on. People say the eyes are the mirror to the soul. When they say it, they mean it's how we look into someone else's soul. But what if the eyes are how the soul looks out, how it reaches the rest of us? I'm trying to figure out what the eyes typically say."

"Why?"

"No reason."

"Right. I think you might do better if your eyes were the mirrors into the brains of someone with an I.Q. over 50."

"Are you critiquing my taste in women?" he asked.

"I cannot critique that which does not exist." By now we were walking on a rooftop. Randy owned one of the highest lofts in the art district, providing us with a good view of a cityscape that included several high-rises, a park, a ritzy social scene where the young and the near-young hung out, and a skid row nearby. Billboards extolled the virtues of plaque remover, being a good father, buying a new car, drinking beer with a pretty young woman, using vaginal deodorant, staying off drugs, eating tofu, and those of Flagg, big-time superhero fellow.

Flagg was, of course, our schoolmate, Jason. The billboard emphasized a man who had muscles on his muscles; Steve Reeves had been a ninety-pound weakling in comparison. Jason/Flagg had red-white-and-blue shields on his shoulders and knees, a red-white-and blue cape, a red-white-and-blue helmet—hell, he was just red-white-and-blue all over. I delude myself into thinking I'm just as patriotic as any individual, but in designing his costume, Jason had taken patriotism to pathological levels. He was proud to be a superhero, and the Nexus Corporation was only too proud to sponsor him, just like they'd sponsored the billboard. However, their ad committee wasn't too swift in the brevity department. It was the wordiest goddamn billboard I'd ever seen. Maybe it'd been written for pedestrians to read at their leisure, rather than drivers trying not to hit the car in front of them. The billboard read, in part:

IT'S NOT ENOUGH TO PLAN FOR TODAY.
IT TAKES A SPECIAL KIND OF COMPANY TO PLAN FOR
TOMORROW . . . AND PROTECT THE FUTURE.

BORN IN FIRE

NEXUS CORP IS LEADING THE WAY,
WITH A HERO FOR TODAY
PRESERVING THE PEACE AND POSTERITY OF TOMORROW.
FLAGG!
DOES A BIG COMPANY REALLY CARE ABOUT HEROES?
NEXUS CORP DOES.

A banner had been hastily pasted over the name FLAGG.
It read:

SEE OUR NEW NAME SOON!

"Nice night," said Ravenshadow, walking on a wall.

"Yeah, it is. What happened to the billboard?"

"Didn't you hear? It was all over the news today. Jason
has to change his superhero name. Turns out some guy
named Chaykin has the rights to the name Flagg. Nexus
has to remove all the ads with his old name. Doesn't have
a new one yet, I hear tell."

"Chaykin? I used to read his comics before he started
writing television. He was good."

"You can be good writing and drawing comics. It's
more difficult to be good when you write television. Anyway, I told Jason I thought it was a stupid name from
the start, even if the focus groups did like it."

"Too bad Captain America and Uncle Sam were already taken, eh?" I asked.

"I have this feeling Jason would have been happier
being called American Maid, but don't quote me. I came
up with Ravenshadow all by myself by the time I was
twelve. I had a direction in life. I didn't need a corporation to give it to me."

"Randy?"

"I know. Lee Jackson." He jumped down and sat on a ledge. He looked me in the eye. At least, I presume he looked me in the eye, because his mask, two pieces of metal stitched together with soldered staples, had a thin layer of metal where the holes for the eyes should have been. The layer was punctured with a series of tiny holes, through which someone with Randy's heightened perceptions could presumably see, but which allowed no one, not even one as sensitively attuned to the cosmos as myself, to glimpse the soul inside. "You're right. I have done some special research regarding what happened to Lee Jackson. Research performed via my own special idiom, I might add. Took me years to put it all together. Hell, we were just kids when the first incident happened. What the hell did we know?

"We certainly didn't know Lee had been molested by that same counselor at that same camp the summer before. Didn't know why he was wound up so tight all the time. Didn't know why he was so scared. Until he looked at that guy . . . and burned him right down to the ground. We also didn't know if Lee had set the cabin on fire personally, with his powers, or if it had been just the fire of the counselor spreading as though he had gasoline flowing in his veins instead of blood.

"When Lee ran off—we were too afraid to stop him, and the adults were too confused and unsure of themselves—he had an expression of fear on his face that I haven't forgotten to this day."

"Is that why you wear a mask that hides all your expression? So you won't be like Lee?"

"I will *never* be like Lee. After the counselor had been investigated and it was learned he'd been suspected of molesting children at the camp, well, that's when my father started referring to him as that sonuvabitch. The revelation created a small groundswelling of sympathy for Lee and his parents. For all the good it did them. One thing about a free society, John, or at least one that purports to be free: you can be the most sympathetic criminal in the world and you'll still be a criminal.

"Lee's folks took off with him that same night. Doc Welles had the feeling, I think, they'd already suspected the nature of their son's power, just as they'd suspected the trouble he might have been in. They couldn't do anything about Lee's exile to Camp Sunshine—the case was still working it way to the courts—not without arousing the same suspicions they'd hoped to deflect from their son, so they were prepared, just in case. They were very smart, really, and they must have had balls of steel, because when the time came to run, they didn't hesitate. They disappeared into an underground network of social protestors so narrow and so deep not even the liberal activist press had suspected its existence. The underground provided them with help, but not much. Just enough to help them keep moving. Otherwise, they were on their own.

"When public opinion started turning around—slightly, thanks to the salacious revelation about the 'victim,' Lee's folks remained steadfast in their determination to protect their son. In some ways, they were the smart ones. The incident had given certain advocates in the Government the excuse they needed to clamp down on we Specials. Lee didn't have to put up with all the bureaucratic crap that followed. But believe me, over the years he endured a hell of a lot worse.

"I don't how the Jacksons did it, at the beginning. Granted, this was years before the debut of *America's Most Wanted*, but somehow they slipped through the most thorough dragnet in the history of the country. Every tollbooth, every bus stop, every train station, every airport was a potential trap, and somehow they avoided them all. Some survivalist manuals were found at Lee's house, in his father's study. They all offered advice about what to do when you're on the lam, when the Feds are after you because you got mad when they tried to take away your freedom. Fringe stuff, but the practical advice must have been well-founded.

"Anyway, the whole country was looking for him. Lee was proof of what everyone privately speculated (even if only a few did so openly): that we—the specials—were dangerous and ought to be locked up. Lee most of all. Whether he was right or wrong, whether it was murder or self-defense, he had proven his ability to kill with the power of his thought.

"For about two years Lee and his folks went from town to town. Changing jobs and names every few weeks. They must have changed their appearance, too. I don't know how they did it, either. It probably got easier to hide as the furor died down—the Specials weren't the only crisis in the world, you know—but in most respects it must have gotten harder. The running man gets tired. And after two years, Lee's folks must have gotten very tired. One night they checked into a motel . . . As for what happened then—well, there are two possibilities, and I don't like to think too much about either one of them.

"The family was about out of money and a long way out of hope. It's possible that Mr. Jackson was thinking they had nowhere left to run, that authorities were closing in. That there was only one honorable thing left to do.

"And it's true Mr. Jackson smoked. The ashes of a cigarette were found at the point where the blaze was determined to have begun. So it could have been done deliberately, as an act of defiance, or desperation; or it could have been an accident. There are ways of possibly finding out, as you know, but I suspect like me you'd rather not. It doesn't make any difference anyway.

"According to Doc Welles, a pyro like Lee needs special training to keep his abilities under control, because the force manifests itself though thoughts, rather than one's physical movements. Therefore the power in question can manifest itself through the urgings of the subconscious as much as the conscious. Anything can set it off.

"Fear. Paranoia. Excitement. Puberty.

"All these factors were acting on Lee while he and his parents were on the lam. Maybe even, in addition to all these: a dream.

"Imagine Lee, asleep, restless but bone-tired, sleeping in a bed beside that of his mother's, having a wet dream while his father smoked and wondered how they were going to get through tomorrow. Who knows? Maybe his father even contemplated turning them all in.

"Imagine how Lee must have felt, waking up to discover that he was surrounded—floor, walls, and ceiling—by flames. His mother and father undoubtedly already incinerated. And himself lying in the only safe zone, evidence of his control. He hadn't even known he was doing it, until it was too late.

"Sixteen people died that night. By the time the police realized the infamous Special Lee Jackson might have been involved, it was too late. The fire had been devastating. One floor of the motel had collapsed into the other; what was left of the human remains were so mixed up that even the forensic scientists couldn't tell who was who.

"The authorities assumed Lee was dead. They wanted to believe it, and nobody on our side was willing to argue. We needed people to believe it as much as the Feds did, and take some of the heat, if you'll forgive the term, off all of us. A few of the Feds believed privately, though, that even if Lee had somehow survived the fire, he wouldn't be able to survive in the big bad world all by his lonesome.

"They didn't know Lee. He'd inherited his parents' stubborn streak."

Randy took off his mask. I always liked those claws at the end of his metallic gloves. They looked like they could slice open an elephant to the heart. I don't know why he took off his mask. I guess he wanted me to look into his eyes, for a change. "I don't have much information on what happened over the next few years, but I can make some educated guesses," he continued.

"Guilt-ridden over the death of his parents, on the run, scared of being captured, scared of who he was and what he could do, Lee grew up on the streets . . . panhandling, stealing, selling blood . . . and prostituting himself. We had the Doc to help us understand who we were and what we could do. Lee had nobody. He grew up hard, he grew up fast, and he grew up alone. It twisted him around. I think on some level he wanted to make the world into what had twisted him.

"And who could blame him? Most of us are living fairly successful lives, and Lee had to watch us from afar while he was sleeping in a cardboard box in an alley. I've always visualized him wandering the street wearing some filthy coat he'd liberated from a trash bin, and coming by a display of TV sets while Matthew Bright was getting his medals for rescuing his partner from an assassination attempt by expatriated guerillas who formerly belonged to Peru's Shining Path Communist Army.

"I can imagine what Lee's worse fear was. He knew he

could never come out of the shadows without facing multiple charges of murder—and a trial that could bring the nightmare of persecution back to the rest of us. We had to—*have to*—show the mundanes we are heroes, that we could help people, that we could handle each other, keep our own kind under control. They could sleep easy at night, knowing that potential monsters wrought by the Force were accounted for, in jail, or dead. With one or two notable exceptions.

"Tell me, John, who do you think would have won a superhero slugfest—Lee, or the Special Formally Known As Flagg?"

"Jason could pound the bejeezus out of Lee—" I said.

"Yeah, but Lee had that ability to induce spontaneous human combustion with but a thought," said Randy. "And you know he would have used it. A man—even a good man—doesn't stay on the run as long as he without becoming ruthless."

"So why do you think it all started with him?"

"Patience, patience, my friend." He gave me a weary look. "Learning the fate of your childhood friends is like fine wine—it must be anticipated before it can be fully savored. A few years ago I think Lee got tired of running. It took a lot of interviews, sometimes with people who didn't want to talk or with folks who knew what they knew only through hearsay, but I think I got a handle on why it went down the way it did. It was toward the end of spring, and the winds had died down in the old apartment district where Lee had decided to sit for a spell, on the front steps of a building in an area where seniors on fixed incomes tended to live.

"People noticed him because he sat for a long time and showed no deference to the toughs who occasionally wandered by. They gave him a wide berth, as if by instinct. But Lee treated them same as he treated everybody else: he ignored them.

"I'm sure Lee didn't look like your typical homeless felon on the lam. As a child, he took pride in his appearance. And he tried to stay clean cut as an adult. Even so, he was still dirty, his trousers were still torn, and he needed a shower and shampoo, desperately. And talk about down on your luck. When you think about it, Specials such as you and I have abilities that would make it easier to fly under the radar; all Lee had was the ability to set people on fire. Not exactly the sort of stunt you can use discreetly. I got the impression that Lee had been connected to several quasi-revolutionary groups that not only spent a lot of time discussing the possible ways and means of overthrowing the United States government, but also knew how to make a person disappear underground. However, there'd been a falling out between Lee and the group, and he'd never really trusted them anyway. He'd been under the group's wing for five years, and now he was on his own again, with no particular place to go, nothing in particular to do. Knowing Lee, he was probably wondering why he'd ever been born. I don't have that problem—I like my life—but if I'd been in Lee's shoes, I'd have probably felt the exact same way.

"Anyway, something changed inside him. Something he hadn't noticed. But it was there—the awareness that there was always a possibility in life, if you could remain open to it. Furthermore, he was tired. Tired of being a monster. Or maybe he was just tired of being alone.

"He didn't know it at the time, but her name was Eleanor Hamilton. She was 67 years old, she lived alone in a house a few doors down, and she was a retired schoolteacher. She had a fierce independent streak, so she'd refused assistance from the bag boy at the supermarket to help her carry her bags home. I have no idea if she noticed Lee as she walked by. Like I said, there were some toughs in the neighborhood, who enjoyed preying on the defenseless. Eleanor was by all accounts a feisty old dame, but she wouldn't look a punk in the eye unless she had to.

"But Lee noticed the peach rolling out of her bag. It stopped directly in front of him.

"Eleanor turned and hesitated. To get the peach, she would have to put down the bags. And she might have to look that stranger in the eye.

"He looked first. He asked her if she needed help.

"She knelt and because she didn't want to set down her bags, spilled more fruit. She protested, she didn't need his assistance.

"But Lee insisted. Gently. She felt obligated to accept his assistance and as a consequence gladly looked him in the eye. And was surprised at the terror and loneliness and, yes, the gentleness she saw there.

"Lee carried her bags and walked her home. He never asked for money, never asked her for anything. He just wanted to help someone.

"And she asked him in. She knew he was hungry and needed a place to stay. She fixed him supper and together they watched television. She had the distinct impression a comfortable evening spent watching TV was a novelty to him, and that he was having trouble feeling at ease. She mentioned that she needed some work done around the house tomorrow. Lee said he'd be glad to help. The next night she fixed him supper again. She didn't ask any questions, and Lee liked that. But she did read poetry—the classics, probably—and Lee liked that, too. He'd probably never before experienced the power of the spoken word.

"Well, from then on they were inseparable. At first her friends and neighbors were worried; one guy was afraid a *Harold and Maude* thing was happening. But their relationship was deeper than that. I suppose you could psychoanalyze the whole thing. She represented the mother figure fate had caused him to lose, and he represented the son she'd lost in Vietnam, her only child. According to the neighbors, he was helping her out for two weeks before she found out he was living in the streets—and cleaning up and showering at the YMCA. That's when she offered him the use of her spare bedroom.

"I can imagine how Lee must have felt. The room was neat, but dusty. The books on the shelves were from the '50s, and an American flag was on the wall. Lee didn't know much about contemporary bedroom decor, but he knew those Western-motif blankets with ranch and ranchhand patterns hadn't been manufactured since the '50s as well. This room had belonged to her son.

"In a drawer beside the bed he found her son's posthumous Medal of Honor, and the letter she'd received from Uncle Sam, regretting to inform her of the death of her son, Richard. He loved this woman who had become like a mother to him, and he recognized the responsibility he had taken on himself. But he already knew, thanks to the example of his parents, that with great love comes great responsibility. He was by all accounts a model houseguest for the year he stayed there—"

"Wait—you keep saying 'according to the neighbors' or 'by all accounts.' Why didn't you just ask this Eleanor woman?"

"Wine, John, fine wine, that should be savored. It wasn't *all* in the paper. In fact, very little was, mainly because a lot of the people felt ashamed and they didn't want to talk about it in the immediate aftermath.

"Apparently he'd been working all day, and by late afternoon he was exhausted. He needed to take a nap. I guess Eleanor decided to surprise him, and get some ice cream and cake from the store. She'd discovered it was a dessert he really enjoyed, one of the things about normal life he'd missed during the mysterious past she never asked him about.

"Lee never liked it when she walked the street alone. He had good reason. A lot of gangbangers had been infesting the neighborhood lately, and the police were too busy worried about some crisis of national security to care much about what was going on in their backyard.

"Unfortunately, I can imagine all too easily what happened next. Four gang members crossed the street ahead of her so they could stop her just a few doors from her house. I guess they had a hankering for some ice cream. And whatever was in her purse. But when the leader drew a knife on her, Eleanor ran. She held onto the bag of ice cream and cake and she ran.

"The neighbors saw it. Some of them dialed 911 but they knew it would be over with—however it ended—long before the police came.

"The punks chased her. They caught up with her, too. According to the police reports, she only had about twenty dollars in her purse. She should have let them have it, and phoned in a complaint later. Not that the police would have done anything about it, but at least she would have been alive. As it was, they cut the purse from her hand and then they cut her throat.

"And then they ran. They ran just as Lee, having been awakened by the noise, came outside, and saw the only friend he'd had in years bleeding and dying on the street like a timid, defenseless animal. I don't know if something snapped in Lee at that moment, or if what happened next was simply the next logical step in his emotional progression from outsider to outlaw. In other words, Lee was a fundamentally good man whose path in life—which he had not chosen, it had been chosen for him—had dictated he be forced to bend, then break the law. And who knows what strange alliances he'd had to form to stay underground? Who knows how long the escalation had been moving toward what he did next?"

"Oh, my god," I said. My gut sank like the *Titanic.* "That's when—"

"You got it. I want you to think of this in terms of a crane shot because that's how I see it. He's kneeling there, in the middle of the street, holding the dead body of the only person who'd offered him unconditional kindness for years, this person who was dead because she lived in a neighborhood rife with crime. And he's crying, he hasn't cried for years, he grieves for her and he grieves for the whole stupid waste that has been his life. And that's when he decides what he must do.

"He arranges her body in a dignified position, then he stands and his bare arms and face begin to smolder. At first just smoke, then tiny flickers of flame.

"Everything had been really quiet before, as if everyone in the area had paused to listen for a traumatic change, the way the birds will go strangely silent just before the onslaught of an earthquake. Then someone trips over a garbage can. He looks in the direction of the sound and we can see his eyes have begun to glow.

" 'Where are they?' he asks.

"He has seen a trio of street punks—not the ones who'd committed this crime, but who had just come to watch—and gets a pretty good idea who he wants to talk to first.

The one who has fallen down has twisted his ankle, he's going to have trouble getting away.

"Lee asks the question again. The flames are spreading all over his body, covering but, significantly, *not* consuming his clothing. For the moment Lee is in utter control. He stands over the punk and asks the question a third time. The punk cannot answer—who knows? Maybe he really doesn't know. And *that* is when Lee crosses the line.

"He spits on the man. He spits fire. One small ball of fire that emerges from his mouth like a missile and lands in the punk's eye as if it'd been a spittoon. That moment was captured on amateur camera and was shown worldwide within an hour of some cash exchanging hands. That was the moment when everything changed and the whole world—including we Specials, I might add—understood for the first time how a Special could threaten the world order.

"What happened next showed just how inhuman a Special could be—because as the man was screaming and trying to put out the flame with his bare hand—Lee laid *his* hand on him and set the poor bastard ablaze. It turned out the guy was no angel—there was a third strike warrant out for his arrest—but nobody deserves to die that way."

"Except maybe the guy who killed Eleanor Hamilton," I said.

"That's the problem with the anti-death penalty argument—there's always some bastard so low on the evolutionary scale he gives traditional murderous snakes a bad name." He lit a cigarette.

"I didn't know you smoked!"

"There's a lot of things you don't know about me, John," he said, offering me one. "But you do know what happened next.

"Lee stalked the city. It happened to be on the West Coast and there wasn't a Special who could conceivably stop him for a hundred miles around. I remember thinking that's the first time the authorities ever had that type of problem.

"Yeah, blowback from bad social engineering. Blowback in the form of Lee stalking the streets like an avenging angel from Hell. Setting afire buildings and cars and parks and even a hospital. The footage is incredible—there're shots of lone policemen and citizens locking, loading, and taking dead aim at him—but the bullets melt before they get there. The street at his feet is molten, yet he walks on it like a prophet walking on water. And through it all he only has one question—in fact, he spares a brave TV reporter who jams a mike into his face so he can ask the question: *'Where is he? Where is the one with the knife?'*

"When the SWAT team showed up, they cut loose a barrage of gunfire—didn't even faze him; by now bullets did more than melt in his general vicinity, they *evaporated,* at his command. By now Lee had left a swathe of burning buildings in his wake, and God knows how many innocent people died, and God knows if Lee was capable, would ever be capable of caring again. He kept asking the same questions: 'Where is he? Where is the one with the knife?'

"So perhaps the town fathers, from the commander on the scene to the mayor in his bunker, can be forgiven for having an idea when the officers investigating the scene where all this started—to try to learn how to stop it—learned about Eleanor. They understood his motivation. Those who'd suffered knowing a murder victim, or having a beloved one killed in a senseless manner, could relate to the desire to rain down hellfire and brimstone upon the cityscape that had caused such senseless pain. But relating to a desire and actually indulging it are two different things, and they had a responsibility to their entire community.

"So yeah, maybe they can be forgiven making a bargain with the devil. After all, the devil was on *their* doorstep."

For the first time I realized what had actually happened. Like everybody else, I thought the last killing had simply been, well, the last killing. "They sacrificed him."

"If by *him* you mean the heinous scumbag who cut Eleanor, then you are correct. Since everybody in the city was riveted to their TV sets, it was a simple matter to communicate to the populace that a certain reward would be provided—plus pardons and a new identity via a witness protection program if necessary—to anyone who knew the man who killed Mrs. Hamilton, and where they could find him. You realize how fast a million dollars talks even in a crisis situation? The authorities had the identity and the whereabouts of their man less than thirty minutes after CNN got the facts. The leader of the SWAT team got the thankless task of talking to Lee via a loudspeaker and steering him toward his man. The plan was to help Lee get what he wanted, then hopefully take advantage of his distraction or induce him to flame off, and take him out. "

"The leader of the SWAT team eventually committed suicide over this, did he not?" I asked.

"Yeah. The man had a bad conscience, even though he was a hero to many. Too bad for him. Anyway, it turns out Lee had been walking in precisely the opposite direction he needed to in order to find his man. His man—and his family—lived in a nearby housing project. The man—does anybody remember his name today?"

"I remember now. His name was Mick Piker."

"Very good. Piker knew he was about to pay for his life of crime in the most horrible way possible and he tried to run, but police snipers on rooftops kept him discretely penned down inside his building. Piker knew who and what was coming after him. He tried to hide in the basement but by then Lee appeared to have a sixth sense that was leading him directly toward his prey.

"A prey who'd gone to a storage room in the basement to cower and hide. Lee walked straight toward the room, and then toward him. A boy of about seven, perhaps too naive to know the dangers his curiosity was pulling him toward, had followed, and was hiding at the top of the stairs, when Piker sank to an even lower depth than the ones he'd plumbed already and begged for his life. 'I didn't mean to do it,' he said. 'It's not my fault. She fought. If she'd just given me what I wanted, she'd . . . *It's not my fault!*'

"I don't know if there was a right thing to say, under the circumstances, but that was definitely the wrong thing."

"And that when Lee burned him," I said.

"Yeah." Randy tossed his cancer stick off the rooftop. "He burned up good, real good."

"So what do you think happened after that? Was Lee's rage finally over?"

"To a degree. The flames died out on his body. His clothes weren't singed, and he didn't even seem to have worked up a sweat. But I doubt seriously that at that moment he thought a human life was worth more than a flea's.

"Then he saw the boy. Cowering. The boy said, simply, 'Don't hurt me.' And y'know, I wouldn't be surprised if another boy in the past had said that exact same thing to a man he thought he was supposed to trust at summer camp.

"That was when Lee rediscovered his humanity, the unseverable bond between himself and his fellow man, between Special and mundane. 'Run,' he said to the boy. "Get away. Quickly.'

"The boy did. He was the last to leave the building."

"And that's when Lee did it," I said. Recounting this story, in this detail, had brought back the numbing shock and the spiritual desolation of knowing our friend, a good kid and, later, a man who had tried to be good, had been out there all alone in the world for nearly a generation, and we had done nothing about it. True, there had been nothing we could do about it, but that didn't make me feel any less guilty.

I remembered that once, when we were kids at Camp Sunshine, me and Randy and Lee and Chandra and Joshua were lying on the grass, looking up at the stars. We were trying to grasp the fact that each one of those little pinpricks of light represented another sun—or another galaxy—peeking at us from the distant past. Lee said:

"I want to be a star."

"What? A TV star?" Chandra asked. "A movie star?" Amazing, how her character was already solidly in place.

"No, a star," Lee said, pointing at the sky. "I want to be free."

I couldn't help wondering if Lee had recalled the same moment from his past, in that instant when he decided that he could live with what he had become and released all the force that was inside him, exploding in a vast ball of flame that sent pieces of the burning building flying for miles around.

"So," I said, "Randy, this burst of nostalgia is very touching, but you really think it has something to do with the two murders?"

"The day Lee died I noticed something that—well, maybe it'd be best to explain it to you in the Shadow-cave."

" 'Shadowcave'? C'mon, Randy, you don't really call it that, do you?"

"Sure. You got a problem with that?"

Yeah, I thought it was silly. But once I was inside, below the official basement of the building where Randy's loft was located, in an artificial cavern filled with the latest in hi-tech equipment and several changes in Ravenshadow's uniforms, I had to admit I was impressed. "Pretty elaborate, Randy. Painting pictures paid for all this?"

"People like to see the world through somebody else's eyes. They pay a lot more to see it the way one of us does. And thanks. It's not as fancy as what some of the others have, but it lets me monitor my abilities. Normally I can bench-press 2,000 pounds. It's not a muscle thing, it's a force thing. But recently, right up to the night Lee died, I noticed something—"

"You?"

"Well, I had some help from some physicists and doctors I allow access to my inner sanctum occasionally."

"I can tell from the Victoria's Secret decor over there."

Randy gasped and removed an interesting pair of pink panties from the back of a chair at a console and hurriedly tossed it in a nearby plastic trashcan. "Ahem. It's not what you think. Very little recreation goes on down here."

"What did you notice?"

"A slight decrease in the figures; it'd started a few years ago, but until recently had been barely perceptible. My strength and other areas were in a gradual decline. Basic physics: energy can neither be created nor destroyed, only transferred to other states.

"Each time I used my power, I transferred it to strength or flight. In so doing, I used up a slight amount of it via kinetic transference. It's been a slow process, but if it's a continuing phenomenon, it's possible my powers—and yours, and everybody else's—may one day do a slow fadeout. So you'll understand why I was surprised to see that, the night Lee died, my bench press went up. Suddenly I could press 2200 pounds.

"There were additional increases in all other areas of my metabolism. I'd not only regained strength and power, I increased substantially across the board."

"Did you gain any new abilities?"

"No, I just got better at the ones I already had. My composition even improved. Our energy does not die with us, John. It's transferred to the rest of us. When Lee died, we got $1/112^{th}$ times stronger. Now we're $1/111$ plus $1/110$."

I was dumbfounded. I prided myself on my self-awareness and yet—"I never noticed."

Randy shrugged. "Why would you? Only those of us who lift weights regularly or take some other measurement would, and at this rate of change, a lot of other explanations seem more reasonable."

"Does anyone else know about it?"

"No. I've kept the information to myself. I figured, if it got out, some of us might—"

"—Try to accelerate the process."

"Judging from the recent murders, someone else noticed."

"So why'd you tell me?"

He shrugged again. "I figured it's time."

He had that right. I left realizing it would have been one thing if the force had dissipated naturally with the passage of time before the Specials started kicking off on a regular basis; but now we were dying young, when we were still strong. More force to go around.

As I left I heard Randy exclaim *"Eureka!"* He'd solved his current artistic problem.

I was glad he'd solved his problem. I didn't know it yet, but I had begun to solve mine.

This was the end of everything that had gone before. An end, and a beginning, of understanding, and of a battle that would soon engulf us—mundanes and Specials—all.

9

MASQUES

One warm summer evening, Cathy Holmes had a long conversation with a guy from the office. His name, not that it's important, was Harold, and he was a new programmer at Synthesystems, Inc., a dot-com that had made its mark in the virus protection industry. The conversation occurred toward the end of the Roger Clinton Presidential years, when the country was coming off a cocaine scandal in the Oval Office, and the economy was riding nearly as high as the President had been on that fateful night when he'd been videotaped by the DEA. (The scandal enabled Republican John Ashcroft to win the next election in a landslide.) Cathy held a prestigious position at the firm; it was her job to defeat their new protection upgrades.

Cathy was known as the Angel of Death, an appellation meant not only to give respect to the vast intellect she brought to her job, but to comment on her general good looks. Cathy's body was like a platypus, in that it was put together from the female parts God had left over from when he created other women. Instead of the endearing ugliness one associates with a platypus though, God's leftovers conspired to create a charming and imposing monument to feminine possibilities. She was tall and slender, but her shoulders were broad, she was well-endowed, and she had short black hair. She liked to wear a pair of granny glasses like the kind Roger McGuinn wore when his name was still Jim. Overall, she was the kind of woman any man would be glad to look at twice, or a hundred times, and whom any nerd would gladly worship.

Cathy first noticed Harold toward the end of a day when she'd outfoxed an office rival's most recent protection program yet again. Harold was being escorted by hunky Jim Bamforth and a few members of his development clique toward the elevator. "—Far as I'm concerned, you're a lifesaver, Harold," Jim was saying.

Harold looked embarrassed. "Well, I didn't—"

"Don't give me that," said Jim. He was very good at insisting a person accept a compliment. "Nobody else in that office could get that system back on line. You did it in less than an hour. It's a pleasure to have you in the company."

That's not true, Cathy, no doubt, thought. *Nobody asked me!*

Even so, Jim was being nice and it was difficult to criticize a guy who could do that. Especially when he leaned over the top of her cubicle and said, "Hey, we're going to O'Malley's and celebrate Harold the conquering hero. Come on, munchies are on me." He knew better than say the drinks were on him.

"Be right there," she said, waiting for the—

—Punch line. "And bring the book."

"Jim, nobody wants to see that. He doesn't even know me—"

"Doesn't matter. He'll get a kick out of. C'mon... bring the book."

"It's around here somewhere," she said, pretending to rummage about. Actually, she knew exactly where it was; she didn't even have to glance at it: A folder with a blank spine, but clearly marked *Pederson Memories* on the front cover. Sighing, she tucked it into her purse.

At the bar, Harold quickly discovered something that Cathy was more than the office Amazon. She had a unique pedigree to boot.

"I don't believe it!" he exclaimed. "You're one of the Pederson Specials!"

Jim, who was standing over them at their table like a frat house yenta, said, "That's excellent! A Pederson Special! Sounds like a sandwich! A hero sandwich!"

"So funny I forgot to laugh," said Cathy, not without affection. She had a slight crush on Jim; too bad he had been experimenting with his homosexuality for the past four or five years.

Indeed, a flirt from the company next door named Mike caught Jim's eye, and off he went to talk to him, leaving Cathy and Harold alone.

Harold, eyes shining, stared at her. "I can't believe you're a Special and no one told me. Do you have a—? I mean, can you—?"

"They didn't tell because they respect my wish to let people form an impression of me before they know, and no, I don't have a power. I'm the same age as the others and I was raised with them until we graduated Sunshine High. I was *in utero* when the Big Flash hit, but in all these years I never manifested anything more than a cold.

Probably the Flash just didn't take. And I'm an ordinary woman."

"Well, I wouldn't say ordinary," said Harold. "From my perspective, from *any* perspective, you're impressive. Not only are you a programmer extraordinaire, but you're beu—beau—beaut—"

She leaned closer to him. He was blushing. "Go on," she said.

"What's in the book?" he asked hastily.

"It's a printout of my scrapbook. It's actually only a fraction of the material I've collected, scanned, and stored down through the years. I started keeping the original when I was a kid because they were my friends and schoolmates and many of them were already famous. I knew, even then, I was seeing something no one else would ever see in quite the same way. You want to have a look?"

"Sure! Where the stuff on Matthew Bright?"

"At the beginning. Nearly everybody asks about him first."

Harold opened the book to a scan of a newspaper clipping containing the well-known face of Matthew Bright. It was a chiseled, square-jawed face. The guy was wearing a police uniform, and appeared to have muscles on his muscles. Cathy sighed as she looked at the page, which to her was upside down.

"So what's he really like?" Harold asked.

"For one thing, he's a lot like his father," she said. "Next to Doc Welles, who was always sticking up for us when it could have gotten him fired, Matt's father Monroe was the most important mundane hero we had. He was a cop, a guy who liked to follow orders but liked even more to see justice done. After Lee Jackson burned that molester, the Feds threatened to take us away to an Army base and sever our familial ties through legislation. Mr. Bright organized a class action suit, went to court, lost, lost his job, appealed, lost another job, and appealed again until we went all the way to the Supreme Court, where we won. Big time. *He* won, because it was an open secret that Mr. Bright, more than anyone else, kept everyone spirited and motivated when things were darkest. He ensured that we were able to visit home on the weekends, that the parents had an important say in who was allowed to teach classes and what the curricula was, and made sure the Feds were liable for any and all fees that the families would under normal circumstances be responsible for. Meaning that the Feds had to pay our health insurance bills, our accident insurance, and even, to some degree, any fees that might result in a wrongful death suit brought against us or by us in the future.

"The Supreme Court decided that Mr. Bright had been unfairly terminated from his job too. He could have taken the settlement money and run, but he returned to walk the beat again. Being a cop was in his blood. And he always liked to say that the entire affair renewed his respect for the law during an era of rampant cynicism. I think Matt got his love and respect for the law from his father. All kids love their father, but Matt worshipped his. What's more, we all felt pretty much the same way about Mr. Bright. He'd ensured we Specials would get equal treatment by the law, and we would have an opportunity to live as normal a life as possible. True, some of the kids, those who could fly or had other abilities which could result in unpredictable and/or dangerous behavior, had to have a Federal Agent staying over at their parents' house with them on the weekends, but that was a small and not unreasonable concession to make. Besides, most of the agents were nice. They were a bit more suspicious of us, perhaps, but looking back on it I now see they enjoyed seeing us getting the chance to be just kids.

"Anyway, Matt was amazing. He was one of the first who discovered he could fly. He was stronger than just about anyone else in the group, and it took a lot to hurt him. The mandate from the Supreme Court included the school's obligation to assist those whose abilities had kicked in the proper training to use them as effectively as possible—this, on the one hand, while the Feds on the other were doing everything in their power to see we rarely used those abilities while out amongst the general population.

"Well, most us didn't mind phys ed. much, but training was a bore. The kids with the abilities were put through their paces, while the rest of us did mundane exercises. The fliers had to learn precision and agility in the air, and so had obstacle courses of loops and other shapes to fly through. They generally hated it, but Matt performed every training exercise as if he was training for a championship—which in a way he was. We all knew, even then, he would be a special among Specials.

"I guess we were fifteen or maybe sixteen when Mr. Bright died. In the line of duty. Killed while chasing a guy who'd robbed a liquor store. We were all devastated, but Matt more than most, naturally. He swore to pick up where his old man left off, to become a cop, just like him, and make a difference, just like him.

"Unfortunately, what we'd be able to do professionally once we were emancipated—and the Supreme Court's ruling had implications on *that,* too—had yet to be determined. Because the Feds still thought, for some reason, we could be dangerous, we weren't allowed to join any division of law enforcement.

"Matt rejected this restriction. So he took off. Literally. We watched him go. It was the first time anybody had gone that high since Willie.

"The Feds clamped down on the rest of us. All weekend leaves were cancelled and the fliers were kept on-site at all times just in case somebody else thought about a copycat deed. Not that anybody was motivated. We'd been pretty well indoctrinated by that point into believing the mundanes were all so afraid of us that one of them might do something stupid and shoot one of us in the back. That was only partly true, and a lot of people felt precisely the opposite way, but that's another story.

"Anyway, Matt was gone. Disappeared as if he'd gone into one of those other dimensions a couple of us were capable of glimpsing. Turns out Matt was smarter than any of us and was hiding in plain sight. Also, it turns out he wasn't above breaking the law in order to enforce it, but I think we can chalk that up to the indiscretions of youth. He got some fake I.D., lied about his age and faked an educational background, and joined the N.Y.P.D. Although he couldn't conceal that marvelous physique, he acted in all respects like a mundane. He concealed his strength and refrained from flying even when it would have helped catch a suspect. He was popular on his beat, especially with the children, even the troubled ones. He never patronized them. He knew what it felt like to be an outsider.

"Furthermore, he was well-liked by his fellow officers. It seemed he was always around when backup was needed, and his fellow officers were always willing to buy him an off-duty beer. His career was assured. He was a shoe-in for promotion.

"Then it happened.

"One day a tenement meth lab blew up during a police raid. Matt was on duty that day, and the lab had been located, without his knowledge of course, on ground covered by his beat. So it was no surprise he happened to be nearby when he was needed.

"The fire was the result of a booby trap, of course. Some criminal mastermind had rigged the device so whoever was inside would be surrounded by a circle of flame that prevented access to all exits. Maybe jumping through a window was an option, but they happened to be ten stories up. The cops were just trying to figure out if it was time to panic yet when a wall crashed down on 'em. It was curtains, for sure.

"Now if anybody else in Matt's shoes had been there, they might have just called the fire department and let the professional mundanes take over. After all, that's what any mundane worth his common sense in negotiable bearer bonds would done. It would have been suicide to go in after 'em. Besides, why would Matt want to destroy the very life he'd spent so many years—and so many lies—building? Anyone else—maybe even any other Special—would have walked away.

"But Matthew wasn't like anyone else. He flew through a burning window, picked up a huge segment of the wall and tossed if off the penned cops like it was a beachball, then flew them all out of there, one or two at a time, until everybody was safe.

"Well, all of the cops were safe, that is. A few of the lab technicians were trapped inside, but Matt didn't have time to save them. Building collapsed too fast. He did save some people on the street corner from debris, though.

"Paulson—*Paulson*, that sick bastard—wanted Matt fired, placed under arrest, and probably executed. Paulson couldn't stand the fact that any Special had defied him, and defied him so brilliantly.

"But Matt had saved the lives of a dozen cops, not to mention those on the street corner. The press was with him. Talk radio was with him. So was the N.Y.P.D. and politicians of both parties. Paulson got a court order stating the N.Y.P.D. lacked the authority to give him a badge.

"Paulson got the shaft. The N.Y.P.D. said 'Screw you, we're not only giving him a badge, we're making him a frigging detective!' He got a badge, a uniform that combined his twin aspirations of becoming a police officer and a superhero, and had the first professional job of any of us. He was on his own, out in the open, for all the world to see. Today he assists the law enforcement community of this nation and about sixteen others, in his spare time."

"You must be proud of him," Harold said.

"I didn't have anything to do with it, but I know what you mean. Like I said, I never really any particular talent to make me part of the group. I was just lucky to be there. It was nice, to be a Special, even if only for a while."

Harold shook his head. "I think you're special," he said, slurring a few words. "You may not be one of *the* Specials, but I think you're . . . you're . . ." He blushed. Again. He rifled a few pages of the scrapbook. He put his finger down on the picture of a blonde kid who, in his years of being a Specials' fan, he hadn't seen or heard of before. "Who's that?'

Cathy smiled sadly. "Jacob Polachek. A sad story.

Jacob was a mundane high school kid who claimed that he'd done something 'special'—I forget what, he floated or something. Doc Welles checked the local medical records (which were quite extensive, and covered pregnancies a year before and a year after the target period) and determined that Jake had been conceived a few days too late to have been affected by the Flash.

"Jake insisted he was Special, and even took his case to court. It was winding its slow, inefficient way up the legal ladder when something happened to Jake—he pushed a friend out of the way of an oncoming truck. The friend lived, but he died. He wanted so much to prove to the world that he was special, but instead he was a loser and liar. And then he showed himself to be the kind of hero even Jason and Matt aspire to be. Like I said. A sad story. You know her, of course?" She pointed at another photo.

"Oh yeah. Paula Ramirez. 'P. Ram,' for short. I've been to three of her concerts. Least, I think they were concerts. But she was the most amazing singer I'd seen—er—heard. Whatever. When P. Ram's on stage, the audience is completely quiet. She has no band, no microphones, she doesn't even open her mouth. She just stands there, closes her eyes, and does—whatever it is, she does. Three times I've seen her, three times I'd forgotten all the lyrics, the melody, I don't even remember what her voice sounds like, if she has a voice."

"Oh, she does. It's dark and husky."

"I mean, a singing voice. She spoke before and after her set. If you could call it a set—"

"I get the picture."

"You know what she sounds like. It's beautiful."

"What she does doesn't work on tape or CD either. It

can't be broadcast," Cathy said. "Doc Welles thinks her power is telepathic in nature, though I assume, like so many others, you found the concert to be a quasi-religious experience?"

"No 'quasi' about it. Who's this?"

"That's Johnny Simon. Actually, he always hated 'Johnny,' always wanted to be a 'John.' He's serious like that."

"What's he do?"

"He's a writer. Writes poetry, literary criticism and tomes about social and philosophical problems. He's reviewed regularly, but I don't think his writing is particularly . . . brilliant. Maybe I just don't like the way he slings words around."

"No, I mean, what's his power?"

Cathy shrugged. "Something to do with the ability to bend wavelengths. He never actually demonstrated it except occasionally, when he didn't want to be seen in a photograph."

"Then what happened?"

"He wasn't seen. Oh yeah, he also tried his hand at writing a popular series of pulp detective novels, but they weren't very suspenseful. Too much talk, not enough action. I hope he's learned something about human nature since then. He was standoffish as a child, rarely intermingled with anyone. He was always off to himself, reading, or writing in some journal. That's how he got his nickname: Poet."

"Then you two weren't friends while growing up?"

"No, not really. He wasn't friends with anyone but Doc Welles. He was the doctor's favorite. He wasn't in any of the cliques. Always sat by himself during the football games, with his nose in a book between plays."

"You had cliques?"

"Hey, sure, a lot of us had powers, but we were still kids in high school. For a long time, until the social barriers started breaking down, the strong kids hung out with the strong kids, the fliers hung out with other fliers, and down to the low rung of the social ladder, the near-mundanes, where I was."

"What caused the social barriers to break down?"

"The games, for one. And my figure, for another. Excuse me—!" She'd spotted Gary Foster, her second favorite hottie and, she recalled with some pleasure, a functioning heterosexual to boot.

"Cathy!" said Gary, as they collided and embraced. "I just got in town."

Cathy thought she saw someone blush out of the corner of her eyes. "Harold," she said, turning not too gracefully, "this is my friend Gary. Gary—this is Harold. He just joined the company."

"That's nice," said Gary, not really caring. "Harold? People still call their children Harold?"

"They did thirty years ago, when I was born," said Harold.

"That's nice," said Gary, again. "Harold? Sorry man, that's a tough cross to bear." He turned toward Cathy. "Say, I was headed toward Mel's for some dinner when I saw you through the window. Want to join me? Nod-nod-wink-wink-say-no-more."

She was tempted. Then she looked toward Harold, who was stammering something, trying desperately to stay in the running, and at that moment she realized something deep and dark and probably not so rational about herself. She might be attracted to hunks, but she liked, *really liked* nerds. "I can't, Gary. It's kind of an office party. Maybe later?"

"Maybe, babe," he said. "I'll call ya. See ya! Bye!"

"You, too. G'night," she said with a sigh.

"You were talking about the games?" said Harold, hoarsely.

"Uh, right—right." Then she remembered. "Close, actually. During games such as football, the Specials were obligated to turn down, turn off, or somehow deflect their powers. The slightest violation meant a penalty. Because on the game field, all Specials were equal, and all Specials had to be the equal of mundanes. It all boiled down to what you really had, what you would have had if it hadn't been for the Flash. A nice ideal. Impossible, of course, but a nice ideal. Guys like Peter Dawson couldn't play because he was invulnerable and couldn't turn his power on or off. He didn't have a talent for any non-contact sports either, unfortunately."

"Yeah, I heard he died, and I remember thinking 'Too bad' but not knowing too much about him. You didn't read too much about him in the fandom press." He looked down and saw her fingers touching a Jason Miller page. "He was a football star, wasn't he?"

"When I think of Jason, that's how I think of him," Cathy said, with an involuntary sigh. She remembered, fondly, one of the many times he plowed through the defensive line of an opposing team. He was running for the touchdown, as usual, smiling like he didn't have a care in the world. As usual. She wanted to tell Harold how Jason was always flying, even when he wasn't literally. She wanted to tell him how it felt to be standing alone at the edge of the football field, hoping to see the look of victory in his eyes, and hoping—against hope—

that he would see her and share his victory with her.

But his teammates always carried him past her—and he always stopped to pick up Chandra or one of the other cheerleaders. Usually, though, at that stage in his life, it was Chandra. And Cathy had always felt uncomfortable getting close to him, or speaking to him, because she was, as she used to so discretely put it, "underdeveloped" for her age. She'd only begun to blossom when she was a senior, and by then Jason firmly thought of her as a baby sister type. Even so, she sat as close to him as possible all the time, trying not to be too obvious, so she could just listen. She knew all about him, but only because *everybody* knew all about him.

"He was totally free when it came to sharing his thoughts; he held nothing back," she said. "He was still in love with the ideas he'd read in comics as a kid, and wanted to be just like the more self-assured characters. Not the heroes with feet of clay you found in some titles. I learned a lot about comics from Jason, but not to appreciate them, by the way.

"Jason believed we should all be heroes, and he didn't understand those who, even at that early stage, withdrew into the isolation of their outsider status and were determined to be as mundane as possible."

"Did you want to be a heroine?" Harold asked.

"Why, yes, I did." It was her turn to blush. "But it was not meant to be. Even Paulson—that sonuvabitch Paulson—seems to have lost interest in me. After graduation, I went to Midwest State, along with Jason, fifteen other Specials, and a whole lot of private escort. The very day we were registering, the campus was hosting a career day for the seniors, with a bunch of Chicago corporations swooping down on the business and law grads. Well,

Jason hadn't even registered for his first quarter of classes when he walked up to the Nexus Corp booth. I watched him do it. He had this look on his face, as if a burning bush had just called his name.

"It's a funny thing. The media had been talking about the Specials for years but because we didn't look any different from the mundanes, people often didn't recognize us. At least, not back then. So when the recruiters started talking to Jason, they didn't know who they were dealing with. They thought he was another dumb freshman jock with a blonde bombshell under his arm and muscles on his muscles. By the time I'd inched close enough, I heard a Nexus rep say, '—We also offer full medical and dental, vacation with pay, stock options. and a generous retirement package. Now I must have missed something. What was it you said you could offer us?'

"The girl under Jason's arm laughed. Jason said, 'For starters I can bench press 2,500 pounds. They say I have an I.Q. of 250, but they're not sure if they can accurately measure an I.Q. that high. And I can fly. They've got me clocked at about 800 miles an hour now, which means I can break the sound barrier, but I think I can do better.'

"The reps didn't believe him. One shallow suit said, 'Okay, son, fun's over now. We've got serious people waiting—'

"And Jason jumped high in the air and stayed there for several minutes. The students caught on fast that he was a Special—heck, our entrance here had made all the local papers—so they gave him an immediate burst of applause, half-giddy and half-sarcastic, like most collegiate approbation. I loved watching him fly—watching him noticing me."

"You two must have been close."

"Oh we were, we were very close. He couldn't keep his hands off me. Young lovers, you know how it is." She couldn't believe she was lying to the guy, but lying was easier than admitting the truth, even after all these years, that Jason rarely if ever noticed her once they'd left Sunshine High. The most painful, no, the most humiliating memory of all was of the night she came to Jason's dorm room on a pretext of asking if he needed certain notes from a chemistry class she'd known he'd missed.

"I'm surprised things didn't work out," said Harold.

"Depends on what your definition of working out is," she said with a wink. "We were both career-driven, and busy with school—" Or just plain busy. Her memory climaxed, as it were, with her noticing that Jason had left the door to his room open and then, during a moment of weakness, of peeking inside, to see Jason sprawled asleep on his bed next to a naked blonde who said, "Go away, honey. He's taken!" Cathy blushed at the mere thought of it, even though the incident had occurred over a decade ago.

"Anyway, Nexus Corp hired him and made him their corporate symbol," she said. "Sent him all around the world. Gave him the costume he'd always wanted. And they gave him a name. Flagg. Of course now he has to change it. I bet they're polling the focus groups even as we speak."

"I heard they were testing names like Anthem, Patriot, Justice. They'll probably announce the result at a big press conference. That's what happens when you hit the big time."

"They'll probably have a new slogan too."

Harold grinned. *"I'm changing my name, but not my tights."*

"For all the big time," said Cathy, "he still lives in Pederson, in his family home. Married. I hear he has a kid."

"You hear? Don't you—"

"No. Not anymore."

Just then Jim stuck his head between them and said he and the others were calling it a night. Cathy looked at Harold and smiled.

"We're staying," said Harold. "Aren't we?"

Cathy nodded in the affirmative.

"So do you and the rest of the Specials keep in touch?" Harold asked.

"When we can, but it's not always possible."

"Do you know—" and here Harold was embarrassed to note he had become breathless—"Ravenshadow?"

"Oh yeah, he always had a gift. He could see things no one else could. Trail anyone, or follow anyone. But he hasn't stayed close to any of us near as I can tell. Between his success as an artist, his hobby as a rich playboy, and the rest of his life, which he uses to fight crime, he hasn't had the time to keep in touch with the rest of the gang."

"The time or the inclination," said Harold.

"Sometimes I think his art and his crime fighting are the same thing. The art buys him the resources he needs for his work, and his work frequently inspires the content of his art. Both painting and putting a criminal behind bars are attempts to impose a rational order on the rest of the world, and to find meaning.

"Then there's people like Laurel Darkhaven, who by

dropping out of sight have left the distinct impression it's better not to know what happened to them or where they went. She was a telekinetic, meaning she could move things with her mind. Never anything big, just small things—she could spin a toy top, make a tornado out of a stack of paperclips, and make plastic dolls walk. Everybody figured it was a useless power—we were kids then, what did we know? We had no idea why Doc Welles spent so much time with her, asking questions which now, in retrospect, I see were meant to provide her with moral bearings in life.

"I suspect the doctor's efforts were an absolute failure. She dropped out of sight too, doesn't even have e-mail anymore. I think she joined the intelligence community. I asked Randy once—"

"You mean Ravenshadow?" Harold interrupted, excitedly.

"Yeah. Him. I asked Randy why they'd pick her. He pointed out that the carotid artery is a very small object. If you could pinch it closed with just a thought, you could shut down the blood en route to the brain."

"You think she's become an assassin?"

Cathy shrugged. "Maybe. You know, it's pretty easy for some Specials to embrace the dark side of the force, as it were, and Laurel always was sullen and standoffish. Even so, I didn't think she had it in her to kill."

"Not even in the line of duty, for God and country?"

"I guess I'd think about it differently then. I guess." She'd ordered a cup of coffee, and stared at it intently while she stirred in her usual three spoonfuls of sugar.

"Which side do you think Joshua Kane has embraced?"

142

Cathy smiled. "The answer to that depends on how religious you are—or should I say, what religion you happen to believe. Joshua stopped communicating with us the moment he left high school and didn't have to subject himself to the presence of sinners. Actually, I shouldn't say that. His father doesn't allow Joshua to communicate with any of us, and if he'd had any legal recourse during our formative years, he wouldn't have allowed his son to mingle with us in the first place."

"Joshua has the power to fly?" Harold asked.

"The power to levitate is more like it. And he can irradiate golden, yellow, or white light, which enables some, those who are culturally conditioned toward that predilection, to associate him with the divine."

"Sounds like you don't approve."

"Mr. Kane believes Joshua's abilities are God-given, but somehow he can't bring himself to draw the same conclusion about the rest of the Specials. And I include me in that category because as far as he's concerned, I'm just as bad as the rest of my classmates. Jason used to call Josh's dad 'The King of Denial.' Get it? Denial. . . . da nile . . . well, he's got a big cathedral in Montana and his own cable network and syndicated TV show."

"I went to one of his sermons once."

Cathy was surprised. "Really?"

"Hey, it's a form of prejudice to assume you can tell whether or not someone's a Christian just by looking at them. "

"True. *Are* you a Christian?"

Harold shrugged. "No, but I wouldn't be a true Special fan if I hadn't used my vacation time to see a Special in the flesh."

Cathy raised her eyebrows.

"Special sightings are highly regarded in the chat rooms," Harold explained, "and seeing Joshua Kane, hearing him speak the word of God—as he hears it—is unique among Special sightings in that it is guaranteed. All you have to do is make the trip, check into a hotel, put up with some proselytizing, and you have a sighting."

"How many sightings have you had, Harold?" Cathy asked.

"Up until tonight, I thought it was only five. Now I've found out that for the past month it's been six."

Cathy made a note to get even with Jim someday. She liked Harold, but obviously one reason why Jim had invited her to be monopolized by Harold was so the new office hero could have the treat of a one-on-one chat with a Special. She could see that Harold didn't care that her inclusion in that select group was an accident; he'd been hanging onto her every word. Now all she had to do was figure out what revenge would be appropriate to take on Jim. Maybe she could set him up with a female cross-dresser. No, he might like that. . . .

"So what was Josh's sermon like?" Cathy asked. "I've never even listened to one on the radio."

"Never watched his TV show?"

"No," she said emphatically.

"Well, the church is, architecturally speaking, incredible. It's sleek and has hundreds of stained glass windows, so it has the illusion of lightness and some elements of modernism, but inside it's very majestic and Gothic. And spacious. I think it wouldn't be that difficult for one of Joshua's followers to feel the presence of God in that place."

"What was his sermon about?"

"The topic was ostensibly the heinous spiritual traps one can find laid open to him if he succumbs to petty jealousy, but after about fifteen minutes and a few quotes from a dubious translation of the Bible, he latched onto the lack of moral fiber in today's society, exemplified by ex-President Roger Clinton's continuing addiction and the fact that somebody's son was thrown off the little league baseball team for not playing well enough."

"What?"

"Not playing well enough. According to Joshua, it's not whether you win or lose, it's how you play the game. That's how God will judge you. I've given it some thought, and I've decided Joshua's sermons are like a book by Hemingway."

Cathy blinked. "What?"

"Well, in a novel Hemingway will devote as many pages to how much you should tip a French waiter as he will a scene of battle, or a bull fight, or the death of his leading lady. All things are equal, in his universe, in that regard. Big things vs. small things. It's up to the reader to sort 'em out. That's how I feel about the sermon I heard from Joshua Kane."

"Sounds like a helluva way to tell a story, I gotta tell you that," said Cathy.

"I see you have a strong dislike for Joshua."

"It's difficult not to. Everytime he stages a protest at an abortion clinic, the TV news shows up and he puts on his light and levitation act, and he adds another couple hundred deluded viewers to his flock."

"You sound like a feminist."

"Most women think they aren't, but if you look at the way they've lived, they've had no problem taking advantage of the opportunities feminism has provided them.

Starting with the right to vote, I might add. But you're right, obviously, I don't like Joshua. I consider him brainwashed, but he wants to take away my freedom, he wants to control my body, under the guise of living up to the standards set by the old white man with a beard who lives upstairs.

"The last time Joshua came to a reunion, he got into a fight with almost everybody. Called us all a bunch of sinners and said we were all going to hell because we were infected with the force. As opposed to him. Randy called him a fanatic and tried to deck him. It was quite a brouhaha."

"You said he's brainwashed, in your opinion? I read somewhere that young people who are brainwashed by the insidious influence of a domineering person and/or peer group come out of their mental fog after about 90 days or so once they are outside the presence of said peer group."

"Mr. Kane would never allow that to happen."

"I don't think Joshua is the true focus of your dislike."

"That's true. I don't know why, but I think Josh is deliberately hiding something from himself. Maybe he's trying to be an avenging angel to make up for some shortcoming that wouldn't matter to a normal person who didn't have religious fanatic for an old man. Of course, it doesn't help that there are a few unrepentant sinners among us."

"Besides Laurel?"

"Well, if she's killing for democracy, then she isn't a sinner, though my father told me about a book he once read, about an assassin for the Pope. Every time the assassin killed someone, he had to do nine weeks of solitary confinement as penance."

"Wasn't that a Dolph Lundgren movie? He played a modern Knight Templar?"

"I was thinking specifically of Jerry Montrose."

"Pyre. I saw him once. He was speeding through Atlanta on an overcast afternoon. Leaving a trail of flame like a military jet—only jets can't make twists and turns around buildings the way he could." Harold sipped at his drink; suddenly he appeared very sad, as if an era was over. "They say he's dead."

"I don't believe them. Jerry is a slippery bastard who won't stop at getting what he wants. In a way, that was always his problem. I wasn't surprised when he went on the wrong side of the law. Now he has nowhere to go, no place to be but in hiding. He can't communicate with us and he can't blend in with normal people." Cathy sipped her drink. She too felt sad, but that was because she was thinking of the troubled kid who couldn't get along with anybody, even when people wanted to get along with him. "I can't imagine how lonely he must be."

"What about David Mueller? What's his situation?"

"The same . . ."

Mueller was a Special who'd provoked several interesting discussions, rants, and speculations in the chat rooms. He could merge his thoughts with those of anyone within a 20 foot range. He'd go into a trance—or a coma—and what his host saw, he saw. What his host felt, he felt. Harold had taken part in numerous discussions about what it would be like to vicariously live someone else's existence for a short while. He would see it as an adventure, an opportunity to perceive the world as does the opposite sex, an chance to expand one's mind and broaden one's horizons.

"You sound like you don't care for him very much,"

he said, after it belatedly hit him that she indeed had sounded that way.

"I don't. Maybe I should. But we suspect—and Doc Welles would never confirm this—that David honed his power until he could make his host do things and not remember them afterwards. I always suspected he was using his abilities in ways he shouldn't have."

"What do you mean? He wasn't taking over the minds of the girls, was he?"

"Several of us had blackouts. We'd wake up naked and discover evidence that we had . . . pleasured ourselves, long before we had the inclination to do it on our own. A lot of the mundane girls had the same problem over the weekends. Doc Welles tried to help David, I'm sure, and he certainly protected him from the authorities. I don't think he wanted to find out what would happen if David was alone and frightened in a jail cell somewhere, around hardened criminals. You get the idea. David could do some harm in someone else's body, but during that period his own body would be comatose. Helpless."

"Sounds like your Dr. Welles had a lot of tough decisions to make."

"Who knows what the right thing to do was. I guess we all had to forgive David, when it all went bad. His mother, you see, was an alcoholic. She was suicidal when he wasn't home, but when he was over the weekends, she was usually in a drunken stupor. She was a mean, self-pitying drunk too. One Saturday night David slipped out of the apartment to go a movie. When he returned home he saw his mother standing on the edge of the roof of their building. A 12-story building. She was weaving back and forth. He wasn't sure she really wanted to jump, but as I got the story, when he yelled at her, she said she wanted to die.

"I can only imagine how David felt at that moment. I doubt he liked his mother very much—he dreaded going home, and the frequency of the blackouts slowed down considerably (they never really stopped) after Doc Welles threatened to keep him home during the week too—but she was his mother. And David had human feelings. He must have loved her as much as anyone loves their mother."

"But 12 stories! You said he could project his mind for 20 feet."

"You're a good listener. I like that."

"Yeah, and I think on my butt too."

"And you're charming," Cathy replied. "And you *are* correct. David could only project 20 feet. But that was his mother up there. He had to try. I'm sure he did try. But we'll never know what happened next. Whether David successfully projected his mind but lacked the control to keep his mother from falling off the roof. Or whether he only projected himself into her body when she was falling and was finally only 20 feet away. Of course, by then, there was nothing he could have done about it, except get out, and we don't know if he ever learned the skill of getting out of another mind fast. Either way, he was inside her when she died."

"But he didn't die."

"True, but she still took him with her when she went. He's in a hospital up north. Catatonic. But probably okay. The Feds pay for his health care. It's the best. They turn him often, to keep the number of bedsores down, and exercise him everyday, and he's got a great view where he can watch the grass grow. At least, that's what Randy says. Must be a terrible way to live."

"Not live," said Harold. He shuddered. "Exist."

And they were right. It was a terrible way to live. To exist. What they didn't know—but what I found out later, irresistably noting the irony—was that while Cathy was being so concerned about that wretched little pervert David—and while he was catatonically enjoying the view in his hospital window—he was being stalked by somebody he had known since childhood. He was being stalked by someone he could have protected himself against if he hadn't succumbed to that one moment of weakness, that one temptation to sacrifice himself for the good of another that had left him a glorified vegetable at a VA hospital. I don't know how much of David's mind was actually working at that moment. A mundane mind would have been asleep. But a squirrelly, squirmy mind such as David's still had possibilities. Perhaps it was a mere specter of its former self, an ember forever dying. So even if David had been aware of the stalker, *his murderer*, he still would have been too weak to prevent it. He still would have died, a shattered heap of mangled human flesh thrown out a five-story high window.

Thrown through some bars, by the way, bars that had been bent apart by a pair of gloved hands.

I have on good authority that before doing the heinous deed, the scumbag had the impertinence to say to David, "Sorry. Hope you understand that this is necessary. It has to be this way." Then he paused, waited for the moment of impact below, then added, "Maybe at least now you'll find some peace."

Cathy and all the others, including myself, wouldn't

find out about David's defenestration until the morning. At the moment she was closing the scrapbook with an air of both relief and nostalgia; she enjoyed thinking about the good old days, but she was glad she wasn't living through them any more. "There are over a hundred stories like these, but that's all I can handle for tonight."

"Well, I do appreciate it," said Harold, leaving some money on the table for as a tip. "I really do. I'd never thought about how difficult it must have been for the Specials growing up. I was always jealous of them, I'm afraid, because special is one thing I never was. Well, I'll never look at them in the same way again." And once they were outside, he added: "It's amazing that you grew up with them, knew all their secrets."

Cathy blushed. "Well, I wouldn't say I know all their secrets."

She had no idea that I'd been aware of her presence one day as Doc Welles and I had a private conversation, theoretically locked away from all the others, while sitting on the football field bleachers. Cathy, who was still somewhat skinny and underdeveloped, happened to be walking behind the bleachers just in time to catch Doc Welles reminding me, once again, that the slightest miscalculation made while practicing my powers could be fatal to the entire class of Specials.

I was feeling funky that afternoon. Like many typical outsiders, I was severely bummed by the apparent futility of it all. I asked the doctor what difference it made. Half the world wanted us dead anyway. Maybe if I accidentally killed us all, I'd be doing everyone a favor.

That was supposed to shock Welles, but he'd heard it all a hundred times already, not only from me, but from several of the others. His response to such remarks was always cool, and he never believed us unless he suspected it would be prudent to at least go along with us, for a while. The only thing that was different this time was that he'd decided to shock me back.

He pointed out, not unreasonably, that if it would easy for me to accidentally kill everyone, it would be infinitely easier to kill everyone deliberately. And as for the half of the population that already wanted us Specials dead, the doctor believed that our staying alive was the best revenge we could have on those folks. He reiterated, for the umpteenth time, that whenever I did use my power, my control had to be perfect. The doc had this premonition, you see. Normally he wasn't given to them, but in my case he had to make an exception. Someday I might be someone's only hope. Whether that someone was a Special or a mundane remained to be seen. I didn't believe him, of course, but I appreciated the fact that he was trying to assure me that my existence mattered.

And that is what Cathy heard. She never knew, either, that I knew. And so she told Harold, "Some secrets you keep. Out of respect, fear, affection, or all three."

That's right. She felt affection for me. God knows why. Most of the group did, by the way. I'd remained neutral throughout all the cliquish behavior of the first few years of high school, and I always tried to treat my fellow Specials as if they were my equal, whether they actually were or not. I appreciated that affection. I miss it.

"You sure you don't need a lift?" Harold asked Cathy.

"No, it's fine. I'm just down the block in an apartment. I like working close to home."

Harold cleared his throat. Several times. "I was

wondering," he finally said, "if you wouldn't mind, er, uh, ah, going out sometime."

Cathy knew the question, in some form, was coming, but to her surprise she was more ambivalent then she'd been when anticipating it. "Oh, Harold, I don't know—" she said before she realized she was actually thinking about it. "Sure. Why not?"

"That's great!"

"As long as you don't mind going out with a Special who has no powers."

"Not at all. And besides, how can you be sure you don't have any powers?"

"Well, granted you have to be exposed to a given situation in order for your abilities to manifest themselves, but I expect I would have been exposed to the right situation by now. Besides, I did all the usual jumping out of trees and trying to hold my hand over a flame stunts. Most of us girls were real tomboys at one time or another."

"Come on, your power might be so different from the others' that you still haven't been exposed to the right situation."

"Considering some of the others' powers, I'd hate to think of what that situation might be. Look, I've reconciled myself to being normal. I'm okay with it. Saves me from a lot of responsibilities."

They heard a high-pitched, inhuman scream.

Followed quickly by the sickening crunch of skin and bone being flattened beneath the wheel of a passing car.

A feral cat had just been run over. By a driver so unaware of the unusual bump in the road that he didn't slow down or check things out in his rearview mirror.

Harold grimaced. "The poor thing . . ."

"Poor kitty," said Cathy, kneeling beside the furry corpse.

"Nothing you can do for him. He's dead." Harold was obviously nauseated by being so close to the crushed cat. Of course, he was a guy who couldn't watch the Animal Planet cable station because seeing footage of animals dying or getting eaten moved him too easily to tears, and here he was, getting a close look at a fresh carcass, all because he was attracted to this woman.

"I know. I just hate to see it."

Tenderly, Cathy put her hands on the bloody corpse. "Poor little kitty," she said. "Good night."

She stood up, shed a tear, and then she and Harold walked away. The city would pick up the corpse sometime tomorrow. "At times like this," she said, "I wish there was something I could do, like stop the car, turn back time . . ."

"I know," said Harold, "but there's nothing you could have done. And who knows, if you did have a power, it might've been something silly anyway."

"Like what?" she said with a grin.

"Like turning roses blue, or being able to bend spoons—but only spoons, not knives or forks. Or being able to inflate and bounce around. Wouldn't *that* be useful?"

"Pretty funny. That makes about as much sense as being able to split into two or three duplicates of yourself. You know, I like you, Harold."

Something was happening behind them, something that Cathy, at least, never could have guessed.

The cat realized that something was happening too. One moment he was crossing the street, trying to run under one of the metal monsters, and the next he was inexplicably on the other side, safe and on the sidewalk. He had some red stuff that smelled like it belonged to him on his fur, but he was whole and was in no pain. Oh well. He headed toward the alley, where there was a trash bin outside a restaurant that always had leftover fish in it.

"I like you too, Cathy, even if you don't have any powers," Harold said.

10

THE WORLD BETWEEN

Every superhero has his, hers, or *its* limitations; that's just one of the literary conventions of the genre. And those limitations are frequently challenged straight on; for the hero, there is no avoiding or sidestepping the issue. He must overcome his blindness and attune his radar sense to recognize color. He must adjust his hearing so that he will recognize when a certain gun has been fired, from across the city. He must vibrate his atoms until his body returns to its original form, or he must fight and prevail on a world where he has no superpowers.

Take me, for instance. I'm supposed to be this great writer. My superior outsider status has freed me from the constraints of traditional poetic convention—and by that I mean everybody from e e cummings to John Lennon. My expertise in matters of philosophical and literary criticism has brought me great respect, and my influence has impacted at least four Pulitzer Prize winners. And yet I have this one great failing: it is widely agreed that my grasp of the human character leaves something to be desired. The details don't matter, but one must be realistic while gauging one's impact upon the arts, however painful it may be.

A great and noble sage with a smoking gun in his hand once said a man's gotta know his limitations. John Simon's corollary says he has to know his limitations so he'll know when they are being challenged. Mine were being challenged. It was time for me to rise up to meet those challenges.

And I had the profound example of Peter Dawson, a man who thought of his limitations as a prison rather than as a challenge, to remind me constantly of the price of failure.

In order to solve the Case of the Very Special Murders, I'd have to grasp something elusive and insightful about human nature, and thus far I'd demonstrated to the entire world that when it came to human nature, I didn't have a goddamn clue.

There was only one thing left to do, only one way to overcome a lifetime of little-to-no direct experience with the quiet desperation of the noble and/or ignoble human heart:

I'd have to cheat. I'd have to talk to someone who might have a clue.

About human nature, that is.

I did know one thing, though. I knew it because before I got my first grant, I had to work at a bookstore, because even a Special with an intellect as Special as mine has to work for a living. At this store one of the clerks was accused of skimming the top of the take, and everybody was sure it was him because a) he was a bum, and b) he used drugs and drank too much, and c) he was always broke, and d) a, b, and c combined.

I thought he was guilty too, which ended the matter

in my mind. One of the few times I'd joined a group was when the staff confronted the bum and demanded a confession. Only problem was, the bum was innocent. The culprit was some other bum. Turned out the culprit was the manager's highly respectable new boyfriend, who as it turned out drank too much and was always broke. Everybody was contrite and embarrassed for only a little while—hell, they'd never trusted the first bum anyway and figured it was only a matter of time before he pulled some stunt—but the lesson was plain:

Don't jump to conclusions on matters of guilt and innocence. It's just possible that the guy who drives across town with a loaded shotgun, who parks in front of his intended victim's house, gets out of the car, walks into the living room and blows his victim away before he has a chance to move—that guy just might be acting in self-defense. You never know. You have to hear all sides and wait until all the evidence is in.

Words to live by. Unfortunately, people were dying and I didn't have time for a steady, methodical investigation. I had to start cheating, fast.

I had several potentially unsavory Specials in mind, not to mention the several more who were unsavory already. Most of us had been unsavory at least once, though I hasten to add I was not one of them. It was part of the learning process.

Then there was the possibility that one of us was committing the crimes during a blackout period. Like the alcoholic who awakes to discover he has inadvertently bludgeoned his favorite hooker to death, one of us could be deep in that Dr. Jekyll jive. Heck, it could even have been me; many times I've closed my eyes while trying to think of what my next sentence should be, only to awake minutes or hours later, with no idea how long I'd been out.

Of course, I could always make sure of my innocence by scanning the videos left by my household security devices, but I figured that could wait. The better part of valor would be to narrow down the list of possible suspects, not that I wanted to investigate them immediately, of course. I just needed a preliminary list in preparation for my cheating.

It took considerable concentration for twenty to thirty minutes, but I did eventually narrow the list of possible potential suspects down to seven. It certainly wouldn't have surprised me if the villain turned out to be:

Maximum Hacker, who had ambitions to be a professional boxer but had thus far succeeded in being an enforcer for a small time loan shark. Max's sense of taste and smell could adapt to find pleasurable favor in almost anything edible. In other words, if he'd been the star of *Pink Flamingoes*, he could have pretended the main course at the end tasted like ice cream. Max was bitter about his connection to small-time crime. He'd felt he was destined for better things, stupid power or no stupid power. Rumor had it he took out his bitterness on down-on-your-luck cardsharps.

Thijs van Ward, who could read body auras, and who had set up a psychic reading shop in Barstow, California. He enjoyed parting the foolish and the gullible from their money.

Deedee Noonan, a sullen frail of no great physical beauty, damn little intelligence, and absolute zilch charm, who was caught once torturing bugs with her mind by ringing them in a tiny electrical field. Rumor had it she was treating her nebbish husband the same way.

Roy Uttal, who had a sense of touch so sensitive and well-developed, he could close his eyes and read a newspaper with his fingertips. He had become a masseur in Seattle and, rumor had it, a pimp for underaged girls.

Red Lansing, who used his phantom power to sneak into plays and movies. His body had a tenuous grasp on this plane of reality, and his mind was almost as ghostly. The girls said that if he tried to kiss them and was feeling nervous, then his face would slip *into* theirs, giving them cool, unpleasant shivers. He could also transfer his halitosis, an endowment of rather dubious worth.

Gary Feldman had the gift of gab. Literally. He could sell aluminum siding to people with brick homes. Fortunately for the human race, Gary had his limitations. You know the phrase "aim high, shoot low"? Gary aimed low and shot lower every time. He could talk people into doing minor things they wouldn't normally do, but nothing financially or emotionally damaging. Meaning he couldn't bilk a millionaire of a fortune nor convince a virgin to give it up for him. Unless, of course, some part of them already thought it wasn't a half-bad idea.

Bridget O'Miley, though, was another story. She was an emotional firestarter, a woman whose pheromones could arouse such a response that she could make some men jump to all sorts of amazing conclusions, and do all sorts of stupid things, in order to please her. A few dead bodies had been laid at her doorstep in the past, but so oblivious was Bridget to the potential consequences of her most casual remarks that she was just as shocked as the police that (typically) such a milksop could have committed such a cold-blooded act.

Then again, the culprit could easily be someone else. I had to be careful not to jump to conclusions. I needed more data to work with, and I had to be sure that data was accurate.

So why was I so filled with trepidation as I approached the front door of this house with five gables in upper New England? I can't say it was a dark and stormy night—at the moment it was a dank and cloudy dusk—but I couldn't shake my anxiety at what I was about to do. Physical intimacy has never aroused my curiosity, at least not enough to learn what it actually feels like. And what I was about to do was more intimate than that!

Two Specials had the potential to help me. Clarence Mack was the first. His abilities were slow to reveal themselves, but once they did, the school authorities and his parents alike were compelled to give him his own room. Clarence was a dreamwalker, who could enter the minds of individuals when they were asleep. He could see and occasionally interact with their dreams, and he could remember them afterwards better than the individual in question. His interpretations tended to be Freudian, but that was to be expected, since his initial dreamwalking experiences happened in the minds of puberty-ravaged teens such as himself.

Clarence had gotten a degree in psychology and specialized in helping severely traumatized children. He had also written a few books on the interpretation of dreams that sold well in New Age bookstores. He was well-known as a Special who'd done a lot of good in the world, even if his personality was rather, well, abrasive. Forget the talk shows, he bombed on the lecture circuit and on panels at the shrink conferences. He lacked the common touch. Fortunately for the mental health of the human race in general, he only tried to tell jokes and/or be funny in groups of three or more Specials. He was noted among us for his uncanny ability to blow the easiest punch line while being completely oblivious to the concept of irony.

Even so, he wasn't particularly moody like the Specials' other great astral traveler, Lionel Zerb. His was a solitary youth; the only difference between me and him, really, was that I was more polite about it. Lionel had no problem being nasty to as many kids—and indifferent to as many adults—as it took in order to get what he really wanted out of life: to be alone.

Dr. Welles assured me—and, presumably, him—that the desire to be solitary was natural, given as how the Specials' differences from one another only emphasized how different we were from our fellow man, and so it was right and reasonable to be a tad withdrawn. Welles wanted us not to take it to extremes. I made an effort to at least talk to the gang occasionally, whereas Lionel just grumped out.

The parents held these get-togethers every few months, during which they'd get to know one another and talk about the various issues pertaining to the kids— legal, financial, educational, and rearing. All the parents did it; the group was loosely divided into cliques bordering on cells, and then twice a year they all got together for this networking fest and they figured out new ways to get Paulson, the FBI, and both major political parties to trip over their own feet. Some of the parents got to be as devious and twisted as some of their children, but all in the name of protecting us and taking responsibility, two themes which, despite the kids' potential danger, held great resonance with the public.

Neither the Feds nor the kids liked this particular response to Big Flash-related problems, but there was nothing they or we could do about it. We didn't like it because we got sick of one another too, or sometimes just didn't get along, but the parents never took that into account. They couldn't afford to let the personal likes and dislikes of their children get in the way of the practicalities behind their eternal conferencing.

My folks went clique-hoping one afternoon, and so it was I found myself, sullenly clutching a few books from a Lloyd Alexander series, at Lionel's house. Lionel was there, natch, along with a few other kids I normally didn't see over a weekend. The parents didn't care if we interacted or not, just so long as we didn't scare the neighbors or cause any other trouble, so it happened I was reading on the front porch while the others, save Lionel, roughhoused in the yard.

Lionel sat on a nearby street corner, pretending we weren't there. Or so it seemed.

From the corner of my eye I caught Lionel waving his arms and stamping his foot. The others stopped roughhousing. We all looked in his direction.

He was talking. Seemingly to himself, but by now we knew better than to simply assume that. We crept up on him, but tried not to distract him.

His powers had kicked in; the nature of the force inside Lionel would soon be revealed.

Gradually we realized he was talking to the ghost of a dog. The poor animal had been struck on that corner a couple of days ago, and though its corpse had long since been picked up and cremated, its spirit still lingered. Lionel was trying to shoo it away like a live stray. It was bothering him. Barking at him. Trying to tell him something, maybe. Remember that Gary Larson cartoon, about the meaning of a dog bark? No matter what the situation, they're always saying "Hey. Hey. Hey. Hey. Hey!" Lionel was getting that from a dead dog. It was creeping him out.

It creeped us out too. None of us wished to emulate that particular power. We tried to get Lionel to admit he was faking it, but he was just as uncommunicative with the living as ever. It took three or four weeks before he'd admit to Dr. Welles—and hence to the adult community— that he could speak to recently departed human beings as well. Incredible consternation immediately ensued.

Lionel's power had implications, you see. Here was a Special whose power, even at this young age, could be of immense value to law enforcement organizations. Lionel's spirit reading ability was apparently so reliable that no crime scene would ever hold any secrets from him. The police wanted to start using him at once, regardless of his age, and regardless of the adults' concern that he might be too young to deal with the work emotionally. Dr. Welles stuck his neck out on this one and sided whole-heartedly with the parents.

One thing Clarence and Lionel's folks had in common: they didn't worry about instilling their children with job skills. The force had seen to that for them.

Not long ago, Lionel had terminated his contracts with most law enforcement agencies. More consternation ensued, the agencies insisted Lionel assist them, but Lionel got a court order that had the effect of giving him the freedom from gainful employment he so desired. No one knows why he stopped, if it was a particular conversation he'd had with a recently deceased, or if it was the cumulative effect of having been a graveyard reader all these years. Either way, he bought a big house, just as Clarence had, in a small New England town; but unlike Clarence, he saw no one. He never went out, turned down all requests from the law, and rarely turned on the lights at night. His requirements for the piece of property had been quite specific: no deaths on the premises for the past five years. He wanted to be alone. Truly alone. He was the Greta Garbo of psychics.

Both Clarence and Lionel could see into netherworlds. Both could have information on the killer. I didn't know which one to talk to first, not initially, but circumstances dictated it be Clarence, and I could only do that while asleep. Come to think of it, I was feeling a little tired—

The front door was unlocked. I walked into the old house, found the office, laid down on the plush, air-cushioned couch that maximized the subject's physical comfort and relaxation, and promptly proceeded to grab some much needed shuteye. It occurred to me, just before I stepped from the realm of the waking into the dream corridors, that I had no idea whether or not I snored. I'd slept alone since I finally got my own dorm room.

Perhaps the person guiding me through my journey could tell me after it was over. "I've established contact," he said. "Relax your mind. That's it. Just like that . . ."

Before I knew it I was walking on solid land—at least land that was solid wherever my footsteps happened to be. Elsewhere it was gray and amorphous, and I could not help but notice the trees and boulders sinking slowly, slowly toward oblivion. The houses and alleys seemed forever just beyond my reach. The lines in the fog were much more defined. The shapes of horsemen and their horses, of vultures and owls, of abstract cityscapes and ringed planets, hell, of shoes and ships and sealing wax—

all twisted inside out like balloons expanding to the point of bursting—except that the lines changed into other shapes. The air felt stale and my sense of smell seemed dampened, suggesting, perhaps, that there was nothing to smell.

I was either walking around in my mind—in which case I wasn't nearly as colorful and as imaginative as I'd always believed—or else I'd astral-projected somehow into a mysterious netherworld suspended between planes of reality. The place was so cold that the tiny light in the sky—presumably a sun—reminded me of the light in a refrigerator. I found it difficult to believe I'd volunteered to come here. But here I was.

And I wasn't alone.

"So now what?" I said. "What now?"

"You don't have to shout," said someone behind me.

I recognized the voice instantly, of course. It was that of Clarence Mack.

"Looking good, Clarence," I said. "How you been?"

"Good. I've been a productive member of society for the last few years. Even done a little bit of charity work, helping some of the homeless and otherwise itinerant come to terms with their emotional conundrums."

"That's very nice. I usually just give a dollar to the Salvation Army folks planted outside Target."

"John Simon, shopping at a Target store? I had no idea you were so bourgeois."

"I *do* live on a budget, you know."

"Speaking of which," he said, crossing his arms, and eyeing me with the air of superiority one usually sees in someone who thinks he knows you better than you do, "how *is* the writing coming?"

There is no better way to put me on the defensive than

to ask me that. It doesn't happen often, because of my usual penchant for avoiding contact with general humanity on a casual basis whenever possible, but when it does, it arouses my insecurities, and I feel like a great actor forever on the verge of going on stage, where he is fated to give a great performance. The operative words being *forever* and *fated*.

"Fine. Good," I said.

Clarence always had this pinched, smug expression whenever he thought he'd caught someone uttering a *foma*. A "foma" is a word invented by Kurt Vonnegut—a small, harmless untruth we tell ourselves, in order to make life more bearable. Clarence looked at me now with that accusation in his eyes, and I shrugged.

"Really?" he said.

I shrugged again.

The netherworld changed. Again. The ever-moving lines in the fog straightened and assumed the outlines of definite, stable objects. The gray washed out in stages and was replaced by different primary colors, then the colors of the rainbow, then the variety of hues one associates with real life. I recognized the colors and the lines as familiar: they belonged to my office. It held a few shelves of books, a desk lamp, an overhead lamp, and an infinitely dinged second-hand desk made out of some metal alloy that couldn't withstand pressure in the slightest. Probably got most of its dings from a gentle breeze. The phone and most of the writing accessories were in drawers. For me a neat desk had as few items as possible on it, and this desk was very neat.

I was sitting at the desk. Not the me standing and talking to Clarence, but the me of a couple of weeks ago, when I'd been working on some haiku about apples, oranges, and still-life oils, writing by long hand, when I was interrupted by a phone call.

It was the editor of a small literary journal. The editor was a guy who called himself H.H. Holmes, after the infamous turn-of-the-20th-century murderer, and the journal was an underground affair called *No Poems By Dead People*. Real artsy, published a lot of stuff I couldn't read, but it was perfect for what I tended to write in that arena. I had a bad feeling about the phone call, though. The *No Poems etc.* poetry journal had certain rules and standards, even as it proclaimed not to have them.

"Mr. Simon?" said Mr. Holmes (he was formal that way). "I'm afraid I'll have to reject your latest submissions. You know, *No Poems* wants very much to have your by-line on its contents page, but I thought you understood that we don't publish fantasy."

"I think that's probably a fantasy, but actually, I was very careful *not* to send you any poetry of a fantastic nature."

"Stanza four, line two of 'Carl Orff's Dilemma' references a dragon."

"It's an *allusion,* and it rhymes with flagon. There aren't a lot of words that rhyme with flagon."

"Not in the English language, maybe."

"And besides, I was writing about defrocked monks, loose women, and ungodly drunkenness. Flagon is just one of those words that springs to mind."

"Mr. Simon—"

"It's one word."

"Poetry is made up one word at a time."

That did it. Normally I try to be nice and accommodating to editors, because they provide the only general approval I get from society, but this guy was a martinet.

"What if I change it to a wagon?" I suggested coolly. "Will that help?"

"I don't think the world is ready for a fire-breathing wagon, Mr. Simon. Thanks for considering us. I imagine you have files of these poems on your computer, so I can just throw away the manuscripts, yes? I thought so. Good day."

And he hung up, before I had the chance to tell him a few things about his mother. I folded my arms and fumed. What did I care what he thought? I would have only gotten paid in contributor's copies anyway.

Every light bulb in the room exploded. I looked about in surprise: I'd been fuming harder than I'd thought.

"You really need to control your temper," Clarence said to the me watching the scene with him.

The real me. "Yeah, I get that a lot," I replied, wondering if my illusion of myself as an individual with great self-control was only that: an illusion. Even I, with my somewhat debatable understanding of human nature, had noticed there is so often a gap between a person's perception of himself and who he really is. "Look, can we go somewhere else? That's not what I came here to talk about."

Clarence laughed once, sarcastically. "It's your dream. You're in charge, I'm just along for the ride."

I looked him in the eye. I sensed anger, grief, self-pity, but most of all I felt an intense resentment of *me*. Clarence had a narrow face with a nose that was like the beak of an eagle; his eyes were dark and piercing, yet did not convey very much personal strength. He had always been pale, but walking through my dream he looked like he had avoided the sun for years. I'd always suspected he disliked me—it's not like I'd ever shown him

169

any friendship before—but I'd always assumed his dislike for me was on general principles of some sort: I'd no idea it was so personal.

"Where do *you* want to go to next?" he asked.

The question startled me. I'd never before tried to control the content of my dreams. The scene shifted from my office to a vast and desolate landscape. Fog or clouds enshrouded the sky and horizon like a widow's veil, yet the barren land—with its winter trees and tumbling brush—was infused with an unhealthy light, like an iridescent infection. Ah, home again, home again, jiggetty-jig. I didn't remember this place, exactly, I knew I'd been here many times before, during forgotten dreams.

"Nice, John," Clarence said. "This is a bleakness with a difference."

"I didn't ask to meet you because I needed a critique of my dreamscape. It's true that apparently this place is symbolic, somehow, of my innermost, most private self, because I now recognize that I've come here often, but that's not really what's on my mind. Nor is it what should be on yours."

"So?"

"Like I said in my message, I want to talk to you."

He hung his head. He'd been trying to avoid this moment. "About the murders."

"Yes."

He looked over his shoulder. I had the distinct impression he was afraid he would see someone. "I'd rather not," he said.

"We all have to face our problems eventually. And while you'd rather have me face mine right now, you know I have to deal with a bigger issue."

Yeah, I was pushing him, but he pushed back, turning to me with a honest anger and resentment so intense and primal that I was shocked. I would have thought him beyond such petty jealousies by now.

"You think that because I can walk in people's dreams that I invade everyone's privacy, that I snooped around in everyone's dreams and maybe along the way I picked up a clue, or I saw something, or—"

"That's not what I meant—"

"Then why else talk to me? I mean, why are you even investigating this? Why *you*? Why not turn this over to somebody else?"

I knew I had no choice but to get him to vent his rage. Thank goodness he was inclined to do so verbally. But I wasn't used to being insulted so irrationally and I was finding it difficult to suppress my own anger. Anger he could sense, could feed off of. "I have an obligation," I said. "A responsibility."

"That's a load of crap. You're just looking for an excuse to be judge, jury, and executioner. That's the terrible truth about you, John. You don't hate this. You want it."

I rejected that straight off, but held my tongue. Nonetheless, pride swelled deep in my breast, and for the first time I think I knew how a Marine must feel before he steps onto that battle-scarred beach already littered with the bodies of his comrades slain before him. I had justice in my soul and death in my fingertips, and I was not ashamed.

"You've been waiting for this all your life," Clarence continued. "Ever since we were kids, you kept apart from the rest of us like you were too good for us. It was always just you and Doc and that's it. Some of the others, they thought you were just shy or something. But that's not the truth, is it?"

The landscape changed around us. Clarence and I stood on floating crags that jutted out from nonexistent mountains. In the sky or standing on other crags were the images of our fellow Specials. Idealized, heroic images. The silhouette of Flagg had a cape that billowed out for twenty yards, the floating face of Matthew Bright possessed a godlike nobility, and even the silhouette of poor overweight Peter Dawson evoked a sensitivity I fear the poor guy always lacked in real life.

"You didn't get close to the rest of us for the same reason people don't name a sick animal," said Clarence, spitting out the words. "You don't want to know their name when it come times to put them down. This is how you see ... the danger you see in us ... that we're mad dogs waiting to tear each other and the rest of the world apart ... mad dogs that need to be put down. Put down by *you*."

Now the dreamscape about us had to be infected by Clarence's own perceptions and preconceptions, because I didn't remember ever entertaining the kind of vision we were both being subjected to now. Ravenshadow's claws dripping red with blood as he stood over the dying Paula R. Maximum Hacker beating the bejeezus out of Bongo Shankar, a meek guy whose only ability was the power to stretch his body a few inches. Flagg and Matthew beating the immortal crap out of one another. Pyro setting Renee on fire. Lilith, who fancied herself the reincarnation of a reptilian goddess, choking Joshua to death. And even poor Cathy Thompson, who had no powers whatsoever, lying disemboweled on the dirt. I have to admit, this really pissed me off. Just where did Clarence get off, having such a low opinion of me? He was correct on one level. I'd always known I might one day have to protect the rest of humanity from the Specials, but why did he think I relished the prospect? What was the matter with him, why had he become so twisted, so inhuman inside?

Even so, I had to contain my anger. I had to let him talk, and if I said anything, anything at all, it had to encourage him.

The landscape changed. Yet again. Now it was a desolate, deserted city, like Los Angeles in the beginning of *The Omega Man*, but without standing buildings. Cars were overturned, water pipes were broken, and skyscrapers lay in pieces as if Godzilla had pushed them down, and yet there were no dead bodies. No dead humans, cats, dogs, or even pigeons. It was as if the remains of the life that had once thrived here had finally decayed into dust.

And only Clarence and I were left standing. If I had to be alone with a Clarence, why couldn't I have had the one from *It's a Wonderful Life* instead? I needed an angel right about now. Not this Clarence.

"This is your nightmare," said the Clarence I was stuck with. "Your nightmare of the world we will create if left unchecked. Unless there's someone to stand in the dark places between us and the rest of the world. And you think it's you. Dear God in Heaven, you think it's *you.*"

Maybe it was presumptuous of me, but the degree of his anger made me suspect he was somewhat irrational, and I therefore shouldn't take his ill feelings toward me seriously.

"Well, damn it," he said. "Say something."

"Why? You've already said it all. I've got just one question."

"Yeah?" he asked, daring me to stump him.

That was easier than he thought. "How do you know my nightmares," I asked, "if you haven't been walking in my dreams?"

He looked like he had been hit on the back of the head with a hammer in a silent movie. "I—I mean, after you called—I wanted to check you out, make sure you weren't the real killer yourself, trying to set me up, see how much I knew, I—"

"I haven't slept since I called you. I don't sleep much at all any more. I'm still waiting for an answer."

Clarence frowned and refused to look me in the eye. "I am sorry, I am ashamed. I've been holding out on you. On everybody. There's one aspect of my power that I haven't revealed to anyone. Until now."

"And that would be?"

"Distance. Until now, people have believed that, to walk the dream of another, I must be within a twenty-foot radius. The truth is, no such precondition applies. I have been walking through the dreams of both Specials and interesting mundanes for years. Not all Specials, and not at all times. Only when my curiosity overwhelms the principles Doc Welles drilled into me, to always respect the privacy of others. I try to control it."

"And why can't you control it, Clarence? Missing something on your own?"

"How did you know?"

"I know what it's like to live vicariously."

"My God, then you do know," said Clarence, with something approaching friendliness in his voice. "I would prefer my dreams remain a private thing, but the problem is, I can't have them on my own. I can't achieve a REM sleep. But dreams are necessary for the preservation of a sane mind. Luckily for me, the dreams of others provide me with the same mental therapy. Otherwise . . ."

"So, you've walked the dreams of Specials, regardless of distance."

"I happen to have walked yours recently. I hope you don't mind."

"I don't think I have much choice in the matter."

"No, but try to see things from my point of view," he said. "Without walking in the dreams of others, my mind is incapable of releasing that creative tension that inevitably builds up with limitations of existing in a waking state. Without the assistance of others, a brand new day is really just the same old day, devoid of the possibility of refreshment or creativity."

"That doesn't give you the right to invade the subconscious of others constantly."

"Now who's being judgmental? Oh wait, I forgot, it's your mission in life to be judgmental. When did you start feeling that way? Was it the day you realized the nature of your power?"

I figured there was no point in arguing against his interpretation. "No. I've always felt pretty much the same way about my peers, even before the first day."

Clarence nodded. "I'm not surprised. I shouldn't blame you, though. It seems our emotions and basic personalities have been dictated to us as decisively as our talents. Who would have thought the old nature/nurture argument could be applied to those with superpowers as well?"

"Don't tell me you're going to blame your lying on your parents."

Clarence pursed his lips. "I can't say they are people of character. Father is in real estate, Mother is a corporate lawyer. They appear respectable, but I've walked into their dreams, too, before they suspected me and kept me at the school over the weekends. Not that it did any good."

"You concealed the range of your power from the beginning?"

"Of course. Otherwise Paulson would have tried to order the medical staff to administer mind-numbing drugs to protect the subconscious privacy of others. No way I'd permit something like that to happen. What was it Welles said: 'Never give up, never surrender'? And never, absolutely never, put yourself at their mercy."

"He taught you well," I said, a little envious. I don't believe I could have hidden something that significant from the Paulson squad for as long as he had.

"I'm not saying I haven't taken risks," Clarence said. "I've tried to satisfy my curiosity on certain primal levels. Through the dreams of others I have tasted strange cuisine, experienced the endless variety, debauchery, and bliss of sex a thousand times, have learned how to appreciate an endless array of art and music, from the most intellectual to the most inane, and I have truly walked the face of the Earth. I even know what it means to be weightless, John. Do you know of any other Special who can say that?"

I thought about it. "No. Can't say as I do."

"Have I ever told you about Chandra?" he said, with an evil grin. "I know how she felt."

"When?"

"I know how she felt the moment her powers switched on." He laughed, and blushed. "I didn't know it was possible to feel that beautiful. I guess she thought it was a good thing at the time."

I stuffed my hands into my pockets and turned away

from him. I wanted to swab my mind, to disinfect it, to remove any psychic remnants of him. "Go on," I said.

"Chandra was lucky. A lot of us never knew the exact moment when our powers switched on. It could take months or years to figure out. But Chandra knew the score immediately. Not only have I experienced her dreams of the memory, I've heard her talk about it on *Larry King*, and I was there when it actually happened. Say, you weren't there, were you?"

"I was having a session with Dr. Welles."

"Hmm. It was history class. We were taking an exam . . ."

And as I imagined what the scene must have looked like, the dreamscape changed to reflect that scene with utter realism, yet from a skewed angle, as if we watched from the viewpoint of adolescent, inebriated pygmies. We saw rows of wooden school desks, populated by adolescent Specials pondering the subtle enigmas of a multiple-choice exam. I never had any trouble with those.

Chandra sat surrounded by boys on all sides, for it was just beginning to dawn on them why they might want a girl's attention. At the moment, however, they were concentrating on a, b, and c.

Randy was scratching his head. Jason scowled. Clarence was whipping through the answers. Looking bored, Peter stared at the pages. Matt was erasing. Bernie, who affected the odds of games of chance in his favor, covered his eyes and answered the questions almost at random. Max was catnapping, and Jerry was burning the edges of his papers with his fingertips.

"That was when it happened," Clarence said. "The exact historic moment when Chandra became the most beautiful woman in the world to whoever was looking at her."

And I had missed it. Yet one more life experience that others in my peer group might regard as normal, but which through either chance or temperament was denied me.

I was catching it now. Randy stopped scratching and looked like he'd been stung by a bee. Jason got this confused expression on his face. Peter brightened up. Matt got an expression on his face similar to that of Jason; I'd always felt those two were cut from the same cloth. Bernie's eyes got wide, Max woke up and Jerry accidentally burnt his test to a crisp. I remember he had to take a make-up later.

But that was in the future, and at the moment the future was the farthest thing possible from the minds of those boys. The girls sensed the change, too—Stephanie glared at Chandra with loathing and Cathy had this stunned expression, as if she'd just been knocked a few more rungs down the social ladder.

Because, in fact, she *had* been knocked down. So had the other girls. And the boys never knew what hit them, at least not until Doc Welles saw Chandra and the same thing hit him, an hour later.

But right now, in the sky, the boys and girls of the past were looking at Chandra.

Chandra blinked and looked around. She laughed nervously. "What?" she asked. In the dreamscape her question seemed like a stage whisper. She gasped as she realized that the boys' moonstruck expressions, which seemed to me as more stupefied than lustful, were directed solely at her. She blushed, profoundly, as she realized the stares weren't going to stop in the near future.

She was flattered, yet had an undertone of nervousness in her voice as she said, "Guys—what's going on?"

"Like I said, she thought she liked it at the time—being the most beautiful girl in the world, that is," Clarence said. "She enjoyed having boys cling to her every word, and even more, she appreciated the adults doing likewise. Especially that dreamy algebra teacher. But then after a while—and I'm talking just a few weeks here—she realized it didn't matter what she said—whether it was insightful or malicious or off-the-wall or just plain vapid—the male animal was going to pay attention to her anyway. The male animal didn't care about her appearance either, though when she discovered the effect transcended media, and was especially potent on the big silver screen, she made certain she never slackened or got sloppy in that area. Be that as it may, she soon realized that as a result of her ability, there was one thing the male animal would never be able to offer her."

I felt nauseated, the way I always do when I feel an onslaught of sentimentality coming on.

"No man," Clarence said, "would love Chandra for who she was. They would only love her because of her mutated pheromones. Do you know how she lives now?"

In the sky appeared the foyer of a great mansion, one opulent and rococo even by the standards of the bad taste it aspired to. Masked men in spandex tuxedoes walked back and forth, not doing anything in particular, so far as I could see. They were just walking, being men with big muscles. The silver masks concealed their entire faces but for their eyes and nostrils. Their eyes were glazed yet determined. I don't know about their nostrils.

"Between movies and modeling contracts and beauty magazine covers and talk shows," Clarence said,

"Chandra lives in a huge house in Beverly Hills with the wealthiest men in the world. Men who are so in love with her they have given up all aspirations pertaining to their personal lives so they could experience the privilege of devoting themselves to her. There's only one rule: they must all wear masks so they'll look exactly the same. They see what they want to see in her ... and she wants the same thing, to reduce them to ciphers. That way, when she looks up, she sees what she wants to see."

And what I saw, in the sky, was something I had never needed, never wanted to see. I mean, I'm no prude, and I figured human nature alone would dictate that was what was happening from time to time in Chandra's opulent boudoir. It's just that I didn't need to see it, especially not in the sky of my dreamscape. And I despaired at ever getting out of my mind the picture of Chandra in bed, being hammered all the way to China by a faceless minion who'd passed the Charles Atlas course with flying colors.

"And do you know who she wants to see?" Clarence asked.

I didn't want to answer, but the changing face of the masked man in the sky did all the answering for me.

"She sees *you*," Clarence said. "She loves *you*. Can you imagine? All the world to choose from and she loves you, the only man in existence who is indifferent to her super pheromones. I bet you didn't even know."

I did now. For the face of the man to whom Chandra was making love indeed belonged to me.

With an effort of will I wiped the sky clean; the landscape changed into a flat silver plane, upon which green tombstones cast long shadows, and tables with plaid tops had melting spoons and forks dripping over the sides. The sun was a hollow pink, and the sky a pronounced gray. I could not look at Clarence. I hadn't felt this heartbroken since the last time a beloved relative died.

Clarence must have sensed some of what I was feeling, because he sneered and said, "Don't feel sorry for yourself. Chandra lives a spiritually barren existence because she has no choice. You're different. You live a spiritually barren existence because you're selfish and don't want to share yourself with anyone."

"Baloney. If Chandra wants to be loved for who she is rather than for her force-given ability, why can't she find a woman to love her?"

Clarence *tsk-tsk*ed me. "John, I'm surprised at you. Surely such an adroit judge of human character understands a person's sexuality is wired in his—or her—brain. Chandra couldn't become a lesbian even if she wanted to. She's not even curious. Trust me, I know."

"You've checked out her dreams," I said. "Often."

"Well, yeah!"

"Why are you telling me this?"

Before Clarence had had a resigned tone in his voice; now he was angry, openly resentful. "Because when the day comes that you have to kill her, or let her die, or let someone else kill her, I want you to know that she loved you. I want you to know what you could have, but never will." Beat. "And because you let me—" He couldn't get the words out. he tried again. "You let me—"

"Let you what?"

For a moment our minds touched and I felt his memory of a super-powerful fist hammering him once on the jaw. I tried to control my emotions. We were getting close. "You've been deliberately diverting the discussion. What are you trying to avoid, Clarence?"

Suddenly, it was no longer clear who was guest-starring and who was the star of the mind we were in. The landscape twisted into an abstract red configuration that most resembled the rusted ruins of a long-deserted city. The air starting blowing in a couple of different directions, then converged into a tornado that spewed silent lightning and putrid orange smoke that indicated one of the minds in question—Clarence's or mine—was seriously rotting at the core.

Clarence gave me my first clue: it wasn't me. He stood staring at the tumultuous sky like a stricken bird. He had stopped listening to me.

But I could hear him. His memory was saying something in a deep, familiar voice. *"What did you tell them, Clarence? What did you tell them?"*

His memory cowered in a corner while an intruder threw the furniture around his room like it was made of phonebooks.

My own voice emanated from the answering machine. "Clarence. It's John. I need to see you about the murders. Tonight. I don't think we have a lot of time."

I watched the Clarence beside me go so pale the white almost fell off of him. The air and dirt around us had liquefied and the wind had spawned three distinct tornadoes of psychic energy, stirring up the basest emotions and fears from Clarence's subconscious the way you or I might stir a stew.

"You've got to tell me," I whispered.

"I can't . . ." Clarence whispered back. "I can't."

"Yes, you can. You have to."

The ground was liquefying at our very feet. Pretty soon we were going to be sucked down into the tumultuous psychic mush. If things were going to stablize,

Clarence would have to start 'fessing up quick.

I prompted him. "It happened after we talked."

He nodded, reluctantly. "Yes."

"After I told you to wait. To do nothing. You went inside someone's dreams. You suspected something, didn't you?"

"Yes."

I became a camera. I was watching him. Watching Clarence sit in his chair, pop a couple of pills, and go to sleep. Watching him climb up that hill, walk up that road, creep up that ridge, until the naked man sitting at the edge of the ravine was in plain sight.

"You saw something," I said.

"Yes. And I heard something, too."

The naked man's back was to us, but it was plain from his spectacular build that he was a Special. He hung his head low, and he appeared to be shouldering the weight of the world. It was only a matter of time; either he would crumple beneath the pressure, or he would hurl the burden away and watch it crash and burn.

"I'm sorry, it's not what I wanted," the naked man said. "I didn't have any choice."

Already the stench of rationalization insulted my b.s. detector. I didn't have any choice either. I had to stand still and listen to it. So did Clarence, but in the memory his position was a little more precarious than mine.

"They were my family. We grew up together," the naked man continued, sobbing. "But they don't understand. It was necessary, it was—"

The naked man then sensed the presence of Clarence. That was my only explanation for what happened next, because Clarence could tread lightly in the world of dream and intellect when he felt like it, and surely he felt like it while in this sicko's mind. For the naked man looked through his fingers and saw with a shock that he was no longer alone, that his innermost self with its most sensitive fears had been revealed to an interloper. The shock of discovery gave him strength. The fear of social condemnation trumped his doubt, and he turned to face the spy in his world of pain.

He stood tall and proud. He stood wearing naught but the pride of a warrior and the mantle of righteousness.

Clarence cowered before him, and I have to admit, standing outside the dreamwalker's memory, I felt a rush of fear and loathing. Perhaps it was only a fraction what Clarence felt, but it was enough to make me feel as if ice had been poured into my veins.

I take it back. Perhaps only a fraction of the fear, but all the loathing and then some. For now that he had been discovered, any guilt Jason might have felt about any of the murders he'd committed recently, any sensitivity toward the victims, any doubt about his justification was merely tucked away to an even deeper level in his subconscious, where it could no longer hinder him.

Jason advanced on Clarence.

"I knew I had to get out of there," Clarence told me. "I had to get out of the dreamscape, knew I had to get out of my house before he could get there.

"I thought I had time. But he was fast."

I could see what Clarence meant. In one of those point of view shifts that can only happen in dreams or movies, I saw the exterior of Clarence's neo-Victorian home. It was dusk, and the sky was cloudy. Was it a bird? Was it a plane? Or was it Jason streaking through a closed window with a murderous rage in his heart?

I watched Clarence attempt to duck the glass and

splinters inundating the room in the wake of his unwanted guest. I saw the unwanted guest streak to Clarence's side and start punching him like an old balloon. Jason held the poor guy by the collar and simply pummeled the bejeezus out of him. He could have killed Clarence in one blow, if he'd wanted, and truly that would have been the merciful way to go about it. But there was something he needed to know.

"What did you tell them, Clarence? How much do they know?"

I felt sick. I realized that up till now, I'd been lucky. I'd never actually seen a dead body. Not before it had been embalmed, anyway. Now I was watching a murder happen. It was just as hideous as I'd always imagined, but still wasn't anything like I'd seen in the movies, where most murders of any artistic integrity whatsoever have good lighting, dramatic impact, and maybe a few good angles. This was simply banal.

Banal, and repulsive.

Clarence dealt with the situation more bravely than I think I would have. But I had an advantage. It could never happen to me. Not like that. Jason, still wearing just his birthday suit, stood over Clarence and grinned down at his bleeding, broken body. Clearly Jason felt that he was the superior human being of the two.

Clarence didn't buy it. He looked at Jason coldly, disdainfully. His body had gone beyond the state of shock by now. There was little more Jason could do.

"It's a funny thing," said Clarence. "My whole life, I've never been a hero. I never wondered if I was doing the right thing, I never questioned the morality of my decisions. I just knew, I wasn't a hero.

"A hero like Jason. Flagg. *Whatever* his name is now.

He was a hero. He always did the right thing: taking food to starving children in war zones, or fighting crime whenever it happened to be in his neighborhood, chasing Specials who had gone bad, or underground, where they couldn't be watched, or protecting Nexus' oil pipe lines from Colombian rebels. Jason indeed stood for truth, justice, and the path of enlightened self-interest. He was like Roy Rogers and Superman combined, throughout the entire world. Heck, there was even talk once of giving him the Nobel Peace Prize.

"All my life I watched him, and the rest of the group, and I wondered what it was like to be a hero. To know that your presence and your deeds make a difference in the world. Somehow my work of helping a kid here and there just never measured up to what Jason accomplished in the world. He'd affected so many people, so positively.

"I wondered what it was like, not to be afraid. Like a hero. A person who would not be afraid, even knowing the worst was about to happen. I knew, this would be my last chance to find out.

"It was really stupid of me—or maybe I was just beyond stupidity at that point—to say to him, 'They know everything, Jason. They know . . . now . . . that you're the one who's been killing us. You can kill me . . . but you can't kill the truth.'

" 'We'll see about that,' Jason said.

"I think that's when he tore out my heart. I can't be sure. I was already having an out-of-the-body experience by then." He sighed and looked dejected. I guess he had a right to. "Aw, crap," he said.

Now that the vision of his death was over, and the sky and landscape were dark and gray and would never again hold forth the possibility of color and hope, I found it difficult to face him. Thank goodness we were in his realm. Had we been in mine we both would have sinking into an abyss of Brobdingnagian proportions, that's how I felt.

"I'm sorry, Clarence. I got here as fast as I could. I didn't know. I didn't . . ."

"Yeah, yeah. I know. I know. And now *you* know. Let me go, John. You got what you wanted. I shouldn't be here, laying down my dreamscape on top of yours. I should have outgrown the need to dream by now. I suppose it's a side-effect of being dead."

I wanted to put my hand on his shoulder, to reach out and provide him with a little bit of fellowship. Two things prevented me. First, I normally didn't do that sort of thing. And second, I was afraid my hand would pass right through his shoulder. "Is there anything you want me to do? Anybody you want me to talk to, or—"

"No. Nobody. I wish there were. Things are going to go further downhill, you realize that, don't you, John?"

"Yeah, I kinda gathered that."

He began walking away from me, not into a bright white light, but rather into a diffuse silver fog. He was headed toward neither heaven nor hell, it seemed, but purgatory.

"Lionel," I said aloud.

"Yes?" said a voice on the plane of reality.

"Let him go," I said. "I'm coming out."

"Understood," the voice replied.

"Goodbye, Clarence," I called, as he had almost reached the edge of the swiftly receding dreamscape. "For what it's worth, for that moment, you were a hero, Clarence. That's all anyone can ask. I just want you to know that."

"Yeah, whatever."

My words evidently failed to uplift his spirits. His shoulders remained slumped—and I'm certain there was a frown on his face—as his body dissipated in the fog.

And he was gone. Then so was I, but I awoke in a familiar, albeit dark place, the study of Lionel Zerb. The sun had just set, yet he had not yet switched on the lights. Maybe he liked sitting in the dark. I, after what I had just seen, did not relish the prospect. But I was still too groggy and disoriented to do much about it.

"Did you get all that?" I asked.

Lionel nodded. He had grown into a thin man with stark features. He wore a black sweater and a pair of jeans that appeared to be in their tenth or twelfth straight day of use. He had a profound case of b.o. as well, but there were reasons for that. Most of the people he hung around with couldn't notice. "Most of it," he said. "Enough." He ran his hands through his hair until it stuck straight out. Evidently it had gone unwashed as long as his clothing. "Jason. Jesus, of all of us, why the hell did it have to be Jason?"

"I don't fully understand his rationale—or his character flaws—yet, but otherwise it makes sense. Jason has all the assets of Nexus Corp behind him. He's constantly under high-tech medical supervision, if not high-tech medical surveillance. The Nexus doctors would have the resources to discover that his power had been declining, only to come back up again whenever one of us died."

"That's only part of what I meant. Jason's the strongest one of us all. I don't know if even Matthew could take him in a fair fight."

"I don't think they have any intentions of a fair fight."

" 'They'?"

I reached for my jacket. "Jason knows we're on to him now. He knows we'll come after him, alone or together. But Jason, for all his idealism, obviously knows a thing or two about *realpolitik*. He's going to start pulling together allies, to give himself a tactical plus a public relations advantage. Clarence was right. Things are really going downhill from here."

"Why not take him down right now?"

"He'll stay low so we can't find him until he finishes gathering forces. Besides, we'll need to get others on board, and that's going to require proof.

Lionel nodded; then it struck him there were implications. "Just a second. Why do we need proof?"

"To avoid going to jail for what we do. Dreams aren't exactly admissible in court. Taking Jason out is only part of the next step. Staying alive and out of jail make up the rest of it."

He nodded again, but this time with a decided air of resignation. "Yes, yes, I know," he said, sullenly, as if it was all my fault.

I realized I was partially mistaken about Lionel at the moment. He was also slightly ... distracted. "He's still here?" I asked.

"Clarence. Yeah, he's still here. Takes a while for the dead to let go, even when they've been given permission to go. It's just my luck that the person they choose to hang around with the most is me. Must be my sterling personality."

"What's he saying?" I asked, though I wasn't sure I wanted to know.

"He's wishing you good luck."

I approved. And I was slightly surprised. Clarence had generally possessed a defeatist attitude. I did not learn, until much later, what Clarence had really said:

"You couldn't even save me. What the hell makes you think you can save the rest? *What?* You're not our savior, John. You're the goddamned angel of death."

Not that knowing Clarence's true opinion of things would have altered the course of what was going down. As I left, I said, "Well, we're going to need luck, that's for sure."

"Where to next?" Lionel asked.

"I haven't decided." Or I just didn't want Lionel to know in case Jason showed up and beat the answer out of him. "Still thinking about the idea of hunting down the lion in his own den. You should get out of town. Go as far as you can. Lay low until this is over."

"I will. But I don't get it, John. What the hell makes you think you're got what it takes to bring down a turned Jason? The only thing you can do is foil cameras."

I turned and smiled. "The better to sneak up behind him. Lionel, thanks. If you need someone . . . if you need someone to talk to, you know how to reach me."

Lionel laughed. "Don't worry about me, John, I'll be fine. It's not like I have a shortage of people to talk to."

"Hmmm." I could see he had a point. I closed the door, leaving him behind.

I have a pretty good idea of what he did next. He sat down in the middle of his study and tried to find a center inside his body that would remind him of what it was like to have peace and quiet. To be alone, if only for a little, pleasurable while.

Inside his study he had a television set, a VCR, books to read, and CDs to listen to. And yet he availed himself of none of those things. He just sat there.

And listened. To the voices of the dead:

"He'll never stop Jason. He just wants his war. You watch, he'll get everyone killed along the way. Everyone he ever loved, who ever loved him. Wait and see . . ."

"And I don't know why you spend so much time with him when my story is so much more interesting. It's not like they're not all going to die. We all die, sooner or later, that's what I learned."

"So where was I? Are you listening to me? I think you're not paying attention . . ."

"Darkness, and darkness, a terrible darkness, and teeth. Butterflies with teeth that gnash and chew and it never, never stops, never stops, never stops . . ."

I suspect poor Lionel was rather bored.

11

WHEN BAD THINGS HAPPEN TO GOOD PEOPLE

Well, perhaps it was just as well that Lionel was a solitary creature. Imagine for the moment Lionel as a social creature, one known to spend some time occasionally with a member of the opposite sex. It couldn't be much fun if you knew that if anything happened, you'd be watched.

Watched by a bunch of dead people, for whom the concept of sex presumably would elicit a degree of interest ranging from zero to nothing. Unless, of course, one of the dead people happened to be a voyeur.

Perhaps it was as good as any excuse to be alone. Me, I don't know what my problem was. My view of romantic encounters was roughly analogous to George Washington's advice on foreign entanglements: they were to be avoided. It bothered me that the moment I'd explore the possibility, there would be a snag.

Of course, I was easily discouraged. Could have had something to do with it.

Still, it would have been nice not to feel so alone as I stood in the middle of that crowd on a hot summer afternoon in a downtown Cincinnati park right across the street from the Nexus Corp HQ. There were television cameras and professional football cheerleaders and a high school brass band that had just won a national championship. There was a sophisticated security system in place, including several guards disguised as just plain folk, a slew of corporate bigwigs and stockholders, and a whole bunch of Special sighters, who just couldn't resist the thought of catching Jason, formerly the superhero known as Flagg, introducing himself to the world under his new name.

Jason was hard to miss. He stood on stage with his massive cape being buffeted by the wind (actually, by a wind machine concealed about a mile away), his shoulders straight and proud, his gloved fists on his hips like the poised hands of a gunslinger. His mask covered most of his face, but couldn't do anything to conceal that egotistical half-smirk that had for the past few years been his semi-permanent expression. So beloved was he by the media and Special fans that most people tended not to notice it.

It was a good thing no one had recognized me. Not only was I making my image nonexistent to any and all lenses, I was doing my best to have the same affect on the human eye as well. I augmented my methods by divesting myself of my trademark trenchcoat, and by tying my hair back in a ponytail. I tried to make sure I broadcast the aura of a man to whom no one ever had any reason to pay attention to. It was the only way I could be alone in the crowd. And despite my loneliness, I had *wanted* to be alone, particularly in *this* crowd.

Because I had come here to kill Jason. Like Pierre the noble aristocratic would-be assassin who botches the job of killing Napoleon in Tolstoy's *War and Peace*, I had come to dispatch the tyrant who would deprive freedom of its future.

Unlike Pierre, I would have to act. And succeed.

But first, I had to listen. Listen to Nexus Corp CEO Mike Gramm pontificate on all that Jason had meant to the people of the good old U.S. of A., especially the ones who happened to work for Nexus Corp. Fleetwood Mac's "Don't Stop (Thinking About Tomorrow)" played softly in the background on a loudspeaker system as Gramm wound up his speech:

"—And we are pleased to announce the result of our search for a new name for the man who has represented Nexus Corp so well, for so long. And not just any name. Jason Miller has been the greatest, grandest, most generous goodwill ambassador any company could hope for. Only a name as grand as the man himself would do, and so we employed several focus groups in an exhaustive, no-expense-spared search for just the right name. And you know what we discovered? If you throw enough money at a problem, a solution's bound to present itself sooner or later! Just kidding. I'm sure you'll agree we've found just the right name for Jason that will help him lead Nexus Corp—and America—into the twenty-first century."

I couldn't believe Jason was actually showing himself in public. How could he imagine I wouldn't be onto his heinous scheme? To think that a man who presented himself as a hero to the masses would kill—no, *slaughter*—his childhood friends because he was afraid to lose his physical prowess. I struggled in vain to recall some incident in the past, some clue that in retrospect would convince me that Jason was selfish and weak enough to cross that line with such clarity of purpose and lack of conscience. What did he hope to gain by being a little bit stronger for a little bit longer period of time? This was the sort of behavior I'd expect of a professional basketball player, not a heroic Special.

But then again, the most harm an egocentric ball player could do was to get hurt or help his team lose a few games. Jason soaked up the compliments in Gramm's speech like a sponge lapping up an ocean. We Specials— particularly we who are most inundated with the force— can feel each other's presence like the waves between two distant magnets pulling together. Surely he knew I was there, in the crowd, waiting.

Was I waiting to gather galvanizing evidence, or was I hoping for a pre-emptive shot, the chance to punch his ticket before he could do the same to another childhood friend? Suddenly I wasn't sure.

"A flag in and of itself doesn't say much," Gramm drawled on. And on and on. Was he ever going to get to the point? "A flag can represent any country, any ideal— good, bad, or indifferent. Nexus Corp wanted an image based on a concept worthy of mankind's highest aspirations, inspired by a man who lives a life that has personified those aspirations better than anyone I know." Gramm pulled a sheet from a huge sign on the stage. "Ladies and gentlemen—I give you—the Patriot!"

There was wild applause. I just stood there and simmered. I had my own patriotic duty to do, and if I got caught, the only reward I'd get was life imprisonment, or worse.

Jason waited for the applause to die down. Then he walked up to the microphone and said, "Thank you very much." I could almost hear Elvis saying it. Then he walked away.

"You must excuse Patriot," said Gramm, by way of explanation. "He has to escort a shipment of rice to Central Africa, where, as you know, there's been a lot of starvation recently."

That was nice. Seeing as how Africa's problem was a drought, was he also going to escort shipments of water for the poor starving children to boil their rice in? Why did I have the feeling that Nexus Corp never thought through all their image-building campaigns?

Then Gramm invited everyone inside for refreshments and, presumably, another round of propaganda. Me, I had to go see someone.

To follow someone.

That was easy; I'd done it many times before. I stalked Jason like a fox hunting a lazy jackrabbit, aggressively but carefully. People tended to leave him alone after a public appearance—he'd developed the reputation of a hero who didn't suffer fools lightly—so both the security guards and media simply ceased following after he'd reached the Nexus Corp parking structure. They didn't notice me slipping past them, I made certain of that. They were definitely making things easier on me, though I do recall wondering why Jason wasn't flying off like he usually did.

Oh, well, even a flying superhero still needs a family car . . .

I found him walking down a flight of stairs toward a bright shiny mini-van.

Now I'd reached the hard part. The part of actually acting, which I wasn't used to doing. I was more comfortable thinking about acting.

But I had no choice. For some reason I wanted to reach him before he changed out of costume, even though a better strategy might be to wait until the number of possible collateral casualties was lower.

Besides, the force was already building inside me. It had begun *in anticipation* of my command. I cursed myself for not practicing more—I found practice boring—but not only was there nothing I could do about it, the force had made the correct decision.

I went beyond a wire-mesh fence. I didn't mean to leave a hole behind as I walked through it, but such power welled up inside me, I was lucky not to have melted the concrete at my feet. I was going farther in welling up the power than I'd anticipated, indeed, this was the most powerful I'd ever been. I'd never risked exposing myself this way, but it was the only means of taking out someone on Jason's level.

"Hello, Jason."

He turned and looked annoyed. He held up his hand like a cop at an intersection. "Sorry, friend. No autographs."

Waves of force oscillated from me, rustling a strewn newspaper, rattling a few tin cans, and shaking nearby car windows. "Autographs," I said. "I'm not here for an—"

I noticed he was cowering, slack-jawed, against his mini-van. Furthermore, my waves of force should have felt some resistance emanating from him. I felt no such resistance.

"Wait a minute—" I said, reaching out to him in a non-threatening manner, so he'd think I was backing off.

I grabbed him by the neck and his legs went as limp as wet noodles.

"Who the hell are you?"

"Hey, let go—I didn't—"

"I said, *who are you?*"

"Okay, okay!" he said, his voice quivering. "My name's Jim. I'm an actor. I stand in for Jason at supermarket openings and other events that aren't that important for him to attend personally. It's the biggest gig I've had yet—"

"I'd say so. Jason too busy to celebrate his new name? He must be awfully busy! What's he doing?"

"How am I supposed to know? They said he had the flu and couldn't make it."

"Our kind doesn't get sick," I said, taking off his mask. His chin might have been a perfect double for Jason's but otherwise he looked like a surfer, tan and blonde.

"Good for you, buddy. I'm just doing a job here. If you got a message for Jason, I think I already have enough incentive to deliver it to him personally . . ."

Some of the fear had gone out of his voice. I was pushing him away. The oscillating waves were causing the cans and papers in the lot to scurry across the floor like odd little creatures. Didn't they ever clean this place up?

"Forget it!" I said. "Go on, hurry! Get the hell out of here!"

A message, I'm afraid, he already had. He was long since scarce by the time I'd mustered my strength of will and strove to contain the power build—which at the level I'd achieved was damned next to impossible. By now the waves were visible—they were blue and crackled like lightning and came out of my shoulders and eyes. I had to get rid of the force. I had to discharge it in a safe place—

The ground! I hoped the parking structure would be able to withstand it.

It was easy to perceive elsewhere, at a security check-point, with Jim, *sans* mask, dashing up to a chisel-faced man with a tiny radio stuck in his ear. "Hey, you've got some nut back there," Jim said. "He grabbed me and—"

That's when the whole building started shaking like one of James Bond's cocktails. Poor Jim fell flat on his ass while the security guy discreetly moved into a door-way. The security guy had been in earthquakes before, he knew what to do. It's just that he'd never expected to deal with one in Cincinnati!

From the Average Joe's point of view, the earthquake was over in moments. There were no injuries, little dam-age was done. The Nexus people got a mite nervous though, when they discovered the crater I'd forged in the lower levels. There was, of course, no evidence of my coming and going, and subsequently they made a public relations decision not to hide the incident from the media and the spies of jealous corporations.

I left feeling that that was what *coitus interruptus* must be like. And I was disappointed in myself. It had been too close, I could have thrown away everything, I had risked my relative anonymity for nothing.

I didn't understand how I could have been so wrong—or, to put the best face on it, so intent on my goal that I had allowed myself to be fooled by the simplest decep-tion. Like I said, all of us—particularly the most power-ful—could sense when one of the others is around. Throughout the incident, I could feel Jason's presence.

He *had* to have been around, somewhere. He was smart to have avoided me. I didn't know what instinct or scrape of information he had possessed to make him so cautious, but it had been a wise decision. I just hoped he hadn't spotted me doing my thing.

I resolved to be more careful in the future. No more being fooled by a mere costume. No exposure until I had a clear shot at a confirmed target.

All I had to do now was find the son of a bitch.

The company called him Patriot now, but that wasn't his name. His name was Jason Miller.

He had never thought of himself as Flagg, either. These sobriquets were merely shrouds that he could pull over his soul: they helped him pretend to be braver and nobler, wiser and more considerate than he normally envisioned himself being, and they helped him justify things. But he was well aware that history did not judge men by their disguises. Men were judged by the truths they revealed about themselves.

And the truth about him was that during his career he had saved thousands of lives. Maybe a few million. He had been an effective role model for a generation of children who were growing up to do as they were told and not to question certain core values of society, such as the need for a nuclear family and a house in the suburbs and the economic power of the man of the house to hold onto both.

Jason was spiritual, too. Most of the crimes and atrocities committed by members of the various branches of, say, the Christian faith had occurred long, long in the past, before anybody living was born, and the greatness of the Christian religion, despite its trail of blood, was unquestioned in contemporary society. Jason was hoping history would treat him just as kindly.

After all, he would still be able to save millions of human beings in the future. Surely the sacrifice of a hundred lives was justifiable.

Surely.

*   *   *

While I was walking away from Nexus Corp, Jason was looking down on me from the top of the corporate HQ. I imagine he had been anxious to leave throughout the ceremony and its aftermath, but he'd spotted me—or rather, felt my presence—and refrained from possibly drawing attention to himself until I'd gotten into my car and was concentrating on getting onto the freeway without getting sideswiped.

Then he took off from the high rooftop like a missile. He stayed close to the ground whenever possible—flying Specials were discouraged from traveling great distances without filing a flight plan, and he wanted this trip to remain a secret. The fields, the rivers, bridges, highways and pockets of civilization passed below him in a blur. He barely noticed tearing through a flock of birds. The main things on his mind were navigating by the angle of the sun and avoiding smacking into one of the Rocky Mountains. But passing through them was fun—he loved the weaving and the sudden changes of direction. Doing so made him feel like he still possessed the edge.

The edge he was fighting so hard to maintain, for the good of the human race.

It wouldn't be long before he came to the Sunlight Cathedral. That was the name of the Reverend Kane's home base in Denver. The good old Rev had built quite a ministry in the years since Joshua's emancipation. His followers were estimated at a million. The ministry owned a cable network, oversaw several charities, managed a hundred private schools throughout the nation, and routinely greased the re-election campaigns of influential politicians from both the major parties. Its culture, from my point of view, tended to be repressive and reactionary. I'd observed that people who sought sin were like people always on the lookout for slights and insults—if you look hard enough, you're bound to find what you're looking for—and the Rev was an old hand at finding sin.

On the morning of Jason's flight across America, Reverend Kane was finishing up a sermon while his son Josh floated above his pulpit and irradiated the congregation with immense floods of bright white light. The Sunlight Cathedral had been designed with the spirit of the great Gothic cathedrals in mind—the material had to be heavy, and sturdy, but it also had to present an illusion of weightlessness to augment a visitor's feeling of proximity to Heaven. And the interior had been designed to highlight Joshua's natural skills at illumination in much the same manner as a well-designed theatre or concert hall.

Whenever he floated in the light, Joshua felt at peace with the world. He knew he would be happy if he could spend every second of every waking hour high above the common throes and travails of humanity. Only in the air, high above his father and the congregation, did he feel close to God.

Of course, it helped if he could shut out his father's words, which he was unable to do throughout this service. His normal ability to practice erecting a mental wall had been distracted by a premonition, and the very concept of his having a premonition made him feel dirty, like he imagined a few of his brother and sister Specials who had the ability to foretell certain tiny and trivial aspects of the future must feel, whenever they had one of their own modest visions.

"And God tells us to be ever vigilant," his father was saying, "because the Devil moves among us like a lion, seeking to devour the innocent. Therefore, he gives us signs, so that we might know we are not alone in our battle for righteousness. Signs, portents, miracles, and his divine word, passed down to guide us through the darkness."

Joshua winced at those words. He had no doubt the Lord had a Divine Word which he had bequeathed to mankind, he just couldn't make up his mind about the translation. And then there was the fact that the words had inevitably been filtered through the mind of Man. Poor insular, provincial, intolerant Man; not even the Ten Commandments could claim to exist outside Mankind's limitations.

"Signs like my son," continued the Reverend Kane, oblivious to his son's lifelong desire for modesty, "dearest of my heart, touched by God and made a true light in our most desperate darkness. He is a beacon to the un-believer, who in my son's presence must recognize there is another, even greater light from which we all proceed. At the conclusion of our services—"

Here it comes, Joshua thought.

"—We ask that you make a sign of your own—a tes-tament to your faithful resolve, that you contribute to the furtherance of our ministry here at the cathedral of light."

We take Visa, Discover, and Master Card . . .

"As the deacons move among you, I ask that you help us to continue spreading the word and fighting the forces of abortion and godlessness—not just here, but across the world—and help us expand the Sunlight Cathedral Net-work into every corner of every country. Especially the Islamic ones. They really need our help . . ."

Then he broke into song, leading the choir and con-gregation in that nostalgic chestnut "Shall We Gather at

the River?" The singing in the service always deflated
Joshua's feelings of proximity to God somewhat, not because it was bad, but because the hymns were nearly
always ancient in character, sometimes dating back as
far as 300 years. His father and the congregation seemed
to enjoy the link with tradition, but Joshua was desperate
to hear a little bit of praise music now and then. The
blacks had it right, God gave us the capacity to feel
rhythm and elation along with all the other things, and
it was a sin not to express that as well.

More than a sin. A waste. Fortunately, this was his
cue.

He floated into an opening in the ceiling.

The opening led to a platform in the middle of the
steeple of the Sunlight Cathedral. At the end of the platform was a door leading to a level that took one along
the length of the cathedral. He walked through the door
and found himself bathed in the real sunlight, magnified
by its passing through the many stained glass windows
that lined both sides of the corridor. The glass throughout
the cathedral had simple, basic color schemes, and some
portions allowed a wonderful, often inspiring view of the
sky and clouds above the city.

Jason found himself staring through one of the clear
windows. His mind was more disengaged than usual. He
had discovered over the years that the best way for him
to get through the day with his emotions semi-intact was
to be as disengaged as possible. Particularly when his
father was angry with him, or if his father was just rant-
ing on general principles.

He could hear the echoes of the final hymn—or was it
the multi-level hum of several hundred leaving cars?—as
he watched the clouds swirl like the sun was stirring them
with a red-hot whisk.

Joshua sometimes wondered at his ability to feel isolated. Here he was, expecting company, and never had he felt so alone. Why was it he felt like he was about to devoured by one of those lions his old man kept talking about?

He reached out and opened the latch to window. Then, shoulders slumped, he walked away.

He was totally oblivious to the great ball of fire that had emerged from one of the clouds.

A ball of fire that was streaking directly toward the Sunlight Cathedral.

A ball of fire that was assuming the shape of a man.

A man who was flying into the open window. "Hey, Josh," said the man as he came to a landing.

Josh turned. He felt his entire body go red from the heat coming forth from this man, and it was a wonder this interloper wasn't already setting the Cathedral ablaze. Then he remembered that the Special known as Pyre, unlike some other firestarters, had complete control over the effects of his flame on other objects. "Jerry?"

Meaning Jerry Montrose. a.k.a. Pyre. On Emancipation Day, he'd hitched a ride cross-country and wasn't seen or heard of again until years later, when he emerged as muscle for a few shady Las Vegas characters who were now serving twenty-to-life for a multitude of crimes, most having to do with guns, money, and thieves.

Josh felt conflicted. Jerry could hold and control his flame indefinitely, but would turn it off if asked. Inside the Sunlight Cathedral were hundreds of priceless objects—at least, priceless now that they'd been paid for—and Joshua didn't want to take a chance that Jerry might let his control slip for a moment, just to keep everybody on their toes.

On the other hand, Jerry couldn't control his flame sufficiently to protect any clothing he might be wearing. He was always naked beneath his flame, and that made Josh uncomfortable.

"Love your show, by the way," Jerry said. "I was in disguise. Your dad really knows how to wind an audience up, doesn't he? Mine just knew how to wind up a punch."

"What are you doing here?" Josh asked. "If you've come looking for sanctuary, I told you before, we couldn't harbor a known criminal. We can only harbor people fleeing a dysfunctional, secular human background."

"That's what you call sanctuary? That's pitiful. Wait a minute—weren't you told I was coming?"

Then it struck Josh. He felt embarrassed, profoundly slow on the uptake. "No—I mean—I was told to expect someone, but not that it would be you."

Jerry nodded and folded his blazing arms across his blazing chest. "I betcha I'm the last person you expected, too."

"Okay, look, I don't know what's going on here, but—"

"Hey, boys, looks like we're together again, just like the old days." Jason Miller, a.k.a. Flagg, a.k.a. Patriot, was sitting on the windowsill. He'd silently flown up and simply slipped in before they noticed. "Relax, fellows. Forgive me, it's really good to see you two again."

"You're kidding," said Jerry. Pyre and Flagg had had a few memorable street brawls between them in the last couple of years. They inevitably made the news, and were broadcast live whenever possible.

"Remember," said Jason, "when we were going to form a rock band, the Three Jays?"

"Yeah, then Josh's dad decided it was the Devil's

music, and no way!" said Jerry, the old resentment more apparent in his voice than he'd intended.

"Look, Jason," said Josh, "I don't know why you're here, or why you wanted to see me, but I don't want any trouble. My father isn't well, and—"

"It's okay, Josh. There won't be any trouble. At least not now. But we have to talk, and I think your dad had better be there. It involves him, too."

"I don't see why," said Jerry. He'd never liked Joshua's old man, but then again, he rarely liked anyone's old man.

"He has to be there!" insisted Jason, giving Jerry an *I overrule you* look.

"All right, I guess," said Joshua timidly. He could never resist Jason when he was being forceful. But he gathered up his nerve, turned to Jerry, and said, "But you're going to have turn off the fire. My mom just had new carpets laid down in this entire cathedral, and if they get scorched . . ."

"All right, all right," Jerry said, already flaming down. "Eyes front, soldier. Got a bathrobe?"

The next few hours were the most difficult of Jason's life. There wasn't a lot of trust between the four men as they sat at a table in a conference room filled with fine objects of religious significance, many dating from the early Renaissance. The stained glass images depicted the Virgin Mary and various angels in a more traditional style, and the plants were all green plastic. Still, they added a nice softening touch to the decor. The men sipped coffee and tea as Jason talked.

The more Jason talked, the more Joshua and Jerry relaxed. Only Reverend Kane maintained his air of suspicion. But he was the only one who wasn't a Special. He was the only one who didn't belong to the club. He was the only one who didn't immediately understand the significance of Jason's theory that the Force was finite, that it wasn't perpetually self-renewing, as so many scientists had believed. He was the slowest to grasp the implications of Jason's theory that the Force, and the Specials, were winding down like old clocks, and that when a Special died, his remaining power was allotted, proportionately, to the rest of the group.

Jason told them what he had done. He told them, wringing his hands like Lady Macbeth, while claiming to have a clear conscience. He tried to convince them of the correctness of his logic, that it was right and proper to take back the power from those at the low end of the spectrum, those wasted souls and ruined lives, dead to any kind of potential, wasting what was not theirs to waste.

Joshua took umbrage at this characterization. Was it not up to God to decide whose lives were wasted and whose were not, on the Day of Judgement?

Reverend Kane instructed Joshua to be quiet, to let Jason to go on with his explanation.

Jason told them some of the Specials least worthy of humanity's trust had discovered the limitations of the Force, and that as word got out to the selfish ones, it would only be a matter of time before the killing began in earnest. Then Jason pointed out that in the final analysis, there wasn't a Special left alive who wouldn't fight to keep what power he or she had, regardless of how little or great it was. Many of us would be reluctant to wait for one of our group to try and kill us first. Many of us would prefer the preemptive strike, and to claim the extra power for our own.

All things considered, they took it pretty well. Jerry kept smiling involuntarily, the unsettling prospects of the immediate future excited him, while Reverend Kane just sat stone-faced. Joshua was pale. Quite pale.

"Jesus Christ on a crutch," Joshua whispered, thinking he was speaking only to himself.

"Don't take that name in vain, son," snapped Reverend Kane. "Not here." Then he turned his attention toward Jason. "Something I don't understand. Why come to me with this? And why bring that criminal into my house to do it?"

The Reverend did not know it, but his words stung Joshua. Was this house not *his* as well, in addition to being the House of the Lord? And was not Jason confiding in *him* as well as in his father?

"The way I figure it," said Jason, "as word of this gets out, we're going to start choosing up sides real fast, and we've still got the mundanes to worry about. They have to decide who to believe, which should be a trick because deep down most have never really trusted us."

"It may be a little late to ask for their trust now," said Joshua. Everyone glared at him, and he hunkered down for a moment, hoping they'd forget he'd spoken.

"I've got some credibility thanks to Nexus Corp," Jason continued. "They own senators they haven't even used yet."

"We might own some of the same ones," said Reverend Kane, with a sly smile.

"But what about me?" Jerry asked. "I'm not exactly a poster boy for credibility. Hell, Jason, you and I have fought almost nonstop for, what, ten years now?"

"Exactly. So for the two of us to get together on something, especially after all the times we've mixed it up, well, that sure as hell sends a message. Now we just have to figure out what the message is, what'll serve all of us the best in dealing with the rest of the world, and each other."

Joshua ran his fingers over his neck. It occurred to him that it could be crushed rather easily if it was being held in the hands of the right Special.

"Perhaps I'm being obtuse, Jason," said Reverend Kane, "but what I still don't see is why I have any vested interest in getting involved to this extent with either of you."

"I'm well aware you think we're all evil," said Jason, "although how your son gets to be an exception to that little rule escapes me. But look at it this way: If anyone else in our little extended family thinks like I do, they're going to figure out that the best response is to eliminate those among us who are low or middle-powered, because they're the easiest targets. Sort of clears all the pawns off the chessboard so the real powers can slug it out. And lighting up and floating in the middle of a room, well, it isn't much of a power when it comes to a fight, Mr. Kane."

Joshua felt a sinking sensation in the pit of his stomach.

"I see," Reverend Kane said.

And Joshua felt himself go down a few more notches in his father's respect. He didn't even blame him. He knew his power was good only for show. Or to be more precise, show biz.

"I think we'll need to discuss this privately," said

Reverend Kane, nodding toward his son. "We'll pray on it. Come along, Joshua."

Jason and Jerry watched Reverend Kane put his hand on his son's shoulder and guide him from the room, into a small private chamber. The door closed behind them.

The last several times they'd met face-to-face, Jason had been in uniform and Jerry had been on fire and they had each tried to demolish the other by way of doing their bit in the eternal struggle of good against evil, or the eternal battle of law vs. lawlessness, which is not necessarily the same thing. Even so, they knew that regardless of what happened next, the mere fact that Jason was out of uniform and Jerry was not on fire and was wearing clothing borrowed from Joshua, clothing that more or less fit him, indicated the rules of engagement between them had changed forever.

"So here we are," said Jason with a smile. "I just might make an honest man out of you yet."

"Just what is this curious bond between the three of us? I mean, including Josh. I'm finding it terribly easy to forgive you."

Jason shrugged. "It's the nature of childhood bonds. They can withstand a lot of strain."

"If what you say is true, and with each of us who dies, the rest get stronger, then the fights are going to get a lot tougher, and the stakes a lot higher, the deeper we go into this."

"I know it, Jerry, I know," said Jason, nodding. "And forgiving is going to become a lot more difficult, too."

Meanwhile, in the private chamber, Joshua and his father were having a word. Perhaps a more accurate description would be that his father was having a word and Joshua was trying to get one in edgewise. "I don't think we can do this, Dad. It's wrong," was about as far as he got.

"And just who the hell are you to decide what's wrong?" answered Reverend Kane, sticking his finger in Joshua's face. "Get this straight, Tinkerbell! I made this place. Built it on my back. All I ever asked you to do was float in place and glow, and you can barely get that right!"

"Dad—"

"Don't interrupt me!" said Reverend Kane, pushing his son against a wall, getting into the young man's space, big time. "You think I didn't see you crying the day we shut down that abortion clinic last month? You can't fool me! I know you disapprove of my methods and I don't care. I know what's right. I really wouldn't care how much you cry, if it wasn't for the fact that the rubes—I mean, the followers—ask questions. I had to make all kinds of explanations, that it was God weeping through you for the sake of all those unborn lives. You, Joshua Kane, are a weakling. You've always been a weakling. If I had what you've got, I could've made this place ten times what it is. But by God, if you think I'm just going to stand here and let it all fall down because you don't have what it takes to do what needs doing, you are seriously mistaken! We've been saying for years that we're in a war, a spiritual war, a war of possibilities, one world or another and nothing in between. Well, that war has come knocking on our front door, son. It's time to take up sides, and that's just what we're going to do. And I don't want to hear another word about it out of you! You hear me?"

Joshua nodded and tried to hold back his tears. He knew there was only one way to Heaven, and that was through the love of his holy father. His human father, that is. "Yes, I hear you," he managed to say, though his effort at holding back tears wasn't nearly as successful.

Reverend Kane stared at his boy. The lad should have been excited—life-long dreams and nightmares were finally becoming a reality—and all he could do was slump in a chair like a wet noodle. To think that his only son, so talented, so gifted, should disgust him so! He turned, walked away, and rejoined the other two. He remembered them vaguely from Joshua's youth; the poor deluded child had babbled on about his friendship with them until he finally figured out his father wasn't interested. Reverend Kane recalled bitterly the sense of relief he'd felt when Joshua finally graduated from the high school that devil Paulson and his government cronies had made Josh attend—as if his boy was on a par with those tainted Specials! Oh well, at the moment Joshua's boyhood pals were tainted Specials he needed. After all, it wasn't just a spiritual war coming up, it was opportunity.

"My apologies for making you wait, gentlemen. We've prayed on it, and we've come to a decision."

"We?" asked Jerry. "Where's Josh?"

"Resting upstairs. Services take a great deal out of him. And he has to pack."

"Pack?"

"We have a long and difficult journey ahead of us. As Joshua pointed out, we are facing a war. A war for the future of those God has blessed, and the future of the world itself. Wars require extreme means. Wars require sacrifice, and from time to time, in any war, people die."

"So what's your point?" Jerry drawled. It bothered him—though not enough for him to actually say or do anything about it—that Jason and Reverend Kane were a little too eager to carry on this war metaphor.

"It is unfortunate, it is a sad thing, but it is inevitable. People are going to die no matter what we in this room might prefer. Better to be on the side that wins, and lives, than the other. But we will need allies with other kinds of power. And there I can help. Now, I suggest you get some sleep. We leave before dawn."

His suggestion was more like an order, but the promise of a comfortable bed was too enticing for Jerry to resist; he was often deprived of such luxuries. The only bed Jason wanted to sleep in was the one where his wife was sleeping, at his home, with his child in the next room. Furthermore, if he'd wanted, he could have flown home in less than half an hour and met them at their destination tomorrow without any trouble. But he sensed solidarity was important right now, especially if he wanted to keep this coalition together. It was, after all, built on the mere scraps of residual childhood friendship. So much anger and indifference had occurred since then.

"Is there a place around here where I can get a few burgers first?" Jason asked.

"Could you buy me a meal tonight, Reverend Kane?" Jerry asked. "I'm busted. Can't carry too money around when you go around flying naked all the time."

The Reverend Kane simmered. He was a tall, balding man whose demeanor was stern; he tended to be stoic around those not in his immediate family. Yet he sensed these two would test him as eagerly as they would test each other.

Fourteen burgers, six orders of fries, and several milk shakes later (the most powerful Specials had big appetites to help them replenish all those calories they burned up whenever they used their powers), Jason and Jerry lay awake in twin beds in a small room in the ministry. The ceiling was built at a 45-degree angle, and there were crosses on all four walls. Through the window they could see the moon, but the brightness from outside was cast entirely from city lights.

"Kinda like old times, isn't it, Jason?" Jerry asked. "You and me, and Josh, bunking together."

"Well, yeah, except that Josh's in another room. Even so, I was thinking the same thing. It's a long way since then, Jer. A long, long time."

Jerry couldn't argue with that. They both stared in silence at the ceiling for several minutes. Jerry knew Jason wasn't asleep—the man's breathing wasn't regular enough—so he asked what he hoped was a pertinent question. "Hey—you think Joshua's still, you know, *that* way?"

"Naw, not in the world he has to live in."

"You sure? In my experience people's leanings are hardwired into their brain and there isn't much they can do about it."

"Yeah, but you hang out with robbers, muggers, and thieves."

"Real cool people. But I understand. You're probably right."

"Hey, Jer, you know how I knew you were never really all that bad?"

"How?"

"You never told anyone what we found in Josh's closet that night. I always thought that was a real stand-up thing for you to."

"Yeah, well, you know, I'm a good guy."

"No, I'm the good guy. You're the bad guy, remember?"

Jerry sighed. Truth be known, he felt he was neither good nor bad inside, but somehow neutral. Not unlike the character Alan Ladd played in *The Glass Key*, an enforcer for a crooked politician; even though both characters were corrupt, you liked them. They stood for order, somehow. "Right. I forget sometimes."

" 'Night, Jerry."

" 'Night, Jason." He hoped the bastard didn't snore. He always had, back when they were bunking together.

Perhaps Jason and Jerry wouldn't have been surprised to learn that Joshua still kept the same secret thing hidden in a suitcase under his bed. He did not sleep well that night. And he said little the next day as he, his father, and his Special friends took the ministry's private jet to Washington, D.C. Actually, little was said between them, period, but theirs was not an awkward silence; they were all simply lost in their own thoughts. It so happened that Joshua was just lost a little deeper.

He spent much of the flight wondering about his name, and if it was somehow an omen of his destiny. His father had christened him Joshua—he figured his mother had had little say-so in the matter—because, depending on your definition, Joshua meant the salvation of God. Of course, there were those who believed God was the salvation, a slight but significant distinction.

No conceivable definition of) his name, however, had anything to do with how he felt personally. No definition explained his secret desires, his distance from God (at least the God his father spoke of), or his inherent loneliness. He had always had obligations besides taking care of his personal desires, and he was used to living a life that had nothing to do with his personal wishes. Today he had to convince himself that what he was about to take part in also had nothing to do with his genuine, inner self. He had to convince himself he was just along for the ride.

But if that was true, why was it that instead of God's salvation, all he could hear was God's laughter?

Depending on events, and how certain elections had fared, Agent Paulson's career in the FBI had ebbed and flowed like a river in an Ice Age. But through it all, he had managed to stay in charge of the Specials program.

Meeting him face-to-face for the first time in years in the office of Senator Roger McClellan, Reverend Kane felt an uneasy kinship with Paulson—they were both ruthless to a degree, and ambitious to the max. Kane observed that Paulson must have taken his responsibilities seriously down through the years; for his hair was white, his face lined, and his demeanor worn down from the burden he had so willingly shouldered, so long ago.

Neither Paulson nor Kane let on their mutual repulsion as they shook hands. Paulson had never trusted the parents of Specials. They caused too much trouble, made his job infinitely more difficult. And he resented their tendency to put the rights of the individual before the good of society. This Kane fellow he had trusted least of all, because all the other parents, whatever their personal qualities, tended not to exploit their children. If their children chose to exploit themselves—and he was thinking of the special Special issue of *Playboy* that hit the stands when some of the better-looking girls were twenty—that was their own business. But this Kane—well, he might dress like a preacher, but he'd seen Kane's kind long before, barking at carnivals.

Even so, he sensed they were in agreement on issues relating to social and family values. Indeed, if anything, Kane was farther to the right. And he was clearly the more ruthless of the two. Paulson suspected men with Reverend Kane's character had done well in Nazi Germany.

Reverend Kane, for his part, had long since decided that if he saw Paulson burning up on the other side of the street, he wouldn't so much as piss on the man. But Kane's opinion on the subject of Paulson had recently evolved, and now he felt his previous position was un-Christian in nature. A true follower of the Son of God would see a man he disliked intensely burning up on the other side of the street, and he *would* cross that street and he *would* stand over that man and he *would* piss on him. Gladly. Gleefully. Knowing this act brought him one step closer to Heaven.

The three Specials, the three catalysts involuntarily responsible for this unexpected détente, watched in amazement as the two men shook hands. They were reluctant to speak, reluctant to fracture the tableau.

The first verbal exchange between the men was hardly memorable:

" 'Morning," said Paulson. "How are you?"

"Just fine," said Reverend Kane. "How are you?"

"Great. Ready?"

"Sure."

Jason noticed the absence of a secretary in the room just as Paulson knocked on the door to McClellan's office. He wagered there would be no notation of this meeting on the Senator's calendar, either.

A deep voice from the other side beckoned them in.

"I appreciate you taking the time to see us, Senator McClellan," said Paulson, leading the way.

A large, balding man wearing a blue suit that must have cost two grand got up from his office chair behind his desk and gestured for them to be seated. "It's all right, Paulson. Your department has been monitoring the development of the Specials ever since they were discovered. When a man like you rings the alarm bell, even on old firehorse like me knows to pay attention."

"I appreciate the vote of confidence, Senator. You know Reverend William Kane, Archbishop of the Sunlight Ministry."

The Senator nodded. "I do indeed." The Senator had a wide, pink face with eyes that appeared too small and a tiny nose in danger of being smothered by his large red cheeks. He had long thin lips and immense wattles under his neck. "Nice to see you again, Reverend. The last few elections your fundraising efforts helped keep some of our party's favorite conservatives from losing their seats."

Jason Miller could hardly believe his ears. He didn't have any illusions about the comparative gravity of his crimes, but that was just him, a flawed imperfect human being doing what he thought was best for the good of the human race. Until now he'd found it difficult to believe that politicians really did equate money with access and favoritism. He shrugged. Not that it mattered anymore.

Jerry Montrose sat down, crossed his legs, and helped himself to a handful of peppermints in a dish. He couldn't help wondering how long it would take a man with that much fat in him to burn to a crisp. Not that he considered actually doing it, mind you. That was just a mental game he occasionally played.

219

Joshua Kane also sat down. He felt sick and shaken, like a field mouse awaiting a storm.

"Would you be so kind to tell me," McClellan said, "just what's so urgent that it could drag you good people this far just to sit in my office?"

"The mints," said Jerry.

Paulson cleared his throat, loudly, sending a definite signal to Jerry.

"Sorry," said the firestarter.

"I think it would be best if Reverend Kane explained the situation in his own words,' said Agent Paulson. "Please . . ."

Kane nodded gravely. All eyes were upon him. It was a situation he enjoyed. "Senator, you know the identities of the young men with me today. Two of them are respected members of the community, while the third is a fugitive from justice who is seeking redemption, perhaps in the form of a presidential pardon."

"Hey, that's a little outside my league," said the Senator. "But I do confess, I do have the ear of the President."

"That makes two of us," said Reverend Kane with a wink. "However, to get down to business, I suppose you're wondering what could bring together such a disparate group of individuals as the one you see before you. I would be lying if I said it was anything less than enlightened self-interest."

"That's what democracy is all about!" said the Senator.

"Not just for our own safety, Senator, but the preservation of our country itself. Just as we have come together, we know for a fact that many other so-called Specials have united in common cause. And that cause is nothing less than a conspiracy to overthrow the government of the United States. At taxpayer expense, they have trained and honed their special abilities for over two decades, and now many of them—we're not yet prepared to say how many—are determined to use those abilities to remake this country into something more suited to their sensibilities."

"Those are serious charges, Reverend Kane," said the Senator, rubbing his massive hands together. "Are you prepared to prove them, and name those involved?"

"At the proper time. Yes. The problem is one of logistics. The moment we announce that we know what's going on, those who have nothing to lose strike. We must neutralize them before we announce our intent."

Jason quietly went slack-jawed with astonishment. He'd always known that beneath his Christian veneer, Reverend Kane was a devious scumbag, but the man contained levels of treachery your average, humble superhero for hire hadn't realized were possible. Machiavelli had nothing on this guy.

"Further, it is in everyone's interest to ensure that the names of those not involved in this are cleared of suspicion," continued Reverend Kane, "lest the action of some blacken the reputations of all."

And Jason knew whom he was talking about.

"I'm surprised I've heard nothing on this before today," said the senator. "What about the doctor we assigned to Pederson years ago—what's his name?"

"Welles. William Welles," said Paulson.

"Yeah, him," said the Senator. "He was supposed to inform the FBI of any plot to break the laws."

Jason cleared his throat. It hadn't occurred to him that Doc Welles would be dragged into this. "He's a good man. He's always wanted to see the best in us. I wouldn't be surprised if that desire has blinded him to what's going on."

"Besides," said Jerry, "aside from the occasional checkups we still have to undergo, we don't have that much contact with him."

"You have anything to add to this, son?" McClellan asked Joshua.

Joshua blanched. "Hmmm? Oh, no . . . no, sir. I think that what everyone else said pretty much covers it."

"I see." Senator McClellan rubbed his massive neck. "The Supreme Court decision that gave the Specials their civil rights also gave the government certain powers to deal with this kind of situation, should it ever come up. I'll speak to my associates on the Judiciary Committee, set up some private hearings as soon as possible. You'll all have to testify, of course.

"Of course, Senator," said Reverend Kane. "You'll find us more than ready to do whatever's necessary."

The first thing that was necessary was fabricating a story that the three Specials could tell with consistent details. Paulson had already compiled various files on investigations and surveys of Specials' habits and activities, and that provided such a wide variety of raw materials that the Reverend Kane, with his inherent talent for conspiracy theory, was easily able to concoct a believable tale that combined actual meetings between Specials and speculations about what they might have possibly talked about. He had to keep it simple, of course, because he observed early on that his son appeared to have no talent for this sort of thing. Jerry, a.k.a. the firestarter Pyre did, which wasn't surprising, but it did surprise Reverend Kane, and disturb him, that Jason, the newly named Patriot, had no problem with the entire enterprise. Indeed, the Patriot took to conspiracy theory like a cat took to hunting mice.

A week passed, during which Joshua did as he was told, nothing more. I like to think that during that time he contemplated getting ahold of me, or another Special who might have been able to help, such as Ravenshadow, that he might have at least considered doing or saying something that would have prevented the tragic chain of events that was about to come. But the truth, unfortunately, was that Joshua was a defeated individual, one who had not been molded but beaten down by his father, and there was no way he would ever defy him.

So when Joshua was asked to swear upon a Bible, before God, that he would tell the whole truth and nothing but the truth to the members of the Senate Judiciary Committee during a secret session, he tried to tell himself that this was not Joshua Kane betraying his childhood friends, this was only the outer shell of an adult doing what he had been instructed to do. His true feelings had nothing to do with it. Nothing at all.

"All right, Mr. Kane, would you please tell the committee, in your own words," said Senator Specter, "how and when you first learned of this conspiracy by certain of your associates to attempt the violent overthrow of the United States Government?"

"I guess I first got wind of it about six, seven months ago . . ." And he was off. The real lying had begun.

When it was over, the three Specials sat by themselves on a bench in a hall outside the hearing room and commiserated.

"How you doing?" Jason asked Jerry.

"I feel like I need a bath. Or at least a good flame on."

223

"No other way, Jer. It's us or them. You know that as much as I do."

"Yeah, I guess I do."

Meanwhile, Joshua stared at the floor and felt the world spin.

A door creaked open. Paulson and Reverend Kane, who had been speaking together in hushed tones, looked up as eagerly as did the three Specials.

Senator McClellan stepped into the hall. "I thought you should know, Agent Paulson. The Committee has made its decision. It grants you extraordinary powers—an ironic turn of phrase, I thought—to pursue this investigation, and take whatever steps you deem necessary to protect the public and private interest, and to save the lives of any innocent civilians who may get caught in the middle."

"Senator, you understand that the young men with me, and those we recruit later, will have to hunt down the individuals involved in this conspiracy," said Rev. Kane. "It's altogether possible that some of them may resist being arrested or taken in for questioning. Some of them may even decide it's better to die fighting."

"I understand that, Mr. Kane," said McClellan. "Which is why you're going to need a duly-appointed officer of the law to oversee that part of the operation. Someone who is entrusted with saving lives, but who also has the legal and moral authority to use deadly force if necessary. I have secured just the right man for this part of the operation."

A man with the stalwartness of a redwood now followed McClellan into the corridor. He wore a shiny blue, skin-tight uniform that accentuated a body of such muscular strength that it rivaled Jason's. The man had a bright gold badge pinned on his chest, and he looked at his childhood friends and smiled.

"Gentlemen," said Senator McClellan, "I believe you all know Officer Matthew Bright. . . ."

12

THINGS FALL APART

The bill was debated in secret in both the Senate and the House. The President secretly signed it into law after it passed and the Supreme Court upheld its constitutionality in secret. The entire process was unique among Washington secrets in that it remained one: The details were communicated strictly on a need-to-know basis, it was not leaked to the press, and the entire affair was bipartisan in nature. No one really investigated the allegations brought by Reverend Kane and the three Specials, no one questioned the wisdom of why a man who could get rich by reading tomorrow's stock reports, or a woman who could communicate visions of times and events past to whoever happened to be standing next to her, would want to take over the United States Government. No one questioned it because it was what they had always feared. It was the opportunity they had always hoped for.

Agent Paulson and the Joint Chief of Staff, General Curtis LeMay III, oversaw the operation from an underground bunker fifteen miles away from the Pentagon. Under their command were three battalions that had been quietly deployed to Pederson armed with tanks, anti-missile SCUDs, and the latest in anti-riot gear. Their orders were clear: apprehend all Specials. The soldiers were ordered to use force if the Specials resisted, and they were authorized to use deadly force at their own discretion, particularly if the Special in question was about to escape.

The battalions entered Pederson at dawn. Standing astride the lead tank was the Patriot, his incredible cape billowing like a great flag in a gale, his arms akimbo, his hands on his hips, and his wide chest thrust out like that of a great stud quarterback who'd just thrown the winning pass at the Super Bowl. I can easily imagine the sense of triumph Jason savored during those early hours, when they first began rounding up the Specials. From his perspective the difficult part—convincing the authorities of the conspiracy—had already been accomplished. Achieving victory through force had never before been a problem for him, and he saw no reason why things would be any different now.

The Feds came to Pederson first because that's where most of us had stayed—the town where we'd grown up, the town where people were used to seeing us, where they knew us, and where we were more or less accepted. The Feds came for the low-powers first, because they figured they wouldn't get much of a fight. They took mothers and fathers from their pleading families, they took the loners and the losers, they took the successful businessmen and the professionals. They took the Specials regardless of their contributions to society, regardless of any good works they might have done or how many people they employed, regardless of which political party they belonged to or what they believed.

Some of the Specials could do nothing more than float in the air, or lift a couple of hundred pounds, or heat up some leftover toast with just a look. It didn't matter. They were presumed guilty, and if Jason and his co-conspirators had their way, they wouldn't have an opportunity to prove their innocence. They couldn't fight their way past the men and the weapons and the tanks and the super re-enforced paddy wagons, even if they tried. Even if they could risk endangering their families, their children.

But that didn't mean some wouldn't try. Ian Erwin was a flier who made his living as an accountant; he took his biggest clients and the school children for little flights around the Pederson vicinity. When the FBI agent knocking at his door that morning realized there wouldn't be an answer, he told the nearest soldier to break it down. They got in just in time to see Ian's legs disappearing outside a window on the opposite side of the house. "He's making a break for it!" the agent exclaimed.

Some of the low-powers were pretty fast. But they weren't fast enough.

Not fast enough to escape Jason, anyway. He'd made sure he'd be around while the fliers were apprehended. He took off after Ian like a rocket. Effortlessly. Such was his power and control that he did not need to work up to his desired speed; he merely imagined how fast he should be going, and that's how fast he went.

Ian had fled wearing only his underwear. He didn't know where he could go, and had no idea how he might survive as a fugitive even if he should get away. He wasn't really thinking, he was only reacting. "Leave me alone!" he shouted as Jason approached. "I didn't do anything."

Jason smiled. Grimly. "I know."

I would like to think some small part of Jason felt sorry for Ian. After all, up until now, Jason had spent the majority of his life protecting those who were not as strong as the bullies who beset them. I would like to think some small part of Jason felt guilty at what he was doing. But who am I kidding? Ian pleaded one more time— "Jason . . . please!"—before Jason plowed into him with a stiff uppercut to the chin, and then a swift right, followed by a swift left.

Ian hung in the air for just a moment, unconscious, before he began to fall.

And Jason hung in the air for a long time, and watched.

Because everytime somebody ran, or somebody fought, it made it look like the story might be true.

If we stayed, we lost. If we ran, we lost. If we fought, we lost. Anyway we looked at it, we were going to lose.

Jason saved Ian. Caught him moments before impact. I know he wanted Ian to die, he wanted to feel that fraction of fresh force pulsating in his body. But the FBI and soldiers were arresting the Specials in good faith. If Jason had allowed Ian to die so brutally, so horribly, someone might have gotten suspicious and started asking questions.

The operation in Pederson was a complete success. The only problem was, the local TV and radio news picked up on it and the word got out across the nation in a matter of moments. For years everybody remembered what they had been doing, and how they'd found out, that day the Specials in Pederson were being arrested. It was one of those defining moments in one's life's, when one has a connection with the national community. Not unlike how the nation felt on those occasions when Martin Luther King, the Kennedy brothers, and Mick Jagger had been assassinated.

The Specials who lived outside Pederson, in particular, remembered.

That same morning, when the authorities came for Randy Fisk, a.k.a. Ravenshadow, the press was at his mansion in force. Everybody knew that Randy was Ravenshadow, that he was supposed to be one of the good guys. He had, after all, helped put a lot of bad guys away, and though he tended to frighten the bejeezus out of them, he wasn't nearly as brutal as some other so-called good guy Specials I could name.

The Feds sent Jerry Montrose, a.k.a. Pyre, another conspirator who named us as disloyal to save his own neck, as point man when their armored vehicles burst through the Ravenshadow mansion gates. Fire against darkness. Great image. Great PR. Jerry left a streak of flame behind him as he flew, like the trail of a fighter jet. "Stand back," he called to the soldiers rushing onto the grounds. "The Shadow Cave! It might be booby-trapped. I'll burn through."

And he did. He melted a hole in a titanium hatch big enough to fly through. The process took less than a minute, and he was already on the other side before he thought it might not be a bad idea to melt it down some more, so the mundanes could get in. By "mundanes" he meant both soldiers and reporters. He wanted the press to get footage of him exploring the secrets in Ravenshadow's mighty fortress when the time was right.

The press wanted to see if Randy would stand, fight, or run—any of which would prove that he had something to hide—or if he'd quietly surrender. Which just goes to prove that despite their years of Special watching, they didn't know Randy.

Jerry found himself flying around in circles. It took him a few moments, but he finally realized he couldn't believe his eyes.

One of the soldiers expressed what they were all thinking: "The whole place has been emptied out! Everything's gone!"

Indeed. The much-discussed Shadow Cave was empty. Jerry and the soldiers were completely stumped. The operation had been in effect for only a few hours. How could one man, even a Special, have possibly emptied such a large space of so much equipment so quickly?

As it turned out, I never asked Randy. Probably because I've always liked what happened next.

Jerry was flying around in circles, and was thinking fast. His life spent on the edges of crime had taught him that things are never as simple as they seem, especially when they look too pat. Somehow Ravenshadow had tumbled onto their scheme, had figured out what was happening in Washington, and though he hadn't warned the low-powers or anyone else, he had been prepared, and perhaps had been working on this evacuation for a couple of days.

"Not everything's gone!" he said, spotting a metal cylinder in a ceiling corner. "Just a second while I check it out."

His flaming jaw dropped. His burning heart skipped a beat.

The cylinder had a digital clock on it.

The numbers were going backwards.

Only thirty seconds left go.

Twenty-nine. Twenty-eight.

"BOMB! Everybody out! Now!"

The soldiers watched in amazement as the burning man streaked out of the cave so fast it was a wonder he didn't snuff himself out.

"Now! Now! Now!" he kept shouting. "Now!"

And he got as far away from there as possible, as fast as possible.

The men were somewhat slower.

I remember when Randy built the Shadow Cave. It was a dumb name and I told him so. But he loved it. It was just like all those comics he had read when he was a kid. He wanted a fortress no one could ever breach. Funny how things change.

Randy liked his little jokes. The numbers hit zero when the last of the men reached the exit, far too late to escape an explosion. In truth they had ten more seconds. They used those seconds and reached safety, but not before their hearts had stopped at least once, as they expected to be engulfed in the coming holocaust.

The explosion arrived with devastating force. The walls broke apart like popcorn bursting its kernels; the fires and debris rolled out like giant buckshot, chasing the sky, burying itself in dirt and concrete. Fortunately for the stragglers, who'd nearly reached the front gates, most of the debris missed them, so the worst thing they had to worry about were the shock waves, which slapped them to the ground like flies. Everyone else hid behind the front walls, which nearly buckled from the force.

The mansion was rubble. Most of it had fallen into the place where the Shadow Cave had been.

The soldiers and agents waited for the debris to cease falling. Then, with bated breath, they took stock of the situation. No one was injured, at least apparently. That was a relief. Several minutes passed, and once the fear of another explosion had diminished somewhat, they walked onto the grounds and collectively wondered if there was a way to salvage the situation.

Back in Washington, Paulson and General LeMay already knew the answer to that. Of course there wasn't. Ravenshadow had played them like a bunch of violin strings. Granted, his escape had clearly been long and careful in the planning, providing them additional "proof" of his traitorous intentions, but they didn't need that any more. The main thing was the simple fact of his escape. Paulson and LeMay immediately got the sense the roundup was going to be very sticky from here on out.

You could say that. Randy had always figured a day like this might come. He'd never made a big deal about it; he simply didn't trust people in general, so it seemed logical the mundanes might turn against the Specials. Besides, as a kid his favorite comics had been about outsider mutant kids: sooner or later the mundanes always came after them. Anyway, every year Randy took a certain percentage of his profits from selling his art and invested it into creating several secret bases; the Shadow Cave, the most visible of his bases and a secret in social custom only, was also the least important.

Fortunately, he'd made other plans as well, and shared them with us. From the secret HQ on the other side of Manhattan, to which he'd raced the moment he learned of the arrests in Pederson, Randy watched a screen playing the scene of his home, his belongings, every thing he'd striven to obtain, being reduced to rubble. And he smiled. He'd never felt that attached to most of it anyway, and the knowledge that the game was at last afoot exhilarated him.

"Ah, well," he said. "Easy come, easy go. Computer, open phone file for all under heading 'Specials.' Prepare to record message, and deliver by simultaneous speed dial. Begin recording. Listen up, people. The balloon's gone up, if you haven't heard. The Feds are after every one of us. Get out now. Right now. Don't pack, don't tell anyone where you're going, just go. Once you're wherever you're going to be for a while, dial this number, 888-555-1243. My computer will recognize your call and store the number. We'll call you with more updates as we have them. By the way, don't use your cell phones or palm pilots. Throw 'em away. It'll just make it easier for them to trace you."

Not everybody had known about this plan, of course. Randy had discussed it with me before he implemented, and we'd decided some of us had to be kept in the dark, mainly the hard-chargers like Matt and Jason, the easily dominated, such as Joshua, and those who simply couldn't be trusted, or were basically amoral, like Laurel Darkhaven. They would be all too likely to spill the beans, for whatever reason, during an actual emergency. The best candidates for inclusion were those who aspired to a life of mundania, or those like Paula and Chandra who were social successes, at the top of the mundane ladder. Further, Randy had emphasized to all that the secret was never to be discussed—not with husbands or wives, parents or children, friends or family, and certainly not with one another. We had all grown up together, we had watched our parents fight desperately so the government wouldn't treat us like animals, and we knew human nature, particularly our own. We lived in a world where even the good guys couldn't be trusted.

So all those outside Pederson knew to answer their

phones, especially if they'd heard the news. And those who weren't around knew to check their messages at once and then destroy the tape. Randy'd always suggested fire. And immediately after hanging up, they did as they were bidden. They left friends, pets, family, and children behind with their spouses—except in the cases where both spouses were Specials and they had no choice but to take their children with them. They left making their good-byes as brief as possible. They left with their identity bracelets in the trash. And they left with only vague ideas where to go. But usually things got clearer after they'd been on the road a while. Randy had given them a few hints about survival, including the necessity about having sufficient quantities of cash stashed away. He was confident most of them would okay, for the time being.

Then an alarm went off. "Uh-oh . . ." A computerized map of the United States showed a green streak headed across New Mexico and Arizona. Randy knew Jason was still in Pederson; only one other Special could go that fast.

"Computer," he said, "dial John Simon, fast."

You wouldn't believe where I was. I could hardly believe it myself. But after my non-confrontation with Jason in Cincinnati, I found myself profoundly depressed. The prospect of facing the coming storm filled me with ennui. I had no spirit, my will was lost. Only the knowledge that giving up would doom innocent people to death enabled me to trudge on.

The reason for this psychic crash eluded me. But that night, while the real Jason was having his powwow with Jerry and Joshua and the right Reverend Kane, I'd snuck through the security of the ritziest hotel I could find, checked myself in, unbeknownst to the staff, and spent the night in an empty luxury suite. I usually didn't risk exposure by availing myself of room service, but I was feeling reckless on top of everything else; besides, my entire stay was going to be charged to Nexus Corp—I'd already seen to that. So I ordered wine, pizza, and a chocolate cake for dessert and listened to classical music on a cable station. Normally that was great background for writing, but tonight I just wanted to listen to the music. I wanted to experience the emotions inherent in the compositions, in the hopes that they would break down the walls in my heart. Those walls were necessary, but they weren't exactly life-sustaining. I had the feeling I was living, but I wasn't alive.

The music consisted of symphonies by Mozart, Beethoven, and Vaughn Williams. After that, the program got a little vague, because I'd passed out. I awoke with a head-splitting hangover and the conviction that I had to see Chandra. It occurred to me that while I was still living, I still had a chance to be alive.

I took care of a few affairs—mostly dreary things like phone and electric bills—and a few days later had boarded a plane to Los Angeles. Reverend Kane's ministry paid for that trip. Now please don't think I was a common embezzler. By now I'd figured out that Jason would go to Joshua, at the very least, and I thought it poetic justice to use the funds of our enemies against them.

I'd been planning on meeting Chandra when she was making one of her frequent public appearances in LA, but when I was at LAX, I saw on the news that the Specials were being taken in Pederson. I called Chandra at once and arranged a meeting at her Hollywood Hills mansion. Chandra might be the most beautiful woman in the world to whomever sees her, but what Clarence had told me indicated she was still an insecure child inside. That could translate to fear, and we didn't have time for fear right now. I needed her to be strong.

We talked in her big front yard. Her place was a Hollywood mansion straight out of the Harold Lloyd days, with gardens and fountains and brick driveways. Statues of mermen kissing mermaids dotted the place like pylons in a power station. I tried not to stand too close to her while we talked. It was early for her—she hadn't put her face on yet—but it didn't matter. Her features were mesmerizing and she smelled so enticing, I actually seriously considered throwing aside my civilized veneer and kissing her. Even the memory that she liked to have sex with faceless, masked men didn't make her any less attractive. I mean, talk about twisted. Why didn't she just put paper bags over their heads? It would have been less expensive, and the result would have been the same.

"John, there has to be some other way," she said. "I mean, can't we talk to them? Reason with them? If we run—"

"We'll live, Chandra. Right now they're more scared of us than we are of them. They're not in a reasonable mood. We have to get clear and protect ourselves until we can work this out. Is there any place you can go that's safe? Where you can't be found?"

"Yes . . . yes, there's a ranch owned by a . . . well, rich friend. He lets me use it whenever I want. He's out of the country for the next month. The place will be empty."

"How many people can it hold? We need to find shelter for as many of the others as we can, before—"

"You mean—you want me to use it as shelter for fugitives?"

"Yes."

"Okay, I think he loves me at least that much."

"Excellent." I felt both relief and jealousy; the inner conflict was making me crazy. If this was emotion, why did people strive to experience it? Life was so much clearer without it.

She looked into my eyes. She was trying to communicate something, of that I am certain, but such was my inexperience with the opposite sex that either I was afraid or had no idea what it might be. I was short of breath, and I had the distinct impression her face had moved ever so slightly closer to mine . . .

Then my cell phone rang. Randy hadn't included me in his earlier group message because we had both agreed it would be superfluous, but I knew before answering that this had to be serious.

"You called it, John," said Randy on the other end. "We've got heavy-duty movement and it's coming your way. You better get out of there, and I mean fast."

"Is it Matthew?"

"Looks like. The news still has Jason in Pederson."

"Gotcha." I hung up. I had to assume two things: a) I'd been spotted, probably by a Specials sighter, despite my precautions, and b) the story of the mysterious hole in the underground parking lot, which had been picked up by the tabloid press, had been duly noted by Paulson and his pals. Subsequent assumptions included the possibility I'd been spotted there, plus the possibility Paulson and co. might have put two-and-two together and come up with the right answer for a change. "We're out of time," I said to Chandra. "You've got the number. Don't lose it." I was a real tough guy.

"But—"

"You have to go, Chandra. Right now."

"All right." She ran her fingers down my cheek. Her touch was light, but my skin felt like it was on fire. She held back a smile, and I was hoping it wasn't because I was blushing. "Life is too short, John. It's a crime against nature to waste it. So when this is over, I'd like very much if we could talk. Some time. Do you think we can do that?"

"I think I'll like that. I certainly wouldn't want to be an accessory to a crime. Now go on. Please."

I watched her drive off, alone, in the cheapest, most nondescript automobile in her possession, a mid-'80s Mercedes Benz. I believe it had been her first car. Her staff and entourage had been dismissed the moment she'd heard the news, so now I was alone on the opulent grounds. Clarence had told me that while he was walking in her dreams, he discovered Chandra that loved me. I have no idea why she loved me. Perhaps it was because I was unobtainable. In any case, I never knew, never let myself know, and now it was too late.

I got a hold of myself. I couldn't think that way, couldn't let myself be distracted. Otherwise, the Specials wouldn't get out of this. They would have no chance.

I went into the house and raced up the stairs, headed for the roof. I suppose I should have been on edge. I wasn't used to responsibility. But this was what Doc Welles had trained me for, all those years. I was determined not to let him or the rest down.

Matt was almost at the mansion. I could feel him. I'd figured they'd send him instead of Jason. I was convinced

Jason took the job as point man for arresting the low-powers because basically he had the soul of a bully. He probably didn't even know it, he'd convinced himself to be such a good guy down through the years. But bullies always took on the low-powers, rather than guys who might give them a fight. That's why Jerry and Matt were picked to do the hard work.

I watched Matt come down from the clouds. His descent took him directly toward the mansion. He could feel me as easily as I could him. Again, it was the psychic-magnetic bond between Specials. His descent slowed as he closed in, but he didn't look like he was going to stop until he was almost parallel to the roof. The clouds behind his back lent him the illusion of wings, so he appeared as an angel as he hung there, his fists clenched, his costume seemingly sprayed on, so that every bulging muscle and vein could be plainly seen. Those weren't the biggest bulges, by far. Matt was a man who didn't mind showing you what he had.

"Hello, Matt," I said, with a wave.

"John. You're under arrest."

"Hmmm." I knew he didn't want to kill me, but what he didn't know was, I was afraid I'd have to kill him. "I didn't think your authority extended beyond New York."

"It didn't, until now. I have a warrant and I'm authorized to take you into custody—"

"On what charge?"

"—in connection with allegations that you and others have joined forces to subvert the government, suspicion of having murdered several of our—"

"Jason did it!" I snapped. I couldn't stand hearing those words out of Matthew's mouth. So sanctimonious, so righteous! "He's using you! He's using everybody!"

"He said you'd say that."

I shrugged. "It's true."

"Can you prove it?"

"Clarence showed me after he was killed."

"I can't believe you said that."

"It's still true. You know what he was capable of. He saw the truth in Jason's mind, in his dreams."

"John, even if I believed you, you and I both know Clarence was a psychic voyeur and a complete fake. No court in the land is going to take the word of a dead guy, given after he's dead. You'll have to do better than that."

"Sorry, I don't accept your interpretation of Clarence or the facts." My hands were behind my back, I released the force into them. "Clarence told the truth. I can't prove it, but I know it's true. You're working on the wrong side of the street, Matt. You should be with us, fighting this."

"I'm supposed to take your word for it? Sorry—it's not my place to say you're right or you're wrong. I'm a duly authorized officer of the court, and my job is to take you back to trial. Everything else is up to the court to decide."

"Don't you think more than a few Soviet policemen thought exactly the same thing, as they carted off guys on charges trumped up by the party?" I could feel the force building inside me.

"Look, John, we both know you can't take me. Playing with electronics and TV waves doesn't give you the power to stop me from taking you if I choose to. I'd rather do this peacefully. I don't want to hurt you."

"Thanks for the thought. But I'm not going."

"I'm sorry to hear you say that." He tilted and flew toward me at deliberate speed. He was confident I couldn't run away—indeed, he was so confident, it never occurred to him to wonder why I *wasn't* running.

241

I didn't show him my fists until the last possible nano-second. They glowed with a cool blue flame that left trails in waves. Matt had just enough time for his jaw to drop in surprise before I put the whammy on him, connecting with a right cross that sent him spinning around like a toy top. He crashed into a skylight on the roof of a nearby wing of the mansion. Indeed, he went through the sky-light, came out on the other side, and landed in a small roof garden.

I stood my ground and waited. I knew he wasn't hurt, not really. Just that damn super-Special pride the high-powers tended to nurse until it was abundant. It still took him several seconds, nonetheless, to regain his orientation.

"How in the hell—"

"Did I do that?" I had asked Doc Welles, one day when I was ten and he had taken me on a hike into the woods. No one ever thought anything unusual about that. He'd often taken me for walks, and everyone figured I was his favorite. I don't know how I felt about him; love for adults was never one of my big character traits, though I had to make an exception for Mom. I never knew, until that day, that our time alone had merely been part of his plan. I was never his favorite, he'd just decided I would need extra attention. And he wanted the rest of the world to believe there was nothing exceptional about the day when he finally talked me through what I could really do—

—Which, the first time I did it, consisted of reducing an entire tree to a stump in about fifteen seconds, thanks to one application of concentrated force.

"You don't want to know," I told Matthew.

*   *   *

"You're different from all the other Specials, John, in one important regard," Doc Welles told me that day. "They control the powers inside them that were created by the force that struck this town while they were in utero. You control the force itself, inside you."

"So what're you saying, Doc? That I'm faster than the others? Stronger?"

"Not faster, necessarily, or stronger. Just deadlier."

Meanwhile, back in the present, Matt shook off wood and glass fragments and stood up. His eyes were steely, and if his jaw had been more set, he'd have been eating through a straw for the rest of his life.

"Go back home, Matt, while you still can."

"You know I can't do that." He got ready to spring.

"How deadly?" I asked the doc, while I stared at the residual force emanating from my fists in great emerald waves. Now I knew what it meant to be smokin'.

"In my opinion, you can kill any of them in single combat."

"Even Jason? Even Matthew?"

"Even Jason—and yes, even Matthew."

"Is that why the other kids are always talking about me, pointing at me?"

Doc Welles sat on a log and laughed. "No, they don't know. You are an outsider, John, and even the most sensitive kids will pick on outsiders in order to be part of the gang. But this is why you're an outsider—think of it as your natural calling—and we can't let the others or anyone else know what you can do. Because they will try to use you."

" 'They'?"

"The Federal Government. Your friends. The enemies you'll eventually acquire. You'll be just like a famous movie director or star, John. Everybody you meet will want a piece of you." He rubbed his chin. "On the other hand, I think the kids can feel the difference in you, somehow. I wonder sometimes if the force was more directed than we think. Maybe it created one person to be a fail safe, someone who could deal with any of the others individually if they turned bad."

"You think some of us are going to turn out bad?"

"Oh, sure. Of course, what I've been saying is absurd. Energy doesn't think, it isn't conscious. I just can't come up with any other explanation. So you're going to walk a hard and lonely road, John, knowing there's only violence at the end of it. You can never allow yourself to get close to any of the other Specials. Never allow yourself to care about them. Never allow yourself to love any of them, or allow any of them to love you."

Back in the present, I remembered the time that Chandra was staring at me while a bunch of the boys were milling around her, searching for whatever sign of feminine approval boys search for when they're ten. The memory made me uneasy, and I had walked away until I felt safe.

"Because one day," Doc continued, "and I do not envy you this terrible responsibility, you may have to kill them. Because you may be the only one who can."

"How will I know when the day comes?"

"You'll know."

* * *

244

Matthew shot toward me like a dart from a South American blowgun.

I sighed wistfully. Why did it have to come to this?

I struck Matthew on the side of the head and sent him spiraling into a dome. Which he struck head-first. Neither time did he see where the blow was coming from.

I realized I was stronger. I had something that belonged to him. Part of the force.

He came at me again. I knocked him back.

From the corner of my eye I noted a television crew in a newsvan had just pulled up. They'd probably come here hoping to see the most beautiful woman in the world get arrested for treason. Instead, they were going to get a spectacular show that was going to blow what little cover I had left, and there was nothing I could do about it.

I could only do something about Matthew, who had once more leapt into the breach. I caught him by the chest, dug my fingers into that skin-tight suit of his, probably tearing off a lot of skin with it, and held him. The waves of the force pulsating between us became visible, white and blue, and I used his own life-force to beat him into a limp, wet sock.

I backed him against a dome wall. The mansion cracked and crumbled from the waves of force that escaped our circuit. He was limp, all right. Blood flowed from his nostrils and the corners of his eyes. His arms and legs twitched.

"I don't want to have to kill you, Matt," I said, momentarily forgetting the presence of the TV news team, who were catching my every word. "But I will if I have to."

*   *   *

Watching the spectacle on television in his office, Agent Paulson realized he'd left the Pentagon too soon. He picked up the phone.

"Get me the goddamned Joint Chief of Staff—now!"

"I told you the truth, Matt," I said, still punishing him with as much brute force as possible.

"Screw you," he said.

I'd always known he had an attitude problem. One would have thought he would have learned from the example of his parents and questioned authority upon occasion.

The blue waves cascaded from us in tsunami after tsunami of light. Summoning a strength from within that frankly I wouldn't have thought him capable of at this stage of the game, Matt grabbed me around the neck and squeezed with all his might. It was too bad for him that at the moment he lacked the strength to so much as crush a worm, but I had to give him credit for trying.

Down on the streets, I later learned, the media folk and the lookie-loos figured the whole place was going to blow, like Randy's mansion, and they high-tailed it to the other end of the street, where presumably they could watch the explosion from a safe distance.

As it was, only the roof went, but the rain of debris did signify they hadn't been overly cautious.

And when they figured that the worst was over, they realized the blue glow that had been wrapping the two Special warriors had disappeared.

I was just a normal-looking man in a long coat, hanging high in the air like a relaxed hummingbird.

A normal-looking man, holding a semi-conscious super-hero by the shirt.

I thought I'd take one last shot at talking some sense in him. It was obvious I couldn't pound any into him. "If I were the man you think I am, you'd be dead right now," I told him. "Now you know I could do it. I wanted you to know that, so you'd believe me when I say this: It isn't me, Matt. It's Jason. It's Jason!"

And I dropped him. His body, though never as invulnerable as poor Peter Dawson's, and definitely weakened by the beating it had taken, was certainly strong enough to endure a fall of a hundred yards.

He landed smack in front of the reporters—who caught the whole finale on camera—and cracked the asphalt at least five times as he bounced to a stop.

I flew off, in a blue glow. It was the first time I'd ever flown. I'd known that I could—Doc Welles had helped me gain a few feet off the ground and together we figured I'd possessed the proper mobility—but I hadn't indulged myself before simply because I didn't want people to think there was more to my abilities than they already knew. It was best not to tempt temptation, as it were. But soon the entire world would know how badly the authorities had underestimated me. If I was lucky, a few people would wonder why, if I was already a murderer, I hadn't killed Matt when I'd had the chance.

I hoped Matt would listen this time. Check out Jason's story for himself. Plus, I thought that maybe, just maybe, by keeping the authorities' attention on me, thanks to my amazing exit, I was buying time for the others to get away while they still had the chance.

* * *

In his office, Agent Paulson watched me fly away on live television. "I always said they were hiding the truth from us!" he exclaimed to the group that had gathered to watch with him. "Hiding what they could do. This proves it. I want full mobilization.

"And get Dr. Welles on the line. I want his ass in here for questioning. A.S.A.P."

Meanwhile, in his bedroom, Dr. Welles watched the same feed. He was only dimly listening to what the reporter was saying: "And then the suspect flew off, heading east. Authorities aren't saying anything now, but according to sources—"

Doc Welles switched off the TV. He knew what was coming next:

The phone rang. Once. Twice. Three times. Insistently.

He opened a desk drawer and pulled out a pistol. He was afraid he might need it, in a pinch.

13

THE CENTER CANNOT HOLD

I've always had this fear that one million years after a nuclear holocaust has wiped out all life on Earth and turned the planet into a dreary black husk, only three artifacts of civilizations would survive, to be found by alien explorers that would use them as their sole criteria to judge the worth of the human race. The first artifact would be a set of the golden arches; the second, a survivalist handbook; and third, a VCR tape of a car chase from the local news. Just so the aliens would know what sort of lame gladiatorial action the human race was capable of appreciating.

Now, a car chase on the surface of it might not have a whole lot of meaning, but obviously the human race attaches some sort of importance to the phenomenon. In addition to being a great visual attraction for the modern cinema, the car chase is generally considered newsworthy for no reason other than the fact that it happened. You've noticed it when tuning into the local TV news:

"Terror in the Mid-East today. Gunman shot and killed on the White House lawn. She's won an Oscar, an Emmy and a Grammy, but tonight she has been arrested on charges of running a prostitution ring. First, however, an armed man in a stolen pick-up truck led police on a chase over fifty miles on I-5 today, this footage courtesy of our very own Channel 4 chopper—"

And if the guy winds up dead at the end of the story, so much the better. And to think such a lead story could have concerned Doctor Welles, all because of the afternoon that he led the police—augmented by army helicopters!—on a merry chase through the Midwest. But since there were no charges yet against him—the Three Js hadn't wanted to drag him into their false tale of infamy—the Feds decided that rather than risk the moral high ground they'd thus far managed to attain in the PR aspect of their war against treason, they'd have the media squash the story of their capture of Dr. Welles. The media was only too glad to cooperate, thanks to the Feds' promise of exclusive footage of certain Specials with unusual abilities being captured.

I had an opportunity to read Dr. Welles' diary, a long time after he'd passed away and the air of confidentiality about it had given way to the sense that what he had written was history. In this diary he had written:

They came for the Specials. They came for my kids—all right, even though they're not kids anymore, I still think of them that way—on unjustified charges of conspiracy to overthrow the government. Most of them had gone into hiding, and when the police couldn't find them, they found the next best thing.

They found me.

All right, I confess, I was going into hiding, too. Occasionally, when I'd met one of the sweet homemaker types such as Stephanie or Renee, they'd let slip that they'd had caches of money hidden in the house, or that they knew what to do if they ever had to go underground. They'd caught themselves immediately after the slip, would either change the subject or slither on by it, and I knew the only reason they'd erred was because they were used to being so honest with me. So in order to facilitate their honest conversation in the future, I never pursued the matter, never paid much attention to the details of their knowledge of potential life in the underground. That was certainly shortsighted of me.

I made my first mistake when I spotted the roadblock. Rather than heading off into a side street, like I knew where I was going, I panicked and made a blatant U-turn. I'd made it about three blocks before I noticed the two police cars behind me in the rearview mirror. What minor sense of relief I might have maintained dissipated immediately and I drove a little faster.

So did they.

I ran a red light.

So did they.

I broke the speed limit. So did they.

I broke the speed limit in a school zone. So did they.

As I drove up the ramp to the interstate, two Apache helicopters hovered around like giant wasps—I had the distinct feeling they wanted to sting me.

At the top of the ramp was a stop light. Three cars waited their turn. I hit the shoulder and drove past them, almost sideswiped an oncoming car, and put the pedal to the metal.

There were at least six police cars visible in my rearview mirror now. And I mean *at least*. They had their sirens on, their lights were flashing, and the voices on their loudspeakers ordered me to pull over, more than once. I couldn't help but laugh. If ever there was a moment for listening to X perform "Breathless" on the radio, this was it.

My engine started making funny noises. Not good. I knew I should have had that transmission looked at. I figured it would last until I ran out of gas, though.

In the original, low-budget, independent version of *Gone in Sixty Seconds*, directed by H.B. Halicki, our anti-hero protagonist, played by H.B. Halicki, eludes what must be a battalion of state police after a chase that lasts about 40 minutes, screen-time. After about thirty minutes of fast driving I was getting tired, desperate, and saw no conceivable way of escape. Even if I could somehow elude the police cars, there were still the Apache helicopters to reckon with. And if I somehow began to elude them as well, they could still fire a few rockets and put the kibosh on my escape plans for good.

Even so, just because I was desperate didn't mean I could give up. When I got near a certain heavily wooded suburb, I took an off-ramp figuring I might be able to get out of the car and lose myself in a shopping mall or some such place. A lame plan, sure, but it was the only one I had. I'd never considered myself a criminal, until then. Of course, I'd never considered myself a daredevil race driver either.

I vaguely heard a policeman's loudspeaker blare: "This is your last warning!"

I chuckled. A brave, foolhardy, self-conscious chuckle. I was pretty sure I had the picture by now. Of course, I had forgotten that I needed a new pair of glasses with an updated prescription, and so I missed seeing the tire strip laid down on the road before me.

Not that I could have done anything about it if I had seen it. Another U-turn wouldn't have done any good. A complete stop might have made my eventual capture a little neater, but considering the animosity these boys must have built up for me by this time, I couldn't be sure.

The razor-sharp blades of the tire strip blew all four of my tires in about two seconds flat.

And I lost control of my vehicle about three seconds after that.

My car rolled. It turned, too. About 360 degrees. I discovered, much to my surprise, that what people said about being in car accidents, combat, or some other life-threatening situation really was true: time appeared to slow down to a crawl and the mind and body had the illusion of having plenty of time to react and consider options. Only problem was, there was nothing I could do except sit in the car and wait for it to stop rolling.

Which it did, coming to rest, briefly, on its side before starting to slide down to the end of the ramp.

Then it rolled some more, down a hill.

From my perspective, the entire incident took about an hour. Then time caught up with itself and I realized I was still sitting down, thanks to my seat belt. Upside down of course—my car was sitting on its top on the shoulder of an intersection.

My wheels—my bare wheels were still spinning.

I heard a policeman call for an ambulance, and another cop kept telling me to hold on, I would be okay, I would be okay.

Okay, okay, I thought. *Of course I will, officer. You see . . . I've flown . . . before . . .* I realized, with a sinking feeling, that I was going to need new glasses sooner than I had anticipated. That's when I passed out.

*   *   *

"You want to fly with me, Doc?" Matthew asked.

I was taking notes on my ever-present clipboard on a warm summer day. I was also having a total recall flashback, which I was very aware of, but since I was remembering a day when I was younger and had more hair on the back of my head, I surrendered to it.

"You want to fly with me, Doc?"

I looked up into the shadow suddenly cast over my face. Dressed in a pair of shorts and a baseball jersey, nine-year-old Matthew Bright hung in the air between me and the sun. He was a freckle-faced, wholesome lad, without a mean bone in his body.

"Me? No, I can't fly, Matthew."

"I can take you with me," he said eagerly. "I can carry you. You don't know what's it's like until you've been up there, with the birds, not in a plane, or a helicopter. Right beside them."

"I don't—"

"It's not really a problem, Doc. I can carry a couple thousand pounds."

"It's not that—I know you can do it, it's just—I'm not one of you, Matthew. I'm not special. And maybe people who aren't special shouldn't fly. Maybe they don't deserve to."

He laughed. Not in an unkindly way, but as if I'd just said something naive. "Now, Doctor, aren't you the person who keeps telling us everybody is special, in their own way?"

"You know what I mean."

"Everybody wants to fly, just once. And everyone *should* fly, just once."

"All right, maybe, just once . . ."

And before I knew it, he picked me up by the shoulders and I was flying, the wind grazing my temples and my lab coat flapping in the breeze. I can't say I was weightless, but the overall sensation did remind me of a dream I'd once had, when I was but a boy. I never told the kids this, but I'd read comics as a lad too, and so on this night I happened to dream I levitated from my bed and flew through my window to land in a tree a few fields away from my house. It was a ridiculous dream, but the sensation of Matthew holding me as he flew was the closest to the fanciful feeling of weightlessness in my dream as I ever managed to achieve in real life.

Well, there *was* the time I ran my car off the interstate, but that wasn't nearly as pleasant.

I wonder what Matthew would have thought if he'd known what sort of notes I was taking that day. Notes on how the abilities of the kids might be overcome if it ever became necessary to put them down, like animals.

"Doctor Welles?" somebody asked. "Doctor Welles?"

He had a voice like Jim Morrison gargling gravel. And he was irritated. That could only mean:

"Paulson."

"Hello, Doctor."

"I'm surprised to see you here." I was lying on a cot in a military prison. My head ached. On the cot opposite mine sat the big "P" himself. He was simmering like a man whose barbecue had tipped over while the entire family was watching. Over the years his animal magnetism had shown signs of radiation poisoning. His eyes glittered with madness.

"You look like hell," I said. "What happened? Somebody cancel a bund meeting?"

"The doctors tell me you're well enough to talk."

"I just woke up!"

"They promised me," he hissed, leaning toward me. "I want you to answer some questions."

"Not without an attorney."

"This isn't a jail," he said, nodding to the guard standing at attention just outside my cell. "And you haven't been arrested. This is an army base."

"I noticed. Am I being detained under the Ashcroft Acts?" I realized I was holding my glasses. What was left of them, anyway. At least one lens was intact. I fought the urge to touch the bandages on my head.

"We made a policy decision long ago that the rule of law shouldn't apply to a Specials revolt. So you don't get an attorney. You come and go at our pleasure."

"Can I have a drink of water?"

"No."

"In that case, not only do I want an attorney, I also want an agent, a publisher, and a publicist, and a copy of the Constitution wouldn't hurt, either."

"I'm not in a mood to play, Doctor. We tried to access the termination method files for the Specials. They've been deleted. Only a handful of people had access to that material. Including you."

"Deleted—oh, no! I'm shocked! Shocked, I tell you. Why can't you retrieve the data from the hard drives?"

"Because the hard drives were mysteriously demagnetized, totally erased. Well, the files may be gone, but the data is still there in your head. I want that information, Doctor. And I want to know where the rest of the Specials are hiding. In case, you haven't heard, the country is in danger." He had already walked away, obviously hoping his concluding comments would be helped by a dramatic gesture.

"Oh, it's in danger all right!" I blurted out. I tried to get up but quickly learned that while I might be ready to talk, I wasn't ready to stand. "But it's in danger more from what you're doing than what the Specials are doing! I won't give you any information."

"Then we will tear it out of you."

I gasped, and had immediate visions of Argentine torturers smuggled into the country just to meet me. I couldn't put it past the bastard. Nothing I could do about it. I sank against the wall and realized however dire my personal situation might be, the situation was infinitely more dire for him. Jason, in his bid for more physical power, was playing Paulson and all the rest as Grade-A Number One patsies. Did Paulson really think Jason *et al.* would kowtow to him when it was all over?

"Mr. Paulson, call for you." The guard handed him a cell phone.

"Right. Give it here." He snapped his fingers, not that the soldier appeared particularly slow. "Then lock him up and come with me." The word he spoke into the phone as he walked away only aggravated my anxieties. "Where did you find them? Good—good! I knew the wiretap would work out. That arrogant so-called Ravenshadow should have known we'd break through his network shenanigans.—No, don't do anything until reinforcements arrive. I'm on my way."

What was it that Joker says at the end of *Full Metal Jacket*? "We live in a world of shit." Suddenly, I was consumed by the fear that I would soon know exactly what Joker meant, only this would be one tour of duty that would last for the duration of my life.

However long that turned out to be.

I wondered if there was some way I could convince them to put in cable TV. I had the feeling CNN was going to be showing some unique footage in the near future.

I sighed and watched the ceiling spin. It had just about slowed down to a reasonable speed when suddenly my meager effort at reorienting myself was thwarted by a mousy feminine voice coming from the cell opposite mine.

"Hi, Doctor Welles?"

The voice was familiar, but it took me a moment to place it.

"Stephanie? Stephanie Maas?"

She came out of the dark. I hadn't noticed her earlier because the guard had been standing between us, and truth to tell, she did know how to make herself inconspicuous. Stephanie was a tiny little thing, meek beyond words. Her husband was an overbearing control freak, but I had perceived from their personal interaction that he truly cared for her. Perhaps she cared for him too, but she was such a needy type that I'm not sure love ever fully entered into that equation.

"They got you, too?" I said. "But why? In all these years, you've never demonstrated any abilities."

She ran her hand through her cropped brown hair. "I guess they wanted to make extra sure, after what happened with John showing all those extra powers nobody knew about when he fought Matthew."

"Ah. Well, I suppose I can understand that." By now there was enough adrenaline shooting through my system to provide hydroelectric power for the entire state of Illinois. Enough so I could actually stand and pace my cell. I was thinking about things, but I instinctively inquired of Stephanie if she was all right.

"Yeah . . . I think so. Just scared. I mean, I don't know if any of us are ever going to get out of here."

I nodded. Still only half-listening to her. But I knew what she meant.

"But for me," she continued in a ragged growl, "it's great. Because the stress lets me get out a lot more than I ever did before."

My bowels dropped into the fifth dimension. "What . . . what did you say?"

"About what?" Her voice moved up nearly an octave.

"Just now. What did you say?"

"I said, I don't know if any of us are ever going to get out of here."

"All right . . . never mind, then. I must have been mistaken. Thought I heard something else."

"Yeah, Doc, that would be me." The contralto rasp returned as, in that instant, her face changed. Her lips became longer, her nose aquiline, her eyes green and devilish. Her shoulders seemed broader, her hair was suddenly black and spiky, and even her breasts looked bigger. Her overall bearing became strong and confident, two qualities I had never, ever associated with Stephanie.

"Good to meet you at last. That little mouse Steph has told me all about you. You're okay in my book. But the rest of these creeps—first chance I get, they get the treatment. You know what I'm saying?"

I blinked and she had changed back to sweet, scared Stephanie. "What? Why are you looking at me like that?"

Now I was really depressed. As if I wasn't under enough stress already. I'm afraid my response wasn't exactly memorable:

"Oh, crap."

*   *   *

Simon here. The Doctor's notes indicated that by now Paulson had left the base, riding shotgun in the first of five Apache helicopters. I hear tell he claimed to have been thinking of an uncle who had retired from the spy game once the Berlin Wall fell. Figured his life's work was over. Paulson suspected he would soon know exactly how his uncle had felt. Paulson's entire professional career had been leading up to this day. And he was going to savor every second of it.

"ETA for the target area is 1500 hours, sir."

"Outstanding. Once we're on the ground, it's your mission, Colonel."

"What kind of opposition are we looking at?" the Colonel asked.

"These are the last of the low-powers who escaped the initial round-up, so expect some strength, flight, some telekinetics, but not much in the way of invulnerability. A gun will stop them the same as anybody else. That's why we're using conventional forces here. We're saving our big guns and the other Specials who have joined up for the heavy assault roster."

"Sir," said a soldier. "Call for you from base. Dr. William Welles."

Paulson grinned as he took the phone. "Well, Doctor? Did you change your mind?"

"Listen, I can reconstruct some of what you want, but my figures are out of date."

"What the hell you talking about—out of date?"

"I'll need the medical files of all the Specials you've arrested, especially any information about how their powers may have changed, modified, or grown as other Specials had died."

"This had better be on the level, Doc."

Back on the base, Doc would have rolled his eyes, if his head hadn't still been hurting. "Trust me. This information is a matter of life and death."

"Yeah. Right. You'll have the files in an hour."

Returning the cell phone to his guard, Welles figured he'd done everything but paint Paulson a picture. He didn't want to actually come out and say what he suspected because he would only go so far in helping that man. But really, how denser could a modern FBI agent get?

The cars that couldn't fit in the garage were in the barn. No one was outside. Not because it was cold and about to snow, though it was, but because we didn't want to give an easy indication that the Ponderosa-sized mansion was inhabited. The spy satellites nowadays could spot a frog snagging a mosquito with its tongue. Of course, they were going to find us eventually; Randy's plan just called for them to have to work at it for as long as possible, while we plotted a more definitive move.

Of course, they hadn't made the satellite yet that could spot me. I flew in that morning as pretty as you please, landing on the top front porch like I parachuted in every morning. Of course, I had to knock on the window before someone let me in. One of the lesser powers. He glared at me but was cordial enough, and even though I sensed him gallantly trying to conceal his animosity toward me, my mind was really set on seeing Chandra. In a way, it was too bad all these people had to be here. It was inconvenient.

True to form, however, when I did see Chandra, I tried to stick to business. It was difficult. She wore a red gown that showed lots of cleavage and appeared to have been spray-painted on her body. I suppose it just wasn't like her to dress down solely because she was a fugitive.

I met her in the living room downstairs, a living room half the size of a football field.

"How many of us have arrived so far?"

"About twenty of our kind, plus assorted mundanes: wives, husbands, kids. A dog or cat here and there. I have them caged in the basement. You know, until today I never said 'our kind' or 'their kind.' Now—"

"I know, Chandra. You're sure nobody can tie this place to you?"

"Positive," she said, with admirable false bravado. "As I said, it belongs to a gentleman friend. He lets me use it when he's out of the country."

"Chandra, you did dismiss the help, didn't you?"

"I told them if they didn't leave pronto, they'd be fired."

"And you bought their silence?"

"They got an early Christmas bonus, if that's what you mean." She looked me in the eye. "John, what you did at the house after I left—"

"Sorry if I blew something up."

"That's not it. I saw what you did on the news. I had no idea you were so . . . I mean, that you could do so much."

"The Doc said I had to keep it secret because—" I didn't say because I might one day kill some of my own kind. And that might include killing her. "—because he knew a day like this might come."

"It's still hard to believe the government is really after us. I mean, most of the people here have limited abilities. They've never harmed anyone."

"And you?"

She shrugged. "I'm not sure you can call my ability limited. Anyway, some of them just fly. Others make little floating lights. And me, well, there's a big difference between looking beautiful to everyone because of the force, and really being beautiful. I've never felt about me the way *they* do, never felt beautiful. Not on the inside, or the outside. Except a few times, when you and I—"

"Simon! John Simon!" someone called out to me.

Damn, I thought. *Just when things were getting interesting.* I turned to face my accuser. That's how he said my name, as if it were an accusation. "Eli, old friend. Glad you made it—"

Eli was a strapping, dark-haired guy. He was being followed down the stairs by his family. His wife Susan was a Special, too, which is why they had to flee with their children. Eli was a minor league telekinetic, while Susan was a hairdresser, well-known for her ability to transmute another person's hair into a style perfectly suiting both face and personality. Her own hair had certain Medusa-like qualities too.

"Don't give me that 'old friend' crap," Eli said. "I saw what you did to Matthew. Are you out of your mind? I mean, hiding what you can do is bad enough, but then you go and show off in front of TV cameras? No wonder they're after us. Thanks to you, they figured we *all* have something to hide."

"I had no choice."

"Bull. Until you pulled that stunt we could've negotiated our way out of this. It's all some kind of mistake, that's all. But you had to be a big shot, had to fight the number one police officer in the country, and now we're on the run. Because of you." He stuck his finger in my face. I hated it when people did that, especially if they weren't being rational.

"Our kind was being killed long before I did anything, Eli. Because with each one of us killed, the rest of us inherit the left-over energy."

"That's a load of crap. There isn't one shred of proof—"

"Here's your proof—" And I decked him. One solid, extremely satisfying punch to the jaw that didn't even hurt. Eli went flying into the wall, which he struck with a hollow *thunk!* Then he slid down it and landed square on his rear end.

"That punch could have taken my jaw off!" he said, too stunned to be angry with me.

"How about that?" I said, helping him up. "One year ago, if I'd hit you like that, you'd be out for days. Now you can just shrug it off. These conspiracy charges were trumped up by the very people who've been preying on us from the start, to distract everybody from what they've been doing. Our only ally inside right now is the Doc— only nobody seems to know where he is right now."

According to his diary, though, Doc Welles knew exactly where he was:

There was no equivocation now: I was deep in the aforementioned world of shit. The preliminary observations the Feds had made regarding the Specials they'd arrested in Pederson indicated slight increases in abilities across the board. The Feds saw this only as evidence that the Specials had been concealing their true abilities from everyone, including myself, down through the years. Based on what I was reading in the reports, it never occurred to them that perhaps the Specials had not been concealing anything, that their powers were growing.

"Something wrong?' Stephanie asked from the cell opposite mine.

"Oh no," I replied, without thinking. "Nothing you need to worry about."

"I know that tone of voice," she replied, morphing into the body and the personality I'd nicknamed Steph II. "It's the same tone of voice Stephanie's father used when he lied to me. And when he lied to Stephanie's mother about what he did to her."

"Really?" I said. "First, he must have been a casual, confident child abuser, because I was trying to be as nonchalant as possible. Second, I must not have been as good as I thought I was, because I never noticed anything wrong with Stephanie, at least not along those lines. Always thought she could have used more self-confidence."

"She listens to the Carpenters!" snarled Steph II. "Can you imagine what it's like, being stuck inside someone whose musical taste makes you want to puke your guts out?"

"I like the Carpenters."

"I always preferred the Plasmatics. Or Luscious Jackson. You should have seen the look on Stephanie's face, when she discovered she'd bought CDs by *them!* I made her listen to 'em sometimes, she couldn't figure out why she was drawn to them, why she liked them. You wanna know what I make her do with her husband sometimes? You've met her husband, Francis, haven't you?" The way she said "Francis" indicated more contempt than even God had ever seen.

"How long have you been able to come out like this? Does Stephanie know?"

Steph II took a step up the wall. "Her? Nah. She's never even around when I show up. She always used to

265

hide behind me when things went bad at home."

"So you're saying you could see her, but she couldn't see you."

"Yeah." And with that, Steph II walked *up* the wall. "You should have seen her face the time she discovered she was pregnant. Had to give her up for adoption. And boy, was she surprised when she discovered the child's entire ethnic origin. That was fun. For some reason, I'm getting out a lot more these days. I can do things I couldn't before. And I gotta tell you, Doc, I'm liking it big time."

My jaw fell to the floor. I'd seen a lot of strange stuff in my day, but I never expected Stephanie Maas to do anything more unusual than drink her wine too fast, whatever her mood swing. But now I was watching her walk to the ceiling like Fred Astaire on a stroll.

She stood there, her hands on her hips, like she was taking in a breathtaking sunset. "She wishes she could do the sort of things I can. But she can't find the right parts of herself, you know what I mean? Me, I don't have that problem. I'm all power. Well, all power plus all anger. Plus all vengeance, plus all justice, plus . . ."

I'd studied cases like Stephanie of course. But I'd never been privileged to treat one. One of my favorite cases was of a man whose dominant personality was tone deaf, couldn't play a musical instrument, couldn't hum a tune. Whereas personality B, the submerged personality, could play classical piano and compose operas. Of course, the fingers didn't always do what the mind wanted them to do, and the subject's grasp of Italian was pretty weak, but all in all, I thought it was a pretty extraordinary achievement.

"Crap! She's coming back!" Steph II exclaimed, and

did a somersault off the ceiling and onto the cot. Moments later she morphed back into Stephanie, who was disoriented and appeared to be fending off someone unseen. "I'll do anything for love," she said in anxiety-filled, dreamy tones, "but I won't do that."

Well, I thought, so much for my vaunted professional insight into human nature. Like so many cases of MPD, Stephanie Maas had been abused as a child. She manufactured another personality as a kind of guardian. Such responses are typically both creative and desperate. In her case, the submerged personality has the powers. But now the submerged personality was becoming so powerful that it was starting to become the dominant one. A massive power shift in the Force was fueling a transfer of energy more significant, unpredictable, and dangerous than even the reports had led me to believe.

"Plus all death," said Steph II, once again among the living, "all force, all rage, all death, all power, all might, all death, all fury, all death . . ."

"Guard! Guard! I need to speak with Paulson again. Right now!"

The guard, who was initially hesitant, did a double take when he saw Steph II.

"There's a reason for it!" I said. "Now."

The guard saw the wisdom of my request. Paulson, on the other hand, was not nearly as receptive. "You're out of your mind, Doctor," he told me.

"No, damn it, Paulson, you've got to listen to me! Every time one of the Specials is killed, his energy is sent to the rest of them."

"Old news."

"You're hearing, but you're not listening. We've

always suspected there's a threshold that tips a person from low to high, and from high to—"

"I'm sure that's all very interesting to someone, Doctor, but we've got a mission to do, and we're not about to cancel it because you've got some new figures in front of you."

"They're *your* figures! Listen to me very carefully, Paulson. Try to engage your brain for once. I suspect that if even one or two more Specials are killed, the residual energy spread to the rest of them might bring the whole group to critical mass."

Hmm, that's interesting," said Steph II to herself. "Critical mass. Critical mass. *Critical Maas.* I like it. Stephanie Maas and Critical Maas. I've always wanted my own name. Now we can be sisters. First chance I get, I'm gonna take that girl on the town and get her a good shagging."

"What the hell does that mean?" Paulson shouted into his cell phone, into my ear.

I tried not to get distracted by Steph II. I mean, Critical. "I don't know . . . exactly . . . but I do know it could be massively ugly."

I overheard a soldier in the background tell Paulson they were ready to go, sir.

"No go, Doc," said Paulson. "I think you're just out to stall. Buy the others some more time. And as of right now, they're out of time."

"Damn it, Paulson! It's not them I'm worried about. I mean I am, but your men—"

And he hung up on me. I learned later that his squad of choppers had rendezvoused with several hundred soldiers, fifty tanks, several heavily fortified big rigs, and enough weaponry to defoliate and depopulate a small country.

"We're good to go," he told his second-in-command. "Let's roll!"

Simon here again. I was walking in the freshly fallen snow with Chandra. Some of the children were outside playing in the snow, against my express wishes. I certainly didn't want to help the Feds spot us. But of course they would, sooner or later. I was merely hoping the stragglers would join us before circumstances forced a collective decision on all of us.

Then, at least, I might have the proverbial snowball's chance in hell of protecting them.

"I'm sorry about what happened earlier, John," said Chandra.

"It's all right. Eli's scared, and with good reason. We're all scared. Besides, he's got to be worried about his family."

"You don't really seem that scared."

I shrugged. "I might be more powerful than anyone suspected, but I still have my limitations. I suspect I can't take a bullet."

"Though you're not sure," she said with a sly smile. "For a moment there I thought maybe Eli would shoot you."

"I've never exactly been Mr. Popular. I can't expect that to change overnight."

"Well, you've always been very popular with me. Do you know you were the only one of our group that never once asked me out? And you were probably the only one I would have said yes to."

Boy, did I feel like a sap. "I, uh, guess I didn't want

to be like the rest, bothering you all the time."

"Trust me, John, you'll never be like the rest."

"So why are you telling me this now, Chandra?"

"I don't know. Maybe just a bad feeling. Like we're not going to get out of this, and there's no time to put off saying things like this."

"We're going to get out of it," I said, my pitter-pattering heart suddenly turning steely. "I just don't know how."

The conversations among the men and women in the approaching choppers were well-documented in the Congressional investigation that was part of the aftermath of what happened that day. These soldiers were well-trained, they were brave, and they knew the difference between right and wrong. But they had taken their cue from their leaders and from Agent Paulson; they were barely briefed. The rules of engagement were vague, and the potential dangers presented by the Specials were so broad as to be completely nebulous. Certainly they had never been trained for those dangers—what good does a bayonet or a high kick do against someone who can turn into a ghost, then back again? And that was just a for-instance.

A corporal named Trudy Tumball gave the most complete synopsis during the hearings, the most representative of what the soldiers were going through. She recounted that her conversation with Sgt. Masters went something like this:

"I hear some of these can burn you to a crisp just by looking at you. Or tear you to shreds without even breaking a sweat."

"The Colonel said the ones we're after are low powers,"

said Sgt. Masters, giving his weapon one last inspection.

"You think they're going to tell us the truth? You think the military wanted to tell the truth about the atrocities in Vietnam? You think they want us to know that war is an extension of politics by other means? You think they told the guys at Normandy, 'Oh, by the way, those of you in the front row, hitting the beach first? Ain't none of you ever coming home.' Come on. You think I'm gonna risk my life for somebody who ain't even fully human? No way. One of them even blinks my way, I'm taking his head off. And if you're smart, Sarge, you'll do the same."

"I dunno ... maybe," replied Sgt. Masters, when he should have dressed the corporal down for even contemplating firing without an order, and thus providing the Congressional investigation with insight as to how the chain of command failed the common soldier that day.

Knowing a Special was nearby, a Special whom I had not hitherto suspected was in the vicinity, I felt like I was reacting to the hum of an invisible tuning fork being held next to my ear. Knowing Paulson and crew were coming, I felt an electrical current in my marrow, on a level I'd never before experienced. Was this how a criminal felt, knowing his life on the lam was nearing its ignominious conclusion? Or was this how Captain Travis felt, on the steps of the Alamo? Because my foreboding had nothing to do with my being saturated by he Force, and everything to do with my being human.

The foreboding only intensified when a solitary car pulled into the driveway of the ranch house—there were still a few stragglers out there—and a brunette whom I didn't recognize got out on the driver's side.

"Who the hell is that?" I asked Chandra.

"Damned if I know," said Chandra.

Eli answered the question by racing up to the woman, calling out her name. "Sharon! Hey, Sharon!" They embraced, and for a moment I felt like a South Vietnamese villager about to meet Lt. Calley.

"You made it!" Eli exclaimed.

"It wasn't easy, let me tell you!" she said.

"Susan's going to be happy to see you."

"Hey!" I snapped. "Far be it from me to interfere with a tender reunion, but who *the hell* is that?"

"There's no reason to be hostile," said Eli. "This is my sister-in-law, Sharon Casey."

"Hi, it's a pleasure," she said. I sensed immediately that she was a nice though naive person, whose brains rolled from one side of her head to the other like bowling balls whenever she tilted her head, which she was doing now. "How do you—"

"How did she know how to get here?" I asked Eli.

"That's not imp—"

"I said how did she know how to get here?" I punctuated my question by grabbing him by the collar and lifting him several inches off the ground. I didn't know it would be so easy. Like picking up a cat.

"I called her," he said. "We knew she'd be worried sick, and—"

It was all I could do to restrain myself from plunging my fist into his chest and pulling out his heart. "And you called her? *On an unsecured line?* Did you ever hear of wiretaps? With the Ashcroft Laws passed, the President doesn't even need a court order; he can order 'em on his own, on a whim. Don't you think they've got the phones of every one of our families and friends bugged?"

I threw him to the ground. Hard. I would have felt guilty about it had it not been for his quick bounce. He was safer than he knew. I never would have killed him in front of his loved ones.

He stood up, blustering. "You're a freak, you know that? A goddamn paranoid freak! You got no business doing that to me—"

"Who cares?" I sure didn't. My foreboding had gone into overdrive. "We have to evacuate, Chandra. Right now."

"But—we just got here, and others are on the way. Maybe they don't know, maybe—"

One of the kids was playing a radio. I shut it down and listened to the silence. Somewhere, off in the distance, the sound of tumbling kettledrums, rolling across the plain. Or could it be the sound of approaching Apache helicopters, loaded and ready for war?

It's happening! I thought. And in that moment, I realized it was possible I was going to die, and if I could die, then Chandra could die, and if Chandra could die, then so could everybody else, and suddenly it occurred to me that I might not yet be prepared for this sort of responsibility.

The helicopters appeared first, from over the mountains.

"You do as I say," I said to Sharon. "Go inside. Their bullets are not going to distinguish between you and a Special."

She gasped. "What do you mean?"

"He's right," said Eli, pushing her away. "Go inside."

They did, and Chandra went with them.

Eli was standing beside me while the tanks approached. They moved over the big rocks like greased green caterpillars, and they barreled between the trees as if the fingers of God himself were ripping the forest apart.

"John," said Eli. "They're not stopping."

"I noticed. Hold your ground. They're not stupid, they won't shoot first and ask questions later."

No, they weren't *that* stupid, but they came damned close. Most of the tanks remained outside the mansion perimeter, as did the choppers. But three tanks burst through the walls to make way for the officers in their jeeps.

That's when the fliers took off. Twelve of them. Fools. The inevitable standoff had already begun, which under the circumstances I felt was as safe as anybody was going to be for the next few hours, at least. But fliers are a traditionally heedless bunch, and their reaction to fear resembles that of your average sparrow. They got over the helicopters quickly and easily enough, but the helicopters turned like cybernetic hornets and then took off after them.

The chase wouldn't last long. Most fliers can't move in the air any more quickly than they could on the ground, and I noticed a lot of them were out of shape. The helicopters deliberately held back their speed, just as they deliberately refrained from firing on them. Obviously, the soldiers were going to wear them out, and take them back alive.

At least, I hoped that was the plan. If not, then the fliers had made a really stupid decision. But it wasn't their fault. For all their powers—for all our powers—most of us lived ordinary lives. We wanted to be left alone as other human beings were.

But we were all tired of running.

By the time the soldiers warily got out of their trucks

and jeeps, nearly every male who'd made it to the ranch stood with me.

A few steps in front of me was Roy Harper, whom I hadn't seen in eons. He'd been a reclusive type—still was. I hadn't even known he'd made it to the ranch. His abilities had to do with necromantic arts, to the extent that he required the accoutrements of black magic to be able to focus. He had spent most of the last five years in Alaska, dousing for oil. Rumor was he'd found quite a bit.

"Don't do anything rash," I advised him, realizing that with all that had happened lately, I had no idea *what* he could do.

His reply was succinct: "Bite me." He hunkered down, muttered some mumbo-jumbo, added the request "hide us," and gave birth to several blue spirals of force that sprouted from the ground like weeds. Those spirals did nothing to hide us, but I suppose they made Roy feel more secure.

The spirals had the opposite effect on the soldiers. "Gas—they're using gas," I heard one of them say.

"Watch out!" said another. "It's like I heard. They can burn us with a look."

A colonel, hands behind his back, walked toward us. "Gentlemen, you are now in Federal custody. Please surrender and come quietly, and please advise your families to do the same. That way, there will not be any trouble—"

"What's the charge?" I asked.

"Treason. Don't worry. You'll still have rights. After debriefing, you'll eventually be allowed to talk to a lawyer, and the President is open to the possibility that some of your civil rights might be returned to you in the years to come. But there is no debating this matter: you must come with us. You are now in Federal Custody."

It took me nanoseconds to come up with the proper reply, but that was still too late for Moose, who in high school had excelled at the linebacker position. "Get out of here!" he said, pointing at the colonel. "You've got no right."

""He's pointing!" a few of the soldiers whispered among themselves.

Their commanding officer ordered them to be quiet, but their fear was palpable. All their colonel had really accomplished, I'm afraid, was to emphasize how close things were to getting out of control.

"He's gonna do something!" the soldier said.

"Look out!" said another, ducking.

The mere fact that he had ducked was enough to convince one of the men to open fire.

Three short bursts.

Bursts that ripped three holes in Steven Bowers' chest.

Steven went down like a gored ox.

Chandra was the first person by his side. She tried to cradle him, but was afraid to lift his head. His torso had practically been torn in two by the bullets.

The solider, meanwhile, lowered his weapon and became very pale. So did a lot of the other soldiers. It was if they realized an important line had been crossed, and they were actively wondering if there was some way they could go back in time and alter the event.

Even the colonel looked nervous. He was, after all, standing between the two factions.

"He's dead, John," said Chandra, in a wooden whisper. "He's dead."

At that moment my solidarity with my fellow Special was complete. We were ordinary people who just happened to be born with extraordinary abilities. All we wanted was to live *un*extraordinary lives. A dream that had been in a coma, and died completely the moment Steven had.

"Bastards," said Roy, his ineffectual spirals swirling double-time around him, like the spokes of a freaky gyroscope.

I have no idea what thoughts, if any, were passing through my brain at that moment. It was as if my lizard brain had consumed my higher cognitive functions with the fire of its rage and I had become, in effect, a mindless raging zombie.

Great pools of force were building up in my hands, and my anger wasn't going to permit me much restraint.

I charged them.

"Open fire!" someone said.

The bullets bounced off me—wow, I hadn't known I could do that!—but my fellow Specials weren't so lucky. Seven more of us were dead, including Renee, who was shot through the head because she had caught a stray bullet while looking through a window.

I halted in mid-charge and looked around, dumbfounded. I actually thought more than seven had died, because so many more were lying on the ground, wounded.

Fulfilling my fantasy of tearing out someone's heart with my bare hand took on a new urgency.

Especially when I noticed Paulson sneaking from one truck, near the front, to one further back. I remember thinking that this was a man who in Washington always knew how to get out of the way long before the hurricane struck. I had the feeling the identical instinct was helping him now. I was zeroing in on him—

When it happened. When the residual force from the newly deceased seven came into us—striking with a pronounced physical impact—surrounding us with blue circles of pure force that connected us like the atoms in an electrical stream.

The surviving Specials, myself included, were bowled over. The residuals force came into us again and again . . . harder than ever before.

And it enhanced us a second time.

Some of us screamed as we writhed from the pain of the acquisition, but I noticed even Eli, who had been shot in the shoulder and should have been on his knees, managed to stand. And his feet became steadier as more force distributed itself.

"What the hell's going on?" a soldier asked. "This is some kind of a trick?"

I think he was asking the colonel, but the man just stood where he had been, stuck between the factions with this dumbfounded look on his face, like a frightened basset hound unsure of which direction to run first. Agent Paulson had abandoned him in unknown territory . . .

"I don't know," another soldier answered, and he raised his rifle. "But I'm not taking any chances!"

"Wait!" I said.

He didn't wait. Instead, he fired.

And his fellow soldiers fired as well.

We Specials were inundated with an onslaught of bullets. We should have died immediately. But we didn't. I wasn't the only one present who could shrug off the impact of a bullet as if it had been shot from a peashooter. I had company in that regard. Lots of company. Company that included every single surviving Special.

At first everyone cowered. When the soldiers realized

we weren't falling, the stragglers, those who had previously had a prejudice against shooting unarmed civilians, joined in the failing effort at bloodshed.

The mansion behind us was being riddled with bullets. I prayed that the women who'd remained inside were keeping the children and the mundanes safe, somehow. Somehow. For the trumpet had sounded and we had all been changed.

The soldiers ceased firing. They belatedly realized that, to their astonishment, their bullets had had no effect. Now they had no idea what to do.

A few turned their heads at the explosions in the distance. The Apache helicopters who'd chased after the fliers had run into some unexpected resistance.

Then the Specials charged.

I charged with them. "Don't kill anybody!" I shouted. I just wanted to put their weapons and their vehicles out of commission, to teach them a lesson.

My fellow Specials, however, had in mind a more permanent lesson.

I managed to save a few of the soldiers. The rest were torn apart, broken, or just plain frozen in time until their brains died from lack of oxygen. Their vehicles were crushed, their weapons shredded.

It was a grisly scene.

I don't like to think about it very much.

Agent Paulson knew he was running like a scared rabbit into the nearby woods, and he didn't care. The fate of the entire country required his survival. First, he had to figure out how to blame the holocaust on Dr. Welles and start him on the process toward his eventual execution.

Second, he'd have to convince the President that nuclear weapons were their only option . . .

If it wasn't already too late.

Meanwhile, back at the army prison camp, as recounted in Dr. Welles' diary:

I was half-asleep, feeling very depressed, as I waited for the next disaster to strike.

For an instant, it seemed like I was dreaming the walls were coming down around me. I jumped up on the cot and tried to think of where a safe place might be, but since the ceiling was coming down around me too, I figured the odds were against me. Damn, I didn't want to die. Not yet.

Then blackness.

It was only momentary blackness—just long enough for me to wonder if my entreaties to blind existential forces might not be working. But I felt strangely safe somehow. Already someone was lifting one of the large slabs of the ceiling and pushing it aside.

A slender hand reached down for me. "Care for a ride, Doc?"

The hand belonged to Steph II, or "Critical Maas." Her prison outfit was gone, and in its place she wore an unbuttoned flak jacket and trousers lifted from a soldier. The trousers were bloodstained, so I knew the young man hadn't met with a good end

"Time to go," she said, and she picked me up by the shirt and began to fly, taking me with her, lifting me up and over the ruins of our cells.

"What happened?" I said, dazed and confused.

"*We* did. Seems like there aren't low powers and high powers anymore. We're *all* high powers now."

Joining us in the sky were the rest of the Specials who had been held prisoner in this compound. Some of them had changed into wraiths, and more than a few had become pure flame. The gap between thought and accomplishment was nonexistent to this new breed of Special.

"*Now* we get to teach the whole world what fear is," said Steph II. "And power, and rage, and death ..."

Oh, Jason, I thought. *What curse have you inflicted upon the world ... ?*

EPILOGUE

Our kind has never been seen before—and, when the last of us are gone, will never be seen again. Because there is a secret behind our creation, and secrets like this only come around once.

NOT THE END. . . .